CHANNELING CLEOPATRA

CHANNELING CLEOPATRA

ELIZABETH ANN SCARBOROUGH

ACE BOOKS, NEW YORK

CHANNELING CLEOPATRA

An Ace Book
Published by The Berkley Publishing Group,
a division of Penguin Putnam Inc.,
375 Hudson Street, New York, New York 10014.

Visit our website at
www.penguinputnam.com

First edition: February 2002

Library of Congress Cataloging-in-Publication Data

Scarborough, Elizabeth Ann.
    Channeling Cleopatra / Elizabeth Ann Scarborough.— 1st ed.
        p. cm.
    ISBN 0-441-00897-6 (alk. paper)
    1. Women Egyptologists—Fiction. 2. Americans—Egypt—Fiction.
3. Egypt—Fiction. I. Title.

PS3569.C324 C53 2002
813'.54—dc21

                                                            2001046386

PRINTED IN THE UNITED STATES OF AMERICA

10 9 8 7 6 5 4 3 2 1

To Lea Day,
armchair Egyptologist extraordinaire
and to the memory of her father,
Hubbard Day, Jr.

ACKNOWLEDGMENTS

Thanks to Lea for the loan of her library, book hunting, anecdotes, her sense of humor and enthusiasm for the project. Thanks also to Eileen Clare for sharing such detailed information of her trip to Alexandria with me, and to Mike for his anecdotes as well. I also wish to acknowledge Dr. Michael Croteau of the Washington State Laboratory for information about DNA collection and analyses. An especially helpful book on modern-day Egypt was *CULTURE SHOCK! EGYPT!* by Susan Wilson, who generously shared additional information with me for this book.

CHANNELING CLEOPATRA

ꙙPRELUDE

Cleopatra looked at the snake. The snake, its tongue flicking, stared back at her. She apologized to the creature, the emblem of her queenship and the end of it. "My lord, if only Octavius were as trustworthy as you are, there would be no need to disturb you with our concerns. But alas, my protectors are all dead, my beauty faded, and even my hair-dresser and handmaiden have offered their flesh to your fangs for my sake, so I have no choice. If I live and flee, Octavius will avenge himself upon my children. If I live and submit, he will degrade and humiliate my person and position in his accursed Roman triumph, dragging me in chains through the city where I should by rights have ruled as empress. Then he will kill me and destroy my body and my hope for the afterlife. Oh yes, my lord," she said in her tender, singsong voice, the voice of a natural-born snake charmer. The snake swayed, half uncoiled to strike, its hood majestically fanned around its face.

The coils of its body lay still upon the folds of the yellow, red, and white linens of the Isis robes covering Charmion's corpse. Iras lay beside the altar containing the body. Charmion also wore the Isis crown and what was left of the crown jewels. Iras had dressed her fellow hand-maiden's head in the black Isis curls Cleopatra customarily wore when assuming the guise of the goddess. The queen herself had employed her considerable skill with cosmetics to change faces with her look-alike maid. Now, dressed as Charmion, she explained herself to the cobra. The cobra did not mind her humble robes. It knew who she was. She was Egypt, its home, its mother, and finally, its prey.

She spoke to it to clarify her own mind before her death and to delay that same death, for she had long loved life and was loath to leave it, even under the circumstances.

"Yes, it's true. I have it on the best authority. Isis in her compassion has sent me a dream so I may save my body and thus my immortal soul. Whatever lies he tells my peo-ple, Octavius intends to burn me after my death—before it, if he is given the opportunity, I'm sure. So I have chosen my own time. My eldest son has fled the country, and as for my younger children, I am unable to protect them, and moreover, I provide cause for Octavius to do them harm. Perhaps without me to spite with their suffering, he will spare them. And so you must give me my last kiss, my lord. My priests, who know our little secret, will do the rest. In exchange, I grant you your freedom from your du-ties as guardian of this tomb and temple."

She took a deep breath, broke eye contact, and quickly, so as to startle the fascinated snake, thrust her arm at it. Having had its part so considerately explained to it, the co-bra performed its last state service and struck her with a force that staggered her back, away from the altar.

Unhooded and blending with the dust, the snake then slithered out through an open window.

The pain subsided, quickly replaced with numbness. Soon she knew paralysis and death would follow. By that time, Octavius would have received her message begging him to bury her with Antony. She knew he would not, but the message would serve to seal in his mind that the body in her robes was her own. He would expect to see her there, and dead, and that is what he would see.

The stage was set to perfection, except the cobra, in striking, had pulled Charmion's wig askew. Slowly, with a sense of detachment and amusement, as if she had had too much wine, Cleopatra rose and stretched out her other hand to adjust it.

Which was how Octavius and his soldiers saw her when they burst into the room.

She felt Octavius staring hard at her, and she thought for a moment the ruse had failed. Then he said, puzzled, more to himself than to her, "Is this well done?"

The bastard was trying to figure out if her death was to his advantage or not.

She felt herself ready to fly to the afterlife, but she had never been able to resist a good exit line. "It is well done," she said, her voice unrecognizably husky with the dying, "and fitting for a princess descended of so many royal kings."

And so it was that the body of Charmion, dressed in the robes of Cleopatra, was displayed to the people as proof of her death. Later, as Cleopatra's dream had warned, Octavius publicly said she would be interred with Mark Antony but privately, to his lieutenant, he said, "Burn the bitch. The brats may watch."

The bodies of the handmaidens were removed afterward by the priests. Cleopatra's public tomb, stripped of its glories by Octavius, lay empty, as she had somehow always known it would. But by secret passage it connected, down a long and twisting passage with many stairs and a maze of tunnels, with a private tomb concealed deep beneath her palace. In some ways, the tomb was very bare, her special coffin, sealed within three others, the simple alabaster canopic jars with her cartouche and titles and seals of gold, some clothing and toiletries, a prettily carved and inlaid table and chair, a bed, a wealth of lamps. The tomb was for one person only. No place for husbands or children or even trusted servants. Iras's body had been removed to her family's crypt. Instead, the side rooms held Cleopatra's greatest treasure, one that Octavius and other conquerors lacked the wit to covet. But to the queen, for whom the love of erudition was more fundamental than her love of either of her Roman husbands or even her kingdom, her burial hoard was of the most valuable nature possible. It contained the originals to the best, the rarest, the most informed and fascinating of the manuscripts collected by her own great Museon, the Library of Alexandria.

CHAPTER 1

For Leda Hubbard, attending the International Conference of Egyptologists was the next best thing to personally
participating in a dig. When she found a ticket in her mail-
box, she was giddy with joy but curious and also suspicious about who would treat her to such a thing. For the
cost of one of those tickets, you could almost buy a plane
trip to Egypt.

Most of the attendees who were not presenting papers
or teaching seminars had corporate sponsorship. Nonetheless, Leda recalculated her budget six times until she came
up with almost enough to go. Then the urgent need for a
root canal and a new radiator for her car gobbled up her
ticket money.

Cinderella she wasn't, but nevertheless, some mysterious benefactor, secret admirerer, fairy godmother, or possibly a stalker, decided she could go to the ball.

After enjoying a splendid day filled with intellectual
delights, Leda was finally ready to turn into a pumpkin. It
was not yet sunset, much less midnight, but the showroom
had closed, the lectures were over, and her feet felt like

they actually were encased in something as agonizing as glass slippers, which could not have been comfy.

The Portland Convention Center was huge, and she had walked the equivalent of a marathon attending seminars, checking out the goodies in the showroom, and searching for favorite authors of scholarly tomes. She hadn't met any princes, true. But she now had something that was in her opinion much better: a rolling suitcase full of books about pharaohs (and related topics, such as how to identify said pharaohs), now autographed. The only thing better than that would have been to be the autographer instead of the autographee.

Alas, she, who had entertained full-blown H. Rider Haggard/Elizabeth Peters dreams of being an Egyptologist while still an undergrad at Heidelberg, had never fully realized her ambitions.

She had achieved the Ph.D. in forensic anthropology and was a by-Bast doctor-not-of-medicine, though she had probably handled more cadavers than the average M.D. But she had not been able to squeeze in the additional studies necessary to specialize in Egyptology with the time and money allotted her.

The Navy, while debating about paying for her graduate degree while she was on active duty, suggested in their cute little bureaucratic way that Egyptologists were less likely to make it through school without being called into a war zone than, say, their useful colleagues who studied corpses of more recent vintage. In the charming phrasing of the Graduate Studies in Continuing Education financial assistance and career counseling officer, "This is a weird sort of thing you want to study, Chief Hubbard, but the Navy does have a certain limited use for forensic scientists. What we need are people who can put pieces of dead troops back together so the remains can be identified. Most of these troops will not be of ancient Egyptian stock; therefore, if you wish to study any of that elitist crap, you can do so on your own dime. The Navy has no job openings for Egyptologists. Do I make myself clear?"

She had sighed, batted her lashes, and said in the sultry voice that had made her voted by her senior class "most likely to succeed in a career in the telephonic sex industry," "I just love it when you get all butch and masterful, sir."

The officer had blushed. He was about twenty-four. She was thirty-six at the time. A career that had until that time been spent aboard aircraft carriers and submarines dealing with matters that required a top security clearance made her feel much much older.

But the kid had been right about one thing. There were, until very recently, few job ops for Egyptologists who were not Egyptian. This was as true of civilian life as it had been in the Navy. These days, she worked in the Oregon state laboratory, mostly helping law enforcement agencies gather evidence to identify anonymous remains.

Nowadays, there seemed to be a few more opportunities in Egyptology for those who had had the backing to tough it out financially. Some of the instructors her heiroglyphics class used to be able to count on were now unavailable, hired away to digs.

Leda sighed, bumped her glasses up to the top of her head, and rubbed her overstimulated eyes. Always the bridesmaid, never the bride? Screw that. She didn't want to get married. Her father had instructed her in the course of his five marriages just how miserable a charming, sexually gregarious man could make a woman foolish enough to wed him. She was a little slow, but after an ultimately heartbreaking affair with a Kiwi who looked very different from her dad but was his emotional clone, she decided to forgo romance in favor of career. And, like a lot of women who "settled" for the men they could get instead of the ones they wanted, Leda had settled for the practical career with a few readily available opportunities instead of the one she really wanted.

But someone had known that Egypt was to her what Mecca was to most Egyptians and sent her the ticket. So, while she had had a dandy time, she had also acquired a crick in her neck from looking over her shoulder, trying to figure out who had done her the big favor. And the corollary, of course. What did they want in return? She knew her benefactor wasn't her dad, who could have had half a new motorcycle for the price of admission and whose income as a retired cop was certainly not up to it. It wasn't her mom, who would never want to do something for her daughter that Leda actually wanted. Or her brother, who had a wife and two kids to support. So who?

Finally she grabbed a diet Coke and coaxed her homicidal feet to carry her to one of the little lawn tables on the mezzanine of the convention center. She parked the rolling suitcase against the table and sat down heavily.

She was too tired and footsore at the moment to make the trip to the parking lot all in one shot. She sucked down the diet Coke, grateful for the coolness against the back of her throat.

It just didn't feel right somehow, after being someone's guest all day, not to wait around until they jumped out and said, "Surprise!" But that wasn't happening, so she settled back for a moment and spaced out from sheer exhaustion.

As she grew less tired and more aware of how sore her butt was becoming from sitting in the distinctly unergonomic chair, she also realized that the world outside the glass wall of the convention center was dark and full of rain.

Well, it was Portland, after all. Of course it was raining. She looked at her watch. It was close to seven P.M. already, a fact that explained the rumbling in her stomach which was, after forty-five years of valiant service, getting too old to live by fast food and soda pop alone.

The crowd had thinned so that the noise inside the convention center was no more than a footstep here, a voice or two there. Only a handful of people still drifted through the massive corridors. The escalators, so steep that when they were shut down they could have been used as indoor training facilities for baby mountain climbers, were almost empty.

Suddenly, she had the feeling she was being watched. In her family this sort of feeling was not considered paranoid. Both her dad and her brother were cops, and she worked almost daily with the gruesome remains of those who probably should have been more vigilant. She and all of the other adult Hubbards were thus security conscious.

So she opened her big hazel eyes one more time and looked around and up. Never fail to look up, Daddy always told her.

And sure enough, there was a dark head pressed against one of the windows, the face staring in her direction.

That face looked familiar.

She waved. A hand appeared by the face and waved briefly back at her, and then the person headed for the escalator and rode it down to her level.

As the short, slim, dark-haired person dressed in black fashionably reminiscent of Vietcong pajamas surfed down the sliding steps, she recognized them—she thought. Actually, she narrowed the identity down to two possible suspects.

With the sleek black hair and the big brown eyes and familiar smile, who could it be but Chime, Leda's bubbly but brilliant cat-loving friend, a roommate from undergrad days at the University of Heidelberg? But strangely, the person who seemed so glad to see her also looked very much like Chime's equally brilliant but much shyer, cat-allergic husband, Tsering. Leda was startled to realize as the person grasped her hand and hugged her that she continued not to be able to decide which one it was.

"Leda! How very good to see you. You received your ticket, I see."

"Oh, so you were the one who sent it?" she asked, not letting on that she hadn't decided which name to call her benefactor.

"Yes. We arranged to be here along with the recruitment delegation from Nucore, the corporation that sponsors our work. We have a matter of a highly confidential nature we wished to discuss with you—a matter involving your interest in Egypt. If indeed you have continued with your studies and achieved such eminence that our gift was a slight, forgive us. Since your name did not appear on the list of invited dignitaries, we felt that if we sent the ticket, and you came, we could take it as a sign of your continuing fascination with Egyptology."

"Gee, I wish you had sent a note with it and told me how to find you. We could have cruised around together."

"That might have raised questions we were unprepared to answer until now about matters we aren't at liberty to discuss freely. And while here, our time was not our own until a moment ago. However, we were told that you had arrived. One of our security staff made certain that we would not miss you."

Looking around for the other—whichever one it was—Jetsun, she asked cagily, "Is your better half with you?"

"Oh yes, we are both here," her friend answered.

Leda looked around. "Where?"

"Right. Here." The person tapped himself or herself on the chest. The brown eyes twinkled at Leda's confusion. "We are sorry, old friend. It is not fair to tease you this way. We can say no more while we are here."

"I could drive us to dinner somewhere," Leda offered.

"A fine idea."

She half expected her friend to whip out a cell phone and call a third person and end her confusion, but instead, a black silk clad arm linked with hers, and they walked toward the parking lot. The voice was huskier than Chime's had been. So it might be Tsering. On the other hand, there was a silver pendant dangling down over the front of the black silk shirt, so it was probably Chime. On the other hand, the pendant was a handmade silver yin-yang pendant, like some emblem of monkhood, so it might be something Tsering would wear, too. Leda grew more exasperated the more she tried to figure it out.

Once they were safely inside her car, she asked, "Look, I really appreciate the ticket and all—"

"You are welcome. We will be happy, whatever your answer to our question, to see that you always receive a ticket."

" 'We' who?" Leda asked at last. "I don't mean to be rude, but unless you have a mouse in your pocket, there is only one of you here."

When the person in black was silent for a moment, Leda snapped her fingers. "You've had a sex change operation, right?"

The person beside her laughed a laugh that was almost Chime's but not quite. "You might say that, yes. But it did not involve surgery. And we did not change our sex. We . . . augmented it, I suppose you could say."

"You mean you're a hermaphrodite?" Leda asked. She was just kidding, but to her surprise, the person beside her considered her question carefully.

"Emotionally, spiritually, yes. But physically, we are contained within the body of the one you knew as Tsering Jetsun."

"What does *that* mean?" Leda asked.

"Please, could you begin to drive? We will attempt to explain on the way. The parking lot is probably not a secure area, and our person, as well as the information we hold, is of a highly confidential nature, most important to the company that sponsors our work and which, if you agree, may sponsor yours as well."

Leda's eyes widened as she took in that information. "Okay, you're the . . . bosses."

She turned out of the parking lot and rounded the block, onto the bridge spanning the river, and headed toward downtown Portland. The rain, already fairly heavy when the two of them left the convention center, rapidly intensified. It flung itself in buckets against her windshield and rear window. The windshield wipers slapped away only every other bucketful. Then there was the steam rising off the warm car and the defroster, which wasn't working well, not to mention the mist rising from the surface of the river.

"Good thing I am a veteran submariner," Leda told her passenger, who twitched nervously in the seat beside her. She could barely see the headlights of oncoming cars, much less the taillights of the ones ahead of her. One set of headlights followed her onto the bridge and across it, not at all unusual. A little unnerving that they followed so closely in this weather but not surprising. Out-of-towners, no doubt.

"Yes, it is. You continued in the Navy then, after you graduated?"

"Yeah, I retired eight years ago."

"You did not continue your studies?"

"Yes, but I've only been able to study Egyptology informally. I've studied hieroglyphics for several years now with a class sponsored by the museum. We have speakers and that sort of thing. And the Egyptian section of my personal library is bigger than the one in the main city library."

"No graduate school?"

"Oh, sure," she said very casually, as if it didn't matter. "But I got into forensic anthropology instead. You know, identifying remains from fragments found—kind of like archaeology, but more recent remains."

"Oh, that is wonderful! Very useful!" Leda's former friend clapped his or her hands together with satisfaction, as if she had done something very bright.

"Well . . . yeah," Leda said, surprised. She glanced in

the mirror. The headlights were still behind her—two sets of two long rectangular ones, riding high.

"Oh yes, you are already familiar with DNA finger-printing, then, and other skills we will be much in need of if certain discoveries are made. We *knew* you were the one for this task! We hope you will not think it unscientific of us to confess this, but we dreamed we should come here to find you."

"Uh-huh," Leda said, hanging a right onto the Broad-way Bridge and casting a glance into the rearview mirror where the same twin pairs of rectangles still gleamed. "Did you also dream someone would be tailing us when we got together again? Tailing us inexpertly, I might add. Way too close and obvious."

"How annoying. They're just doing their job, but it is confining to have security people tagging along every-where. That is why we asked you to take us away from the convention center. What we have to ask you is not some-thing we want reported back to certain people at Nucore."

"I can probably lose them if you want," Leda said. "Es-pecially if they're not from Portland."

"We think not."

Leda accepted that for a wish to ditch the headlights. She took the exit for Martin Luther King Boulevard with-out signaling, which brought her back to the convention center side of the water, where she'd entered MLK Boule-vard, and she promptly ducked back two streets into the residential district. This was familiar territory to her be-cause she lived here. After cruising for ten blocks or so, she turned back onto MLK and, seeing no signs of the double rectangle headlamps, continued on the road until she once more reached the entry to the Broadway Bridge. She took the bridge onto I-5 south to the Terwilliger exit, ensuring that the other car would lose her. This particular exit had extremely misleading street signs. Everyone moving to Portland from out of state had to spend two or three hours being hopelessly befuddled while following the sign that said south when it took you back north to Portland.

Then she wound her way up the back streets to Hospital Hill, where the University Hospital and the Veteran's Hospital were joined by a skywalk. Pulling into the underground parking at the VA Hospital, she turned off her lights and cut the engine.

"Eating can wait," she told her friend. "Before we get interrupted by your keepers, please explain why you talk about yourself in the plural. It makes me want to get you one of those T-shirts that says, 'I'm schizophrenic and so am I.' You are not, to the best of my knowledge, an editor, royalty, or a head of state, so what gives?"

"You must keep an open mind, Leda," the passenger said, looking rather small, frail, and worried.

"I'm listening," Leda said as patiently as possible.

"As we told you, though this body originally belonged only to Tsering Jetson, it now contains the personalities and memories of both of us: Tsering and Chime."

Leda stared hard in the darkness at Chime's uncertain, diffident smile on Tsering's rather thin mouth. "Okay," she said cautiously. "How did that happen? Where's the rest of Chime?"

"She died, Leda. Or at least, her body died. And when she died, Tsering almost died, too; both of us nearly ceased to be. Tsering would neither eat nor sleep, did nothing but work, until Chime came to him in a dream and showed him how our research could be combined into a process that would allow him to use her DNA to incorporate her genetic and cellular memory—which is far more extensive than formerly supposed—into his own. Since our blending, we have become a new person, Chimera, and are the result of the first trial of this process. As you can see, it was successful."

"If you say so," Leda replied after drawing a couple of long, slow breaths. "I mean, it does seem that your two hearts now beat as one, but other than that, how far does it go, this cellular memory? And how did you—well, transfer—or transplant it? I've heard of organ transplants where the recipient starts having the same vices or food cravings as the donor, but what you're talking about sounds a lot deeper than that kind of thing."

"Oh, yes. It is. In us it is as if Chime's soul has joined Tsering's in a perfect blending of the two of us. We have been very happy ever since our blending. But of course, we were very happy and very close before Chime's death. And we knew each other well, were always in each other's thoughts, could sometimes read each other's minds. Therefore, the transition has been uncommonly smooth and peaceful. Others have not achieved quite the same union, although most have been successful."

"What others? You mean, you didn't just do this to yourself? You've . . . uh . . . already blended others? Did I miss *60 Minutes* the day they aired that episode?"

"Those wishing to undergo the process are sworn to secrecy. Even those we told about it initially were."

"Good advertising strategy. Nothing to get the word spread like telling everybody to keep their mouth shut. And if it's such a big secret, why are you evading your security and telling me?"

"We need help, and we feel that you are the one from whom we should seek it."

"I'm flattered, but it's been a long time since we've seen each other. What made you think of me after all these years?"

"Your interest in Egypt, of course. What we need you to do is represent the company's scientific interests in Alexandria."

Leda nearly hit the roof of her car. "Really? But . . . don't you need an expert?"

"You are already an expert in DNA extraction and fingerprinting. These are main professional skills we require.

What we need even more is someone we can trust. We have never had many friends besides each other, Leda. You were one of the few people in whom Chime confided, and until our blending, Tsering knew nothing of the confidences Chime shared with you. For his part, Tsering was very pleased at your absolute secrecy concerning Chime's surprise birthday party when we were all at university—"

"So it wasn't my high security clearance that told you I could keep my mouth shut?" Leda asked.

Chimera laughed. Now that she knew what the story was with Chimera, Leda felt more comfortable with . . . them.

"That your government apparently trusted you with sensitive information was, of course, another mark of your good character."

"That's right. It's my good character and patriotism. Had nothing to do with the threat of being thrown in prison or being shot for a traitor if I blabbed."

Chimera didn't respond to her feeble joke, just sat looking at her expectantly.

"Okay, so I'm a good egg, and I know how to do DNA ID, and I love Egyptology. You still haven't told me what you need that requires someone with those qualifications. I mean, I'm not even sure I understand why you want to keep your discovery quiet. It sounds as if it's a pretty monumental breakthrough, something that could make your reputation."

"It could. Providing we are able to cope with the publicity, with the ethical objections of fellow scientists who would demand to see our research and deem our process risky. And in the United States at least, we might face prosecution for trying the process on human subjects."

"Oh," Leda said. "That. Yeah. Well, I guess I see your point when you put it that way. I guess I knew that but . . . well . . . the other risky experiments I've been involved with have all been government sponsored, so of course if they screw up, nobody knew anything, and it didn't happen. And of course, I never mentioned anything about it either."

Chimera smiled. "Of course not. In addition to all of those objections, there is the fact that we do not wholly own our process any longer. In order to develop it, we needed further funding, and this could only be acquired from a large company. Fortunately, our old friend Wilhelm Wolfe has been CEO of Nucore and its affiliates for some time. Wilhelm, when he understood what we intended to do, had the vision to back us and in exchange has engaged our participation in the dissemination of the process to others who wish it. We have discussed the ethical considerations of the process exhaustively with Wilhelm, and he is in complete accord with our wishes regarding it. Each applicant for the blending is usually screened by both of us. If either the applicant or the donor material they wish is inappropriate, we will not perform the procedure."

"You mean, like if they wanted to blend with Hitler or Vlad Dracul or someone evil like that?" Leda asked.

"Exactly."

"And these disappointed clients don't rat on you?"

"Not so far. Wilhelm has been able to exercise certain controls through social and economic contacts. Besides, those who wish such inappropriate blendings would perhaps not wish it known to their peers what they had in mind."

"Okay, I can see that. Sounds pretty much like you're going to get discovered sooner or later though."

"Later will be better. Currently, Nucore is engaged in obtaining a wide spectrum of samples of genetic material from historical and celebrated figures who would make desirable donors. In some countries, such as Egypt for instance, the government would undoubtedly disapprove of the ultimate use of the samples if they knew about the process."

"Undoubtedly," Leda had to agree. The present Egyptian government was religiously fundamentalist Islamic, though economically somewhat more pragmatic than some of the other fundamentalist Islamic countries. "So, I still need to know: Why are you telling me all this in secret, and what do you need me for? I would assume with Wolfie's backing, you could have your pick."

"We thought we had made it clear, old friend. We do have our pick, and we pick you." Chimera smiled and actually patted her hand where it rested on the steering wheel. The touch felt familiar and friendly, the hand reassuringly warm. Leda almost expected something ghostly, chill, and ethereal. "Besides, we cannot involve Wilhelm. What we wish you to help us with is something we need to keep a secret from him—at least temporarily."

"But if he's your sponsor, is that legal?"

"Oh yes. We are not planning to cheat anyone. It is simply that this is a personal matter," Chimera said. "We are hoping that the cofferdam Nucore has sponsored across the eastern harbor of Alexandria may yield identifiable remains of Cleopatra the seventh. Gretchen Wolfe has asked to be the first subject to blend with that lady, if a sample becomes available."

"Gretchen? As Cleo-frigging-patra?" Gretchen Wolfe, even in her premed days, had been as unassuming, conservative, and even mousy as her boyfriend Wilhelm was dynamic and magnetic. The contrast, and Gretchen's obvious adoration of Wilhelm, made the rather too-earnest young woman touching and likable.

Chimera nodded, and Leda gave a low whistle, "Well, if she's Cleopatra material, then I'll be the Queen of Sheba!"

Chimera heaved a slightly put-upon sigh and asked, "Which one? Of course, we do not yet have the genetic material from any former queens of Sheba, and it is somewhat beyond the normal range of salary for such assignments as the one we wish you to accept; however, special compensations are not out of the question."

"Chime—Tsering—I mean, Chimera, please. I'm *kidding*. It's a figure of speech, okay? Geeez, I keep forgetting you guys were brought up in Tibet and India. Don't take me so literally."

"We're relieved to hear it."

"It's just that it's kind of a stretch. Gretchen Wolfe to the queen of the Nile, I mean."

"In our experience, that is the point of the blending for most recipients. They wish to become augmented, to supply, through the attributes of the donors, those qualities they feel they lack. In Gretchen's case, she and Wilhelm have become estranged over the last few years, as he travels with the company and she maintains her medical practice. She feels that the ancient queen possesses certain feminine qualities she lacks, and she wishes to use these to hold Wilhelm's attention. But she does not wish Wilhelm to know until afterward. She came directly to us, as a friend. We come directly to you on her behalf and on ours, for the reasons we have already mentioned. You can see now perhaps why we need someone we can trust implicitly to work with us directly if the sample becomes available?"

"I guess you also need someone who knows you—and Wolfie and Gretchen—well enough to trust that you aren't setting me up to commit industrial espionage. Not that I'm sure why that would be to your benefit. But you see the trust needs to go more than one way."

Chimera nodded gravely. "Indeed. As for your qualifications, the line of work in which you've been engaged is the perfect background for learning our process. We will personally instruct you in the next stage of the procedure. The work is well paid, and you will be able to be a part of the large operation ongoing in Alexandria. Besides Cleopatra, Nucore is interested in the remains of Alexander the

Great, Mark Antony, and the many scholars who lived and died in that city. The company can see to it that you are provided with a great deal of corroborative material—samples from relatives whose grave sites are known, for instance. Anything else you think you will need, we will try to provide for you. But you will be working essentially alone and will be isolated in your purpose.

"Thus far, the findings from the site have been architectural rather than anthropological. But if and when the sort of material we desire is uncovered, you must take charge of it personally and conduct all necessary tests. What do you think?"

"Hmmm. Will Wolfie know you hired me?"

"Oh, yes. In fact, we have already discussed the possiblity with him, and he authorized the background check that is a prerequisite of employment. But he seemed pleased that you might join us. Since the assignment calls for only one person, it is good that person will be someone as experienced and discreet as we know you to be. We simply wished to have our own private discussion with you regarding Gretchen's desired blending. All donor material other than the small amount required for her needs should naturally go through the usual process."

"Fair enough," Leda had agreed. The rain still fell beyond the entry to the garage, a glistening beaded curtain crackling as it hit the pavement. Now, occasionally, the dark drops were silvered with the beams of headlamps, as a vehicle drove into the garage. Each time, she apprehensively checked the rearview mirror. No double rectangles. It was almost ten-thirty and the eleven-to-seven shift was just arriving. "I guess we shook our tail. You still hungry?"

Chimera nodded, and Leda headed for the all-night breakfast place where she and her dad sometimes met when he was in town. While they were at breakfast, she thought of one more thing she wanted.

"Look, I would feel better about this situation if I could

have the backup I needed. You say I'll be alone, and I don't much like that kind of odds *so* . . ."

Chimera's slightly raised brows were the only indication of concern about the further qualifications.

"Don't worry. No queens this time. But as you may know, my dad is a semiretired cop. I'd like it if your company would hire him to do security for the job we were talking about."

"Do you think he would?"

She nodded thoughtfully while chewing a bite of pecan waffle. "Yeah. I think so. Laney—that's wife number five—has invited her mom to come and visit, and Daddy can't stand her. The mother-in-law, I mean. Besides, he's been looking a little lumpy and peaked lately. I think he needs a change of climate. Daddy isn't the kind of guy who should get in a rut, and he hasn't changed wives or bought a new bike in over a year. Being bored makes him feel old."

Chimera smiled. "How old is your father now, Leda?"

"Oh, he's only seventy-two. How about it?"

"If he agrees and can pass the company physical, we don't see why not. You can travel together that way. We will speak to Wilhelm."

CHAPTER 2

Duke Hubbard had been in law enforcement since the tender age of fifty, when he finally decided he was getting too old for motorcycle racing and stunt work and needed to settle down. But training for the Nucore security force was like undergoing immigration to a foreign country.

In fact, Nucore and several other of the international conglomerates of similar hugeness and diversity of interests enjoyed much the same international status as a separate country plus some additional perks. It was the security force's job not just to protect the company property but to protect its prerogatives as well.

He was surprised to learn that company security, not customs or immigration in the countries where Nucore had large operations, was in charge of inspecting who and what came into and left the facility in each country. Since Nucore had what amounted to its own private air force, with aircraft flying under the insignia of its various subsidiary holdings, and had in most cases built as many airstrips and roads to supply its own needs as the average army, the arrangement made sense.

All of this he learned in the rookie class in the brand-new Nucore facility outside La Grande. He and Leda were staying with her scientist buddy, Chimera. It was a relief to return to the house, kick back, and have a beer. Leda bought the good stuff. Part of the pleasure of the beer was hearing her yell every time she found another one missing. It was one of their little family games.

She spent a lot of time with Chimera down in the lab, leaving Duke time to read all of the homework for his rookie class. A bunch of it consisted of learning about electronic doohickeys, alarm systems, and security devices that the company employed to guard its premises. Procedural manuals, that kinda thing. He'd be glad when they got to the part about apprehending, knocking down, and cuffing somebody.

The first week or so he was in the class, the younger guys all looked at him like they thought he was some supervisor auditing the class or was getting ready to be an instructor or something. When they realized he was just taking the course along with the rest of them, they acted like he was some pimple-faced kid who'd been held back twenty grades or so. The instructor, a beefy young guy about ten years younger than Leda, called him Pops a lot. Duke was used to that. As usual, the boys who thought they knew everything weren't even in the loop. He knew what this mission of Leda's was all about, and why her old man was the only one she was willing to trust to watch her back. It sounded far fetched to him—Cleopatra, for pity's sake! But it was important to Leda, to Chimera, and apparently to Wolfe's wife, though he wasn't supposed to know that part. It was the clencher for him though. Any lady who would go to that kind of extremes to make herself sexier for her man was alright with him.

So what the other security cops thought of the rookie was their mistake. He was used to smart-ass younger guys being cocky little shits who thought he'd slow them down.

And, to give them credit, they *were* faster with the computerized surveillance equipment used to monitor the Nucore campus.

Duke thought that stuff just caused the troops to relax their vigilance, but he kept his mouth shut and paid attention. He was relieved when the class was over, and Leda and he transferred, along with Chimera, to the Nucore facility on the isolated Greek island of Kefalos, which was the staging area for the Alexandria project.

The island had once been owned by what the Kid referred to as a "shipping maggot" whose taste for privacy matched Nucore's security requirements. Outwardly, the island seemed much like other Greek islands. The postcard village of white, square houses with red roofs staggered along the beach and clung to the side of the hill that was the highest place on the island. The hill was actually the top of an ancient volcano, and ringing the rim were the ruins of an old Knights Templar citadel, a monastery, and the former owner's mansion and shipping offices. Olive trees twisted toward the sky, turquoise waters lapped white, sandy beaches, and the little birds sang from the clotheslines, tra la. Some of the islanders who had worked for the shipping magnate now worked for Nucore instead and stayed as they always had in some of the red-roofed houses. The other houses had been renovated and sheltered other Nucore technicians and employees as well as a few middle-management types. There was even a vineyard or two, which Duke found a redeeming feature.

Here on Kefalos, the security classes were more specific. The chief of security was one Theophilus Agelakos. Agelakos took the attitude that Duke was cute. "So, you go along to Egypt with your daughter, eh? Her poppa make sure she is not carried off to the tent of some pasha."

"Nah, I just want to make sure I get enough camels for her," Duke said, trying to laugh it off. "And be there to . . . uh . . . take her back when the pasha finds out what he's got himself into."

"Very amusing!" Agelakos said. "No need to explain. We understand family here."

Duke had a certain understanding of it, too, from criminal elements he had contact with in Portland, but he didn't want to wreck his amusing-old-duffer image by mentioning it.

"This is maybe not a job for a man such as yourself," Agelakos said. "In Egypt it is not protected as we are here. We have not the alarm systems to guard the company holdings. Much is in the open, on the water, and along the dam."

"Dam?"

"Oh yes, the company has built for the Egyptian government a great cofferdam that has completely emptied the harbor and some of the area beyond."

"Why?" Duke asked.

"Because the government, with the help of Nucore's money, hopes to uncover, raise, and reconstruct above sea level the most important structures of the ancient city: the lighthouse of Pharos, the palace of Cleopatra, perhaps the ruins of the Egyptian Navy and the Great Library's storehouse, continuing the work of the underwater archaeology teams of the late twentieth century. It will be like your American Disney parks—visit Ancient Alexandria in all its glory—a magnificent tourist attraction, you see. A *new* ancient tourist attraction people have not grown accustomed to. This should help bring in the . . ." Agelakos rubbed thumb and first two fingers together meaningfully. "Money, which can then be used, as the company hopes, to repay us. Of course, our corporation also has other more immediate interests in this project, which it will be your duty to protect."

Duke nodded.

Agelakos picked up a stack of DVDs and signaled for Duke to follow him. He opened the door and gave a theatrical bow, bending the creases ironed into his uniform sleeves in the process. The room he'd led Duke to was an office with little more than a desk containing a computer and a chair. "Please be seated," the Greek said with a flourish. "These are English-language newscasts of recent events in Egypt over the last few years, so that you will understand more about the attitudes of some of the people you will be working with and some of the factions who take an unenlightened view of the work you will be protecting. Please study these carefully, and if you have any questions, you may click here." He indicated an icon at the bottom of the screen. "The company expert on Egypt will be available on-line to answer."

This seemed to Duke like one of the smartest things that had been done in this whole Mickey Mouse training course. Leda knew a lot of stuff about Egypt, but most of it was no more recent than a couple of thousand years ago, except for all the scuttlebutt about the archaeologists in the nineteenth century.

Seemed to Duke, during the history part of his lesson, as if no conquerer or invader since Julius Caesar had bothered to kiss poor old Egypt before it screwed her. In fact, the whole thing had been pretty much of a gang bang after the Romans left. Everybody had had a piece of the country at one time or another. Romans, Greeks, Arabs, the French with Napoleon, the English, the Germans—everybody but Quinn the Eskimo had claimed the Nile.

Duke found all of this pretty interesting. After all, if Nucore had more or less the status of an independent state within a country, and he was supposed to be part of a force that represented the customs, immigrations, army, navy, air and police force, it behooved him to know what he was dealing with.

And who. There was the current government, which tended toward fundamentalist Islam, but it was being opposed on several fronts. There was the CCM, Coptic Christian Movement (the Coptic Christian Church claimed it

had no connections with the movement), large and pre-
dominantly black from the southern part of Egypt, where
people were still angry over the flooding of Nubia by the
Aswan Dam over a century before. And there was a pha-
ronic wanna-be group of people who thought the ancient
Egyptians had the right idea and wanted to take the country
back and run it like King Tut or someone. Then there were
the neighbors—Syria, Libya, Turkey—all of them promising all kinds of assistance in exchange for a military toe-
hold in Egypt. So far, the government was smart enough to
see through that one. Then there was the West—Western
Europe and the U.S.—and their economic interests, including Nucore's. That was pretty complicated.

Still digesting the information when the training session
was finished, Duke took the lift to the top floor of the security complex. The main part was inside the crater, accessed
through the ruins of the old Knights Templar citadel.
Someone had a sense of humor. Chimera's villa was down
the road from the mansion and shipping offices where the
lab was located. It was still on the top tier of the wedding
cake shape formed by the volcano cone with its layers of
red-roofed white houses. One of the larger guest houses for
the people who lived in the mansion, Duke supposed, the
villa had a private lab for Chimera built into it. Leda and
her old buddy spent a lot of their time holed up down there,
while Chimera showed the Kid the double-helixed ropes to
his process.

By now, Duke pretty well understood what Chimera's
process was all about, but he wasn't very interested. Why
the hell would anybody want someone else's excess bag-
gage in the way of memories, anyway? He didn't even
want all of his own, most of the time, especially the ones
involving the ex-wives. He sure as hell didn't want someone else to climb inside his skull with him and snuggle up
and yap all the time where he couldn't keep them quiet
when he preferred to be alone. And he had a lot of thoughts

he didn't care to share with anyone. Jesus, the things rich people thought of to keep themselves entertained!

Fortunately, nobody was asking him to participate in the process, just to protect it, which he would do because it was kind of interesting and also, he could keep an eye on the Kid. This was a big break for her. He had never had or married enough money to be able to send her or the other kids off to fancy schools, and of all of them, Leda would have enjoyed that the most. She had to get her education through the Navy, and she did all right. She'd been working with the state lab since she got out. But this kind of thing was what she'd always wanted to do, and he was glad she wanted him along to help her. Of all his offspring, Leda was the one who took after him the most, poor baby.

Hiking down the road in the heat, Duke mopped the sweat off his face with both hands and flapped his loosened shirttails to give his belly a little breeze. He looked forward to one of the imported beers in Chimera's fridge. He was mentally tasting it, feeling it pouring cool and smooth down his throat, when he heard the roar bearing down on him from behind. He jumped aside barely in time to escape being run down. He got up, dusted himself off, and stared down the road at the oddest-looking machine he had seen in a long time. He fell instantly and totally in love and forgot all about the beer. He had to have that bike.

↲CHAPTER 3

About three days after they arrived on Kefalos, Chimera received a phone call at the villa. Leda was dutifully staring into a microscope, though the truth was she was still so jet-lagged she had trouble seeing color until she finished her third cup of coffee.

Chimera, chipper as ever, said into the phone, "Oh, yes, she is right here. Do you want to speak to her? Oh, yes, that would be much better! We will see you soon."

"Let me guess," Leda said. "Was that Wolfie maybe?"

"Yes! He is here to speak to a couple of the board members who wish a blending. One will be arriving soon, and he wishes you to sit in on the interview."

That sounded good to Leda. What kind of a nut, other than most of her friends, would volunteer to be possessed by the soul of some long-dead person who had probably never been all they were cracked up to be to begin with?

Leda tried to look halfway respectable, since they were meeting a member of the board. She put on a clean print skirt and plain T-shirt, and a beaded necklace and matching earrings, each adorned with an eye of Horus, a friend had made for her. Then she and Chimera tootled up the hill to the main offices and lab in a cute little corporate golf cart–esque three-wheeler.

Thinking again of her friends, she asked Chimera, "What do you do if everybody wants to be the same person? I know at least three candidates for Mary, Queen of Scots, two for Elizabeth the First, and you wouldn't believe the number of nutcases who would really like to be Anne Boleyn or Henry the Eighth. And it's a darn good thing for you guys King Arthur, Guinevere, Lancelot, and especially Morgan Le Fey and Merlin were more or less fictional, or you'd need graveyard loads of them to fill the demand from the Society for Creative Anachronism alone."

Chimera considered this a reasonable question and didn't even crack a smile. "First, this is still a very expensive procedure, you understand, Leda. While we obtain as much sample material as we can from each source, often our access is very limited. We were able to obtain a small sample of tissue from Sir Walter Scott, for instance, but we certainly did not wish to desecrate his remains. Sometimes our samples are not taken directly from the body at all but are hair, ancient blood, even dandruff from clothing and so forth. The best samples are from teeth, as you know. But we can obtain more of what we want from what would be considered inferior samples by others who lack our equipment and methods. Even so, it is very expensive."

"So that alone prevents duplicates?"

"No, but of course the first host to request a specific donor, providing the host was suitable, would be blended. Later we may consider blending donors with different hosts. The host personality is not submerged in that of the donor, as we've discussed, but eventually combines to form a new whole, if seldom with the harmony we do. So two blendings from a single donor would not produce two identical blended personalities."

"I suppose not. But what if what each of the hosts wanted from the donor was something very specific . . . like, oh, an exclusive on the secret of whether or not Richard the Third did in the little princes, or the location of buried treasure, say?"

"We would discourage a blending for such reasons, to begin with. A blending is, so far as we now know, a life-long commitment rather than a temporary means to an immediate goal."

"Makes sense to me," she said.

Leaving the cart outside the mansion, they stepped into the great receiving hall. Leda wanted to stop and go, "Ooh, ah," but Chimera led her quickly through to a courtyard/garden, where Wolfe, older, more distinguished and prosperous looking, but still pretty darn cute, sat at a table near a fountain of Aphrodite. He sipped something icy and brown while he spoke with two women.

The older one had a body that, although trim and with as erect a carriage as possible, suffered nonetheless from the crippling effects of arthritis. Her hair was artfully auburn with little wings of silver at the sides where it swept up into a sleek chignon. Her skin was taut, though there were small wrinkles at her mouth and above the bridge of her nose, not quite hidden by her sunglasses, that could only be from pain. Her profile, however, with its Roman nose and square jawline, was formidable. She wore white slacks, an oversized white shirt with the sleeves buttoned to the gold coin bracelets at her wrists, a coral tank top, and a coral, white, and pale aqua scarf swathed her neck. Good brown leather sandals, sturdy and serviceable and at the same time of a graceful, somewhat antique style, allowed her pedicure to show. No coral toenail polish. Class!

The younger woman with her was quite a contrast. Curling dark masses of hair with as much vitality as Medusa's snakes tried to escape the hot pink scrunchie elastic inadequately restraining it. Sunglasses here, too, but the tan was dark, though darker on her hands and forearms, face and neck, than on her chest, elbows, and upper arms. Long legs with dark hairs poured out of khaki shorts, the legs darker at the ankles and feet. She wore rubber sandals with velcro closings, the same kind Leda had. When she sat up and waved as Wolfe greeted Chimera and Leda, her T-shirt revealed the image of Marvin the Martian, Leda's favorite cartoon character, blazoned on its front.

Wolfe stood. "Allow me to present the Contessa Virginie Athene Dumont and her niece, Dr. Gabriella Faruk. Contessa, Dr. Chimera and our mutual friend, Dr. Leda Hubbard."

The contessa's hand should have been dry and cool to go with the rest of her appearance, but it was hard to have anything other than a sweaty paw in such weather, and hers was unexceptional in that regard, except that it was a sweaty paw with rather pronounced knuckles and one gold ring.

Her nod was the cool thing about her. But her niece made up for that with a frank, open grin. Leda answered in kind.

"And who will be joining you, Contessa?" Chimera asked.

"Pandora Blades," she said.

"Why is it that you wish to blend with that lady?" This seemed to be Chimera's brand of small talk in these situations. Leda thought it much more interesting than the usual social babble.

"That should be clear enough," Gabriella Faruk said with an undignified giggle and a light prod to her aunt's snowily clad arm. "She'll finally have all of the talent money can buy! Pandora was, until her murder, one of the finest painters and poets modern Greece has ever produced."

Her aunt allowed a tiny smile to play around her mouth and made a harumphing noise. "Please do not get the wrong impression of my niece, Dr. Chimera, Dr. Hubbard.

She is actually far brighter and more useful than her flip-
pant attitude might lead you to believe. I would hate it if
you barred her from attending me because you feared she
would find some way to turn it into a joke. But to answer
your question, in part Gabriella is correct. I wish to blend
with Pandora Blades because her death truncated what I
believe could be an even more splendid volume of work
than that already produced. I would be thrilled to be a vessel for it. As you may know, Pandora was in constant pain
from the deformities she suffered from polio in childhood
and later, as the result of the terrible accident that impaled
her. My own pain and slight deformity will not, therefore,
be daunting to her. Also, we are of an age, so she may feel
that she is starting where she stopped before. However,
once we blend, she will have far greater financial resources, enabling her to travel, to seek out like minds. She
will be able to devote most of her time to her work without
worrying who will support her or how she is to live."

Gabriella spontaneously squeezed her aunt's hand and
grinned. "Isn't she wonderful? Really? Who else has used
your process to prolong the life of a cultural heroine and
provide for her rather than to elevate their own status? Pandora Blades will not only have a good home with Ginia,
she will also have the companionship of every stray cat and
dog fortunate enough to find their way to Dilos."

Leda listened, slightly bemused, while her mind was
grappling with the niece's very familiar name. Where had
she heard of Gabriella Faruk before? Not here, not as the
niece of a rich aunt. The interior of Powell's City of Books
in Portland, with its rabbit warren of rooms filled with
books old and new—the myth and folklore section, Egyptian, the—

"*The* Gabriella Faruk?" Leda found herself asking with
a squeal of fannish glee. "Author of *The Changing of the
Gods*?" She proceeded to recite the subtitle. *The Metamor-
phosis of the Divine in Egyptian Culture from Ancient*

Times to Present by Dr. Gabriella C. Faruk, followed by a string of distinguished alphabet soup after your name?"

Gabriella's teeth shone white against her tanned skin as her grin broadened. "Guilty of all but the soup. You have read my book then? And you obviously didn't even have it forced upon you by my aunt, since you've just met her."

"Yes, I read it. It was terrific. One of the most insightful books about how Egypt has adapted under the various invaders and their gods, while retaining its essential difference owing to a deep-rooted allegiance to the past. Of course, there was that typo on page 264, but I figured that was the printer's fault."

"Dr. Faruk is also assistant curator at the new Alexandria Museum and on the board of the new library," Wolfe said smoothly.

"Wow," Leda said, "You sound like a good person to know, Dr. Faruk."

"Oh, call me Gabriella, please!" said the young woman—for she *was* a young woman, maybe fifteen years Leda's junior. "I loathe formality. So much is required at home sometimes I cannot wait to get away and kick back. Fascinating as my work can be, some of the people involved in it can be very tiresome."

"That has the ring of a universal truth," Leda agreed, "though I probably shouldn't say so in front of a new employer. Your English is really good and uh . . . it seems kind of American."

"I did my undergraduate degree at UC Berkeley," Gabriella said.

"She was such a nice girl before that," the contessa said with mock mourning, raising her wrist to her forehead like the heroine of a melodrama. "Docile and obedient. Since then, she has been an activist, I believe it's called in America? Here we say *terrorist*."

Gabriella slapped at her aunt's arm, "You mustn't tell all my secrets. And you would be an activist, too, if you still lived in today's Egypt where the fundamentalist Muslims are becoming noisier and noisier and—I beg your pardon, doctors, but I must say it—if one has no penis one is also presumed to have no soul. Now *that* is tiresome."

"Another problem on which I wish to consult with Pandora," the contessa said lightly. "She had a very deep insight into men."

"If you didn't count her husbands," Gabriella said.

Her remark was lost, however, in the general scraping of chairs as Wolfe looked at his watch and gestured to the ladies that the lab would be ready to begin the procedure.

The room where the procedure was to take place looked more like a lady's tropical boudoir. Fresh flowers and tasteful furnishings included a luxurious double bed that lacked a canopy, to Leda's disappointment. The canopies in this part of the world tended to be mosquito nets, and despite its spalike appearance, the room was part of an underground laboratory. Mosquitoes were zapped with electronic bouncers before they could get past the main floor. Netting was unnecessary. Wolfe gestured toward the bed, and the contessa composed herself atop the spread.

Leda didn't see the equipment for the transfer at all until Chimera pushed a button that lifted a panel concealing a computer and what looked like a small magnifying lamp. The panel was right next to the bed, and the device easily extended so that the lens could be fitted to the contessa's face.

"We have streamlined the code transference device, or CTD, from the clumsier ones you perhaps noticed in the labs in Oregon, Leda," Chimera explained.

Wolfe said enthusiastically, "There is even a completely portable one just coming out of production for taking the process into the homes of the clients. Of course, these will be special cases for some time, and the only one who will be authorized to use the new device will be Chimera. But eventually . . ."

"A chicken in every pot?" Leda asked. The idea gave her a tiny chill, even though she knew that wasn't showing the proper team spirit for her new job.

"Only the gold-plated ones," Gabriella whispered to her from behind her hand.

Chimera did the honors, placing the lens of the compact machine over the contessa's eyes and, after a brief fiddle, a computerish beep, and a strobe of light, the device was removed from the contessa's face. The little pieces of adhesive that held her eyelids open were also removed, and without another word, she fell into a deep sleep.

"She wanted me to wait here with her," Gabriella told them. "Any special instructions?"

Chimera smiled. "Only from you to let us know what you would like to eat while your aunt is sleeping. You will find that large chair there converts into quite a comfortable cot. The sleep cycle can be anywhere from thirty-six to seventy-two hours while the blending takes place."

"That long? I didn't know. Perhaps I could borrow something to read?"

"Certainly," Wolfe said. "I'll have someone make a trip to our library for you if you don't wish to leave the room. Dr. Chimera, there is another client due now, and I'd appreciate it if you could attend."

"Me, too?" Leda asked.

Wolfe said quickly, "I don't think that will be necessary."

"Maybe I could go to the library for Dr. Faruk then," Leda said hopefully. She had a thing or two to ask the young scholar about the ideas presented in her book. Besides, Leda liked her. Any fan of Marvin the Martian's was eligible to be a friend of Leda's.

"Perhaps you could prevail upon her to fill you in on the situation in Alexandria also," Chimera suggested.

"You're reading my mind," Leda said.

"And mine!" Gabriella declared. "I would be delighted."

Leda didn't make it to the library before the contessa

awoke. Gabriella was full of amusing stories about Alexandria and the digs and especially about the amazing reclamation project taking place in Alexandria's eastern harbor.

"I don't envy you working with that crew," Gabriella said. "Namid is a pig. An eminent pig, but a pig. And he has chosen other swine to work with him."

"Also eminent?" Leda asked.

"Oh, yes. All of the team leaders are Egyptian, of course, the project being sponsored by the government, though I understand from Virginie that it is Nucore money sponsoring the sponsors, as with so many of the new digs in my country. Without Nucore, the project would have remained one of diving under the water as it was back in the latter part of the 20th century when Jean-Yves Empereur and Franck Goddio were conducting the retrieval of artifacts from the harbor floor. The cofferdam of course enables the study to deepen, layers of interiors to be actually excavated. It would be very exciting if they had found anything new, but so far, they haven't and are still removing the statuary the divers replaced once it had been studied."

"I've heard it's a bit like the military that way—months of boredom with intermittent moments of sheer terror—though I suppose you'd have to substitute excitement for terror in the case of a dig."

"Don't be so sure," Gabriella said. "There have been many politically motivated crimes occurring in other parts of Egypt recently. The dam and the dig are easily accessible from the city. In fact, it's a favorite tourist attraction for local people as well as for actual tourists." She shook her head, the brown curls bouncing and her thick eyebrows drawing together against the nosepiece of her glasses. "Guards are posted, but not enough, I think."

"Not until now, anyway," Leda said. "My dad is going to do security on Nucore's behalf. Archaeologists who worry about the mummy's curse ain't heard nothin' yet. Wait till they hear my daddy's."

Gabriella laughed, and Leda entertained her for a while telling Duke stories about his wives, his bikes, his police work.

Later, watching the contessa sleep, Gabriella asked, "Would you do that yourself?"

"You mean have someone come into my mind like that? I don't think so. I seem to have enough personalities for three people already. Besides, I don't think I could get Daddy to give me away for the occasion. He thinks this is all kind of spooky."

Gabriella shrugged. "It is, really, but fascinating, don't you think? You won't be able to mention any specimen collecting you'll be doing while in Egypt, you understand."

"Oh, no, I've been warned. I hope I can call on you if I have any questions I need to ask without—well, compromising Nucore."

"Certainly."

"So, how about you, would you ever have this done?"

Gabriella's long, spatulate fingers tugged at a tangle of curls.

"Perhaps," she said. "If I thought it would do any good. I mean, you wouldn't undertake such a thing lightly, would you?"

"I wouldn't undertake it at all," Leda said firmly. To herself, she added thoughtfully, *Well, probably not.* As she grew older, she had learned to avoid absolutes. Both women lapsed into silence, Leda wondering who she *would* consider blending with, Gabriella apparently doing the same. Leda thought it was rather like the game of imagining what you would do if you won the lottery. It never occurred to her that her silence might be mistaken for evasiveness.

Chimera was not exactly a chatterbox most of the time, but when Leda returned to the villa, she found the scientist there already, engrossed in lab work. There was a withdrawn quality about her friend she hadn't previously felt. "Hi. How'd it go with the other interview?" she asked.

After a moment, Chimera straightened, took a deep breath, and let it out again. "We hope you will believe us, Leda, when we tell you we came upon our process in a good way, and we intend it for good purposes."

"Well, sure, but then, you can't always control how other people are going to interpret it, what uses they'll want to make of your work."

"True. We are beginning sometimes to feel like Victor Frankenstein. You know, from that movie?"

"Everyone knows that movie," she reassured Chimera. "Why now in particular?"

"Today we had a very important client—other than the countess, who was most delightful, especially by comparison. This was another Nucore board member, however, which was why Wilhelm felt it necessary that we be present."

"Who did this guy want to be? Ceasar? Napoleon? Not Hitler!"

"No, none of those. He probably doesn't consider them worthy to share his mental space. He wanted to use the process in a less usual way. He wished to donate some of his DNA so that his heir could undergo the process."

"Oh, the old 'make me eternally young and beautiful' deal, huh?"

"Pardon?"

"Immortality. You mean this is the first time someone has asked you to do this kind of thing?"

"It doesn't surprise you?"

"Oh, no, I thought all of the egomaniac billionaires would be busting down your doors to do the same thing. They must have been too busy counting their petty cash to have thought of it until just now."

"He brought along several young associates," Chimera

said glumly. "In order that they could attend his interview to hear what he proposed, he paid for all of them to have the process done themselves. Each may choose a donor personality later. It was the arrogance of it all that was so staggering," Chimera said, eyes wide and offended.

"You—both of you—are pretty innocent, in spite of all of the things you've seen through a microscope," Leda told her friend. "What did you tell the guy?"

"No. Of course, no. Wolfe tried to be diplomatic—the man is one of the major shareholders in Nucore—but the process requires a willingness to learn, to grow, to . . . expand. This man clearly wished only to dominate another so that he could prolong his own life and the pursuit of his own desires."

"I guess it works for him," Leda said. "I'm glad you turned him down, though. Sounds like a jerk."

"We worry what will happen when the process becomes better known, when it begins to slip from our immediate control. For what other sorts of perverted purposes will it be used? We are not happy with this, Leda."

"Well, you can comfort yourself that at least so far, governments aren't bidding for it to use for military purposes. Or are they?"

Chimera just groaned and returned to the solace of the microscope.

CHAPTER 4

Alexandria in the afternoon had all of the dubious charm of a Turkish bath, or more accurately, an Egyptian bath. A welcoming committee of heat waves danced up from the runway, enveloping Leda in a sticky embrace as soon as she stepped from the plane. After which she and the pilot spent a strenuous sweaty time unloading large boxes of equipment she would need to set up her lab, the sensitive instruments, the special computer, and her own bags. Then her plane took off again, and she stood sopping in the middle of the runway. The heat was the only thing waving at her. There was no welcoming committee. The airfield was occupied by a solitary helicopter, a mountain of boxes that made the pile she had just unloaded resemble a mere foothill by comparison, and a hangar with a Quonset hut beside it. If there was any ground transportation, she didn't see it.

The people from the site knew she was coming. They knew she'd be bringing lots of stuff. Wolfe had instructed his people to call their people. And yet, nobody. Not a damn soul. She carried her duffel bag to the Quonset hut.

"Hello?" she called, but nobody answered. The computer on the battered metal desk was turned off. She was turning to go, to see if she couldn't find someone to help drag her stuff off the runway, when a door she hadn't noticed in the back of the hut banged open, and a man with hair sticking up in all directions peered out of it like a tortoise from his shell.

"Hi," she said before he could withdraw again. "Are you the guy in charge?"

The man looked at her suspiciously, as if sweaty women didn't come and go from this airport a lot. He could possibly have been Egyptian, he was dark and swarthy, but surely he would understand other languages if he had this job. He continued to look blank as she tried pidgin Arabic, high school French, GI German, and gutter Italian.

"Screw it," she said finally, deciding Nucore must be improving its image by hiring the handicapped, since the man was apparently hearing impaired. Which could actually be an asset, working at an airstrip where, if you weren't somewhat deaf to begin with, the noise of the aircraft engines could wreak enough damage on your eardrums that you soon would be. "I'm calling my dad."

She dialed Duke's cell phone number. He'd been sent here a week earlier, while she received some further instructions from Chimera and Wolfe. A message in three languages told her that her party had traveled beyond the range of his instrument. "Shit," she said. For the benefit of the guy still rubbing his head in the doorway, she added, *"Merde. Alors,"* just for French emphasis.

At that the man shuffled forward. He was barefoot, his shirt untucked from cargo pants with the seat dragging between his thighs.

"You French?" he asked finally in Australian-flavored English. Maybe he was from so far in the Outback he had to think about switching from Bangaroo to People talk. "I thought at first you was a Yank."

"Talk a little louder," she suggested. "If I'm French, I can't understand your question." Then, before he took her seriously, she said, "*Yes,* I am a Yank. My name is Leda Hubbard, and I brought a whole bunch of important and very expensive equipment to work with the crew excavating the harbor basin. Do they have like, a headquarters or anything? I was told they knew I was coming, and someone would be here to meet me."

"Nobody mentioned anything to me," the man said.

"The guy in charge is a Dr. Namid," she told him. "Could you call him, please?"

"Oh, sure," the man said, glad she had asked for someone he'd actually heard of. Then his blank expression turned to one of anxiety. "He won't like it, though. Hates being interrupted. And it's nap time, you know. Nobody'll be working at this hour."

"Oh, right, siesta," she said, remembering belatedly what sensible local people did about the heat that was melting her like the Wicked Witch of the West. "Well, I'm not a mad dog *or* an Englishman. I'm an extremely over-heated German/Blackfoot Indian with a soupçon of Romanian Gypsy, and I want to get out of the hot sun and take a nap as much as the next person. So I guess Dr. Namid will just have to be unhappy as long as he sends someone to get me and several million bucks' worth of equipment baking on the runway."

"Okay, okay, sit down, lady. Your face is red." He fished out a Coke from a cooler under the desk. "Here. Chill." The accent *was* Aussie, she decided. She used to know one of those. Well, Kiwi, actually.

He dialed a number and quickly handed her the phone, "Namid," said a gruff, impatient voice on the other end of the line.

"Dr. Namid, I'm Leda Hubbard, the forensic anthropologist assigned to your project on behalf of Nucore?"

"I have informed Nucore we have no need of another physical anthropologist. Now, if you will excuse me—"

Leda took a deep breath to keep herself from saying things like, "Look here, you horse's ass," and instead said, "I'd be happy to, but I have myself and some equipment to bring to the dig from the airstrip and no transport, sir."

"If you can get ahold of me, surely it is within your capabilities to call a taxi, Miss Hubbard?" he said, and hung up.

"Damn!" she said and the swarthy Aussie smirked.

"Trouble?" he asked.

"Only for him," she said. "Later." Another idea had occurred to her. She dug in her duffel-sized purse for her full-sized address book and shuffled through cards until she found the one from Gabriella. Yes! There it was. And according to the dates the good Dr. Faruk had so considerately inscribed upon the card, she should be in Alexandria and perhaps even reachable by phone, though that eventuality seemed remote, considering Leda's recent luck.

The man opened his mouth to protest. His name tag said Byrne. Didn't sound awfully exotic.

"I'm not busted. I get more than one phone call, right?" Leda asked, not much caring what he thought.

And wonder of wonders, a voice spoke unto her from the other end of the telephone line. "Dr. Faruk speaking," it—she—said.

"Gabriella! It's Leda Hubbard! This eagle has just landed and is stranded. Dad isn't answering his cell phone, and Dr. Namid told me to take a cab. I'm here with two tons of very valuable stuff, and I don't know how the hell to get it there. It's too much for me to move from the airstrip out of the path of passing planes, much less tuck into a cab. Also, I'm in meltdown. Help!"

"Didn't I tell you the man is a swine?" Gabriella asked.

"You poor dear. Hold on, my friend. I will get a taxi and some muscular people and come to your aid at once."

"I will be the grease puddle in front of the desk at the Quonset hut."

"Ciao," Gabriella said and rang off.

Leda was already distracted. Looking up, she saw more evidence of lack of consideration for her tender self. "Hey, Byrne, is that a fan I see up there? Or is it a sculpture? Why is it standing still instead of going round and round, making me cooler?"

Byrne opened his mouth, shut it again, and pulled on the fan cord. The air wasn't cool, but it was different hot air than had been on her before. She was about to sit on the floor and weep for a moment when Byrne gallantly shoved a metal folding chair hot enough to barbeque a pig toward her. He might make old bones after all. She reached into her purse for her sweater (what had she been thinking about bringing *that*) and draped the wrap over the chair. She was wearing pants instead of shorts, fortunately, so she could sit.

To her pleasure and amazement, it was barely twenty minutes before a latter-day caravan arrived, with Duke on the renovated Sopwith riding point, followed by Gabriella in a capacious taxi-van, bringing with her three young men, all Egyptian-looking. For good measure, the van was followed by two donkey carts. Leda, having broadened her cultural horizons while visiting foreign lands in the Navy, didn't bat an eyelash at the donkey carts.

"You poor thing," Gabriella said to Leda, while Leda's Dad gave her a brief wave. Sometimes they were into hugging but not when it was this damned hot.

"Where is your cargo?" Gabriella asked.

"Out there on the so-called tarmac, waiting for things with wings and rotors to run over them," Leda replied.

Duke heard this, and before the young men could react, he had lifted the largest of the boxes and carried it on his shoulder like some sort of golden years native bearer. The young men, not to be outdone, freed the runway of obstuctive, expensive debris in one trip with each of the lads carrying as much as he could. Most of it fit into the taxi and the front quarter of one of the donkey carts. The other donkey cart driver, with great dignity, removed one of the boxes from the front cart and carried it back to his.

None of these people even seemed to be sweating, and in fact, Gabriella was wearing a long-sleeved blouse over a crew neck red T-shirt and a full skirt and sandals.

It wasn't fair.

"Where did you find Dad?" Leda asked Gabriella. "Or did he just happen to hear I had arrived when you did?"

"Oh, no, he actually was in the library when you called."

"Don't tell me he's getting into Egyptology."

"No, hydrology, actually. He's become great friends with the contractor who maintains the cofferdam and wanted to read up on the Aswan project. Also," she said after a bit of a pause, "I think he comes to flirt with me."

"You're female. Of course he comes to flirt with you. But don't worry, you're not his type. Well, not his serious type. You have to be a bookkeeper or an accountant to be eligible to be Mrs. Daddy."

"Really?"

"Yep, all of his wives have been."

When Duke approached, wiping the sweat from his face, Leda asked him, "Do you know where my lab is, Daddy? We'll need to park this stuff once we get there."

"Lab?" He scratched his head. "Namid's people have this place where they wash the artifacts and date them and so forth but—"

"Nah, that's not it. I mean my lab. The Nucore lab. I'm supposed to work it alone. Never mind, I'll give Wolfie's people a call. I don't feel like asking Namid for so much as a cup of sugar." She punched in numbers with the pads of her fingers, avoiding contact between the keys and her unusually long, strong fingernails, now devoid of purple polish. After having her call shuttled through three offices and back again, she had an answer of sorts.

When Duke wandered back, he wore a bemused expression.

Gabriella, having supervised the loading of the taxi, strode back toward them, too.

"It's a beluga," Leda told both of them.

"Whale or caviar?" Gabriella asked.

"Neither. Big white fluffy building that looks like you inflate it with a bicycle pump, but allows for extreme temperature control inside. It's on the mainland, at the base of the Heptastadion," Leda said, referring to the land bridge that connected the Isle of Pharos to the rest of Alexandria and separated the city's eastern harbor from the western one. The eastern harbor had been largely man-made, dug in ancient times from the floor of the Mediterranean to serve as a royal harbor.

A three-story lighthouse that had been one of the wonders of the world had once occupied the Isle of Pharos (oddly enough, the lighthouse had been called the Pharos Lighthouse). Its light supposedly had been visible thirty miles out to sea.

The earthquakes that claimed the royal palaces of the Ptolemys, formerly situated on the opposite side of the harbor from Pharos, had also destroyed the lighthouse. The island's most arresting feature these days was a stockade-type building, a little crenellated and castlefied, called Fort Quait Bay. The western harbor was mostly used by the Egyptian Navy and its teeny submarine fleet. This Leda knew from the boning up she had been doing since Chimera offered her the job.

"I have never seen such a structure at that place,"

Gabriella said, "and I go past the Heptastadion and onto the island rather frequently to check the progress of the dig."

"That's because it's not there," Duke said. "And the reason it's not there, before you ask, is because it's right there instead." He jerked a thumb at the box mountain still rising majestically over the runway.

Leda groaned.

"It's okay, Leda," Gabriella said. "I can't believe no one was told to erect your building before you arrived. I can have Mo and his bros help if you like," she said, indicating the muscular young things who were actually her cousins, Mohammed, and his younger brothers Ali and Sami. Casting a doubtful eye on the mountain of crates, she continued, "If it is a portable building, it cannot be too difficult to set up, surely?"

"I don't think it will be any sweat," Duke said. "I'm pretty friendly with the guy who runs the cofferdam maintenance. He's a hydrology engineer. We can figure out how to put the damned thing together between us. And most of it will load onto the donkey carts now."

"Well, yeah, but I hate to check all this valuable stuff I have with me into a hotel," Leda said. "For one thing, I'd practically have to get a separate room just for it. And something tells me it might get lost or damaged if I left it with Namid. I really don't like that guy."

"I'll put one of my men on it," Duke said. "I'm gonna have to call, anyway. We could use a real truck or maybe another couple of donkey carts, too, to load that beluga up. Once we get it to your site, I'll have my boys guard it till we can put it together. I've got a great crew. It'll be safe with them."

"Thanks, Daddy."

"Until your laboratory is in place and you start work, you must come and stay at my home," Gabriella said enthusiastically. "We will have such fun. I can show you the

city and the other sites, and you can meet my family. And
your equipment will be perfectly safe there, too. Come, we
will get you settled. Duke, you must come to dinner this
evening. Perhaps your friend, the hydrologist, would like
to come, too?"

"Sure, it'd be better than having couscous takeout
again," Duke said. "That's what we usually do at the security barracks."

"Oh, no, our chef cooks Mediterranean dishes I am sure
you will like: a blend of Greek, Italian, French, and Middle
Eastern cooking. Quite tasty."

He nodded.

"I will take Leda home and settle her in. We can plan
how to erect the beluga over dinner, okay?"

"Great. I'll call Pete and see if he can organize the rest
of the transport and some men to load this stuff and get it to
the site," Duke said and winked at Gabriella. "If I tell him
we've been invited to dinner with beautiful women, I bet
he'll come up with something."

"Thanks, Daddy," Leda said. "Love you."

"Love you, too, Kid. See you later."

CHAPTER 5

"I have to go to the market now," Gabriella said, when she and her cousins had helped Leda unload her equipment. They lugged the boxes and crates through the modest entrance, a sort of desert version of a mud room, into a nice courtyard so heavily vegetated with flowers and fronds, palms and cedars that it resembled a nursery. Hard to believe the city was surrounded by desert. This garden would put many in Portland to shame. The only jarring feature was the huge satellite dish, an alien presence on the terra-cotta–tiled roof. They passed through the courtyard into the main part of the house, which was comfortable and furnished largely in the Euro-colonial style. Gabriella showed Leda to a room. Leda noticed right off that something was missing. Other than the door, the walls had no openings to the outside.

"This is the best place to keep your equipment, I think," Gabriella told her. "It is on the opposite side of the hall from the courtyard and, as you see, has no windows. Here, I will lock it, and you take the key. Go ahead, but don't lose the key, please. It's the only one I have, and I'm afraid the locksmiths can be rather risky here. They tend to take advantage of knowing how to open your locks and sometimes make extra keys so they can come calling when you are not at home."

"I need to get the things to make dinner," Gabriella continued. "Do you want to stay here and rest, or would you like to come? I can give you a little tour as we go. This is your first time in Alex?"

"Yep. I'll try to be cool and not a dumb tourist demanding to know where you're hiding the pyramids. Which means, yes, I want to come. Except, doesn't your chef do the food shopping?"

"Oh, yes," Gabriella grinned. "That's what I'm doing now. I'm the only chef here who cooks Mediterranean. My Aunt Saida was going to make couscous as usual."

"Will I be meeting her tonight, too?"

"Probably not until the men have left," Gabriella said. Leda realized that if Gabriella's aunt was a traditional Muslim woman, she wouldn't consider it proper to be seen by strange men, much less share a meal with them. Gabriella herself was so Westernized Leda had somehow expected the rest of the household to be the same, which was not necessarily so, obviously. This was apparently the thoroughly Egyptian side of Gabriella's family. Leda did wonder if it was all aunts, uncles, and cousins. Gabriella was certainly young enough that her parents could still be alive.

"Who all lives at your house besides you and your Aunt Saida and Mo and his bros?" Leda asked.

"Oh, it is quite a large family, but many of the children have grown and live in other places close by. They come and go a lot. There is Aunt Saida, Aunt Naima, and Aunt Layla, Mo and the bros, and their friends, who are always in and out. Then there are my married female cousins Yasmin, Subira—Suzy, she prefers to be called—and Selma. My aunts are widowed. Uncle Omar died two years ago."

Leda didn't ask. But after a while Gabriella added, "My aunties are sisters, and Uncle Omar married all of them. They joke that he didn't really need so many wives, but their father offered substantial dowries for each, and Uncle Omar was an ambitious man." During this conversation, the taxi had arrived, and they were heading east on a broad thoroughfare that spanned the beach and the pit that had once been the harbor. Beyond an enormous dam, the Mediterranean gleamed blue and calm.

"That's amazing," Leda said, turning sideways in her seat to stare at the vast excavation site. "It must be costing billions holding the sea back like that."

"Oh yes," Gabriella said. "We actually hope to raise and replicate as much of what the coastline was once like as possible. Of course, the biggest problem wasn't holding the sea back, actually. Cofferdam technology is quite ancient and was at Aswan while the dam was being constructed and elsewhere. This dam is on a bit bigger scale, and of course, the displacing of the businesses of the harbor is a nuisance, but the commercial inducement was large enough to persuade the government to move the military's naval operations for the duration of the excavation while some of the shipping was transferred to the western harbor."

"Those sound like pretty big problems to me," Leda said, still staring at the hole the sea—and part of ancient Alexandria—had once occupied.

"Yes, but the real pain was rerouting the sewage systems for the city. There were forty that drained into the eastern harbor. They had to be linked with others farther east along the coast. Those who can afford decent plumbing have been most annoyed and inconvenienced. Those who cannot have been delighted by the jobs offering high pay for such lowly work."

"So the city is revolving around this site now."

Gabriella shrugged. "It has revolved around the harbors since its creation, and the site occupies the harbor, so naturally . . ."

Leda glanced across the highway at the stacks of tacky buildings lining the road, called in the guidebooks, Al-Corniche 26 July. On the harbor side of the highway was beach, crowded with people sitting under umbrellas. Their chairs were those molded plastic patio chairs restaurants at home used for sidewalk dining, but here the chairs came in red, yellow, and turquoise, like big bright birds flocking on the beach. "I bet the stock in binoculars has risen just because of local sales," she said.

"Oh yes. You used to see men with fishing poles out here. Now, of course, the enterprising guides and hoteliers capitalize on the easy unofficial access to the what has become the city's chief attraction," she acknowledged. "Perhaps it is all of this which has contributed to Namid's unpleasant disposition. But no, I am being too charitable. He has always been a pig. The stress and importance of his current position have simply worn away the veneer of charm he once used to impress his superiors."

"That's why they need such heavy security, I guess, keeping out the tourists," Leda said.

"That and terrorists, yes," Gabriella said. She sounded rather weary of the subject.

"Well, it all thrills the heck out of me," Leda said. "I can't wait to start work."

Gabriella rolled her eyes. "If the work was all there was to it, I wouldn't be able to blame you. But Namid will make it as unpleasant for you as possible; count on it."

Because of Gabriella's Western mannerisms and expressions, Leda was tempted to say, "Gosh, you're a bundle of cheer," or something else ironic. But she had learned over the years that a sense of humor did not always translate from culture to culture, and although she liked Gabriella from what she knew of her, she hadn't known her all that long and didn't know her very well yet. So all she said was, "Thanks for the warning again."

Gabriella laughed. "I am overdoing it a bit, aren't I? I guess you can tell that when I dislike someone, I really dislike them. Not very *laissez-faire* of me."

"No, honest though," Leda said. Suddenly she wondered if Gabriella and Namid had been romantically involved at some time. Gabriella's wrath about the man was beginning to seem like the grapeish kind—sour grapes. "Where's the market then?"

"Oh, we've passed it already but—" She leaned forward and spoke to the driver. "Turn down el-Nebi Daniel, please, and stop at the corner of al-Horreya."

The driver gave no indication of hearing but hung a right at the next intersection.

"Once we got into the main part of town, we could have easily walked and seen more, Leda," Gabriella told her. "But our time is limited, and I did want you to have a little taste of the city on your first day. Besides," she said, indicating the traffic stampeding around them like herds of buffalo about to jump off a cliff, stopping for nothing and no one, "crossing the street in Alex is an adventure all by itself."

"Yeah," Leda said. "Someone must carry the bodies off every hour, or the streets would be full of them."

"Not really. You get used to the rhythm. You'll learn."

The taxi stopped, and Gabriella said, "This was once the crossroads of ancient Alexandria. Al-Horreya is the former Canopic Way. The name was changed when Nasser nationalized everything. It was Canopic Way since the heyday of the Ptolemys. Nebi Daniel was the main north-south road, running from the eastern harbor to the harbor on Lake Mariout. Along here you would have seen the colonnades, all white, a forest of pillars and fine edifices. Littering was probably punishable by death," she added, only half joking.

Leda was nodding. She had intended to come here anyway. The guide books mentioned it, and she was hoping to catch a little psychic rush from the past, but all she saw were the dreary modern buildings, not very clean and not very well kept up, many of them with graffiti scrawled in Arabic across their walls, and everything smelling ripe with garbage and—aha! The infamous stench of the displaced sewage Gabriella had referred to, now rerouted to another section of beach. "What it makes me think of is one of those postapocalypse movies where everything has gone to hell and gangs roam around, people have chips in their heads, and you sell body parts for spending money."

"We are not quite as technologically advanced as the postapocalyptic people are," Gabriella laughed. "But I understand what you mean. It does feel grubby. That's partly the desert's fault, you know. Even though we're on the coast, everything here gets sandblasted just as it does in the rest of Egypt. Probably even those ancient white pillars and colonnades were grubby-looking, too.

"It is said that the key to enjoying contemporary Alex as a doorway to the glories of the ancient city is a good imagination," she added ruefully. "There's very little left of what it once was. We were so great, you see, so far surpassed other cities, that our invaders were very jealous of us by the time they came and set out to destroy everything. Cultural genocide, I believe it's called now. Then the subsequent invaders thought the remaining treasures were so lovely, they carted them away. Which is why the earlier expeditions of divers tried to be culturally sensitive by replacing everything they pulled out of the sea, laboriously cleaned and examined, right back into the sea where its destruction could be completed. But don't worry, Leda. I promise you, my friend, that you shall see what remains."

"Yes," Leda said. "And fortunately, I do have a good imagination."

"Rue Nokrashi," Gabriella told the driver. "We had better do our shopping and return home if I am to put this dinner together. You may have to entertain our guests while I cook."

"Be careful, or Daddy will be in there telling you how to do it," Leda said. "It'll taste like Chinese by the time he's done with it."

The *souq* was similar to other such markets she'd been to, and sort of a cheaper version of Pike Place Market in Seattle on a touristy Saturday. Nobody juggled the fish, but they did everything else to attract the attention of the buyers, especially prosperous-looking ones like Gabriella and Leda.

"One thing you must have first," Gabriella told her, veering away from the food stalls to a little jewelry shop featuring mostly a lot of Chinese merchandise such as one would see in the finer dollar stores at home. But Gabriella emerged a moment later flourishing a watch with a black plastic band.

"Here, put it on. All of the Westerners on the site have them." As Leda strapped it on, murmuring a puzzled thanks, she saw why. The large black numbers on the dial were big enough to be easy to read, except they were all in Arabic. "It helps you tell prices, street numbers, all sorts of things," Gabriella told her.

Leda was touched by her thoughtfulness. Maybe she would have her sister send over a Marvin watch for her new friend in exchange.

As Gabriella did the food thing, Leda looked longingly over to the next street where yard goods and garments hung. She longed to buy a really pretty caftan and a few fake antiquities to salt around her apartment at home with her collectible toys and books, but then she remembered that she no longer had an apartment at home. Her stuff was in storage, her cats with her sister. Thinking of the cats, she felt a pang of homesickness but then thought, how homesick could she be with Daddy here, and after all, she was in

Egypt, assisting in an actual excavation, field work, no less! And she already had a new friend who had just given her a useful and exotic present.

Still, the crowd and the heat, stifling even now that the sun was past the midpoint in the sky, were making her woozy. She was glad when Gabriella bought her last lemon and they were able to hail another taxi back to the villa.

CHAPTER 6

All through dinner, Duke flirted with Gabriella while Leda and the hydrologist, Dr. Peter Welsh, exchanged glowers across the lemon chicken.

When Gabriella rose to go see to after-dinner drinks, Dr. Welsh stepped on the bare toes protruding from Leda's sandal, dropped a fork, and ducked under the table. She ducked under, too, frowning as hard as he did.

All during dinner she had choked her food down and tried to maintain her cool and slightly comical condescension toward him while being warm to Gabriella and controlling her irritation with her father. Damn him, anyway. Why did he have to buddy up with the last guy in the world she ever wanted to see again? She knew the answer to that but didn't like it.

As for Peter Welsh, now Dr. Peter Welsh, hydrologist and high-muck-a-muck of the cofferdam, he smirked at her, also with condescension mixed with scorn, the worm. She managed to flip a bowl of rice into his lap, but it was small comfort. The damned rice wasn't hot enough to burn or even sticky enough to make him uncomfortable till he could change. But as soon as Gabriella left the room, true to his old form, he pounced.

"What the hell are you doing here, Punkie?" he demanded in a harsh whisper.

"Not chasing you, my dear, that's for damned sure," she said. "I knew they had some dam fool holding back the Mediterranean for this dig, but I had no idea it was you."

"Yeah, well, Duke's a great guy. I had no idea his last name was more than a coincidence."

"Of course not. You wouldn't have known my last name if it hadn't been on my name tag."

"I sure wouldn't have known you now, Punkie my girl. I never expected you'd live up to being my Pumpkin in such a literal way. You've become quite thick through the middle, and you've wrinkles round your eyes and gray hair."

"You're no spring chicken either, chum. And what happened to the surfer boy hair?"

He tried to run his hand across the bald top of his head and rise at the same time. This resulted in a lurch of the table and some of the choice expressions they'd learned, or at least perfected, aboard the same ship. She hated to admit it, but there wasn't much but the baldness she could use to retaliate. He wasn't thick through the middle at all. Still lean and lanky with the bad boy smile, though sometimes he did seem to have other expressions as well when he talked to Gabriella or Dad about the damn dam. Men! Why did only the ones who wanted to spend money and the rest of their lives with you age badly?

Duke poked his head down under the table, too, grinning as if his face would split. "You two already know each other, I guess. Shoot, I could have spared the introductions."

"Daddy, remember me writing to you about Sneaky Pete?"

Welsh snorted. "Shall I explain what I called you to your dad?"

"As if you'd have to!" Leda snapped back.

Her father cleared his throat, no doubt sensing that the responsibility for this, one of her adult relationship problems, was about to land in his parental lap even without the benefit of a daughterly visit to a shrink.

"Children, children," the old man said, downright paternally. "Can't you give it a rest? We all have to work together, after all."

Too, too true, which unaccountably made Leda's blood really boil. She turned on him. "Yeah. Daddy, that's what you always say to your former wife when your new one starts consulting the lawyers about lowering the child support payments. I might have known you'd make friends with this turkey! I think I was only attracted to him because I was young and dumb enough to want a guy just like the guy that married dear old Mom. I forgot that dear old Mom was three wives back before I got old enough to date anybody!"

"Bitter!" Welsh said. "I knew she'd get bitter one of these days. She was too sweet to be believed back in Tasmania."

"I *was* sweet then, you asshole!" she said. "But you cured me of it really fast."

Gabriella returned with a tray of glasses and a pitcher. "Is something wrong?" she asked.

Both men suddenly looked as innocent as if they had been discussing their favorite Father's Day cards, and after awhile, the talk turned to the lab. Much to Leda's suprise, Peter Welsh readily agreed to have his crew assist Duke in erecting her beluga laboratory.

"That is very good of you, Dr. Welsh," Gabriella said. "I could probably arrange for my cousins and some of their friends to help, but—"

"No, no," Pete said with a sharp glance at Leda. "It isn't related directly to the dam, but Nucore has footed our bill, however indirectly. It's the least we can do. Besides, anything to get Punk—Dr. Hubbard here, to earning her keep in her windowless beluga five miles across the harbor from my dam."

This was all said with a charming smile, but as soon as the men had departed, Gabriella poured Leda another cup of tea and said. "Oh my, it is a truly small world, yes?"

"You said it," Leda groaned, sliding down in her chair. "Man, all this stuff with Nucore and past lives . . . I sure didn't want to catch up with my own. And as far as good ol' Pete goes, I thought I had switched that channel off for good."

Gabriella smiled appreciatively in the direction of the doorway where the men had taken their leave. "I can see how that one could have been trouble. I honestly hadn't noticed that he was so attractive before, though, I must say. I only asked your father to invite him so we could talk him into helping with your beluga. He's always seemed a bit of a bore before."

This remark cheered Leda up enough that she was able to sleep soundly beneath her mosquito netting despite the heat. She knew she and Gabriella were going to be really good buddies.

Leda left the construction of the beluga in the capable hands of Duke and *his* friend and their assorted cronies and most unprofessionally allowed Gabriella to show her the sights, especially the archaeological ones. Welsh didn't fail to make a remark in her hearing about women professionals who left all the grunt work to men. But she retorted by saying loudly to her father, "I know from all those Christmases when you let me help you put together your new motorcycles, Daddy, that you can handle 'some assembly required.' And even the most concentration-challenged individuals who can't seem to remember whose bed they last crawled out of can be educable with proper supervision and encouragement."

"Hey," her dad had said. "Watch it."

"I didn't mean you, but if the sheet fits, wear it. After all, there were a lot of Romans in togas here at one time."

Before she and Gabriella took off, Leda said, "I guess I'd better report in, eh? Let them know I'm here, that sort of thing."

"With Namid? You did already, didn't you? It is a courtesy at the most and what courtesy do you owe him now? No, you cannot work at your assignment until your facility is erected, and it is not erected. Besides, you need the background I can give you. Consider this your orientation to Alex. After all, I am the historical and cultural liaison between the museum and the project. Namid is on the museum's board of directors, but my cousin Claude is chairman of the board." She shrugged and grinned mischievously.

Still, as laid back and charming—and young!—as Gabriella was, she had that monied aristocracy born-to-command way about her, like an officer who'd come from a long line of Annapolis grads. Might not know his ass from a hole in the ground but could make you think he did and that it was to your advantage to follow him to hell and back. Or whatever. Leda had no doubt that Gabriella knew exactly which way the local cookie crumbled, or felafel fell, or whatever.

Besides, the clever girl's plan appealed to Leda. Of course, Leda knew that later she would need to make nice with Namid and work with the dig so that she would be privy to any finds of the sort that interested Nucore. Obviously, the archaeologist in charge couldn't be trusted to follow through on his agreements.

Still, what was one day, more or less, and there really

wasn't any place to park her stuff until the boys had the beluga up.

Feeling vaguely that she really ought to supervise but not much wanting to spend time watching Pete wax all competent and engineerish, she took Gabriella up on the offer.

Later, she felt that it was fortunate that the boys had the beluga up in a day's time and sad but also fortunate that it didn't take too much longer than that to drink in what was left of the ancient splendors of Alexandria.

If Leda hadn't already toured Luxor and the Valley of the Kings while she was in the Navy, she might have allowed herself to be impressed by the puny splendors of the little Roman theater and several catacombs and tombs. The Greek cemetery did make her wish she had an entrenching tool handy; those people were buried several deep, and the bottom layer could well hold the remains of some of the scholars whose work had once graced the great Alexandria Library.

The truth was, for all her enthusiasm, it was hot. It was damned hot. And she had been soaking up so much information in the past few weeks she felt as if her brain was a soaking wet, swollen sponge. She found it hard to jump up and down at the sight of Pompey's pillar, which had nothing to do with Pompey but more to do with the Serapeum, which was originally a temple to the religion the Greeks made up to blend their beliefs with those of the Egyptians. It was literally a lot of bull, since Serapis was a bull. The most interesting thing about it was that it had once held the overflow from the great library. You couldn't tell it now. There was nothing but a lot of holes and trenches in the ground and nary a page nor a scroll in sight. Not that she expected anything. She knew that the library had been destroyed some time during or after Cleopatra of movie fame had succumbed to Ceasar, Mark Antony, and the asp, in that order. Exactly who the culprits were who destroyed the library was a matter of debate, but that was long ago and not in her jurisdiction. Maybe if she had found a bit of an ancient library card catalog inscribed on one of the few remaining stones, she would have felt more impressed.

The catacombs had seemed more promising—dead people were, after all, Leda's thing—but although it might have been fun to compare the DNA of the ancient skeletal remains to that of contemporary Alexandrites—no, that was the stone—Alexandrians—she wasn't working that particular corner either. And the paintings on the walls reminded her of graffiti pretending to be pictographs. She almost expected to see a Mickey Mouse heiroglyphic among the ones that were so very un-Egyptian, while pretending to follow the ancient style.

Gabriella picked up on her lack of enthusiasm. "It isn't really terribly impressive, is it?" she said, making a wry face.

"I'm just tired and really, it's a little recent for me. I've always been more into the earlier dynasties. And Greece up to and including Alexander but not so much after."

"No, no, I understand perfectly. If not for Alexander, poor Alex would not exist, and if not for Cleopatra, it would have little to boast of except the soap opera family histories of the Ptolemys before Cleopatra the Seventh. *Our* Cleopatra. She would have agreed with you, too, that the fascination with Egypt lay in earlier times."

"No kidding?"

"Oh, yes, I don't know how much you know about her—"

"I started to read up on her but got distracted a lot back at Nucore. Chimera was always wanting me to look at something new and amazing through a microscope. Most of what I know about her is from the movies."

"She was a genius! A heroine as well and a warrior in the only way she could be. Had she been a man, we would have heard only about her intellect and scholarship and what a great pharaoh she was, preserving Egypt as a political entity thirty years beyond when it should have fallen. Since she was female and had to capitalize on every possible asset, her use of her femininity to preserve her kingdom caused her to be villified and perhaps worse, cheapened, by the history written by the conquerors. She loved all of Egypt and was considered the embodiment of Isis by the people."

"But she was a Ptolemy, a Macedonian Greek, right?"

Gabriella shrugged. "Officially, yes. She was born a Ptolemy and yet, who can say which alliances had been made within that bloodline before Alexander came to Egypt?" Her voice dropped in register and was vibrant with emotion now. "Perhaps some descendant of an Egyptian princess was captured or married for political reasons into the Macedonian royal family before ever Alexander set foot here. Or perhaps the spirits of the pharaohs really did possess living people at times . . ."

"Dr. Faruk! How unscientific of you! Have you been hiding Steven King novels behind the covers of your professional journals?"

"No, no! I am quite serious. What else, after all, is Chimera's process but scientifically induced possession . . ."

"Well, it's not quite that cut and dried. The imported person doesn't always dominate—"

Gabriella waved that aside, and Leda looked around her, relieved to see they were still quite alone. Gabriella shot her a considering look that said she had been aware of their solitude and would not have spoken so freely otherwise.

"Anyway, you must read more about her. She was a fascinating person and a very great woman, much misinterpreted. She loved Egypt more deeply than she cared for either of the men with whom her name is so often linked, and probably more than their children. However, once she was gone, the looting of the country began, and it has not stopped to this day."

"But it's illegal now to remove antiquities, isn't it? Bodies are reburied, that sort of thing?"

"Yes, though it is, as a professor of mine from Texas used to say, closing the barn door once the horses have made good their escape. And it is also true that in the last half of the twentieth century, many of the great museums that housed collections rightfully belonging to Egypt but plundered from us returned many artifacts and remains. This was during a period of politically correct fervor which was ultimately abandoned as unprofitable and stopped short of returning the greatest treasures of intrinsic value. Our own countrymen learned from that lesson. Until the plan was formed to raise ancient Alexandria rather than raze it, as has been done so often in the past, sites were quickly excavated and sifted for items of interest, data recorded, and then some new office building or theater was erected on the site. My own museum is thought to occupy the site where Cleopatra's great library once stood."

"There's not much left, for sure," Leda said, looking around at the ruins, which seemingly could have been simulated in a day or two by a couple of energetic kids with pails and shovels.

Gabriella looked very sad. "Alexandria was in its heyday the most beautiful and cosmopolitan city in the world. Books for the library were commandeered from the many ships docking here. Copies were hastily made and returned to the ships, but the real scrolls remained with us, and many of the scholars as well. The other great cities could not stand it, and when Egypt fell, they destroyed their rival city without regard for the loss to civilization." She sighed. "Of course, that's really only part of it. Most scientists now say that earthquakes caused most of the damage such as that to the structures that are being raised from the harbor.

The Pharos Lighthouse, the palaces, the Ceasarium, whole little suburbs, actually. Our environment has been no less tempestuous than other elements of our history. Myself, I am so grateful to Nucore for funding the restoration of these ruins. The government would never have done it without that money. And it will give new life to the city."

"Yes," Leda said. "It would be a real hoot to go back downtown to the corner of Daniel and Canopic or whatever and see all those columns and pillars you were talking about someday instead of the garbage heaps and graffiti."

On their way back to the villa, she got a call on the cell phone from her dad telling her the beluga was up and ready for business.

So the next day, with the help of Gabriella and the cousins, she removed her equipment to her new air-conditioned lab complete with its own generator. Her dad and some of the security staff he had already appropriated to erect the beluga, four young Egyptian men who acted like he was the president of the country instead of just the head of security, finished installing plugs and switches, cabinets and flooring. Pete popped his head in and flirted briefly with Gabriella, who was, Leda noticed to her pleasure, the reason the flirtation was brief. Gabriella didn't act as if she wanted much to do with old Pete. *Tough luck, fella.*

Good as it was to have a loyal friend and colleague so early in the game, Leda followed the move into the lab with a move of her personal stuff to the Cecil Hotel. This was over the protests of Gabriella and her aunts, who reminded Leda uncomfortably of a sort of summit conference of her dad's ex-wives, had her stepmoms all chosen to wear designer clothes and quite a lot of jewelry in the privacy of their own garden. Dinner with the aunts the night before had been noisy and funny. Gabriella didn't realize Leda spoke Arabic, and Leda was too unsure of her skill to admit to it. But some of Gabriella's translations and the aunts' comments were very funny, and Leda had to suppress her giggles until Gabriella told her what was allegedly being said.

Gabriella's Westernisms were generally frowned upon by the aunts, according to her, though they seemed extremely indulgent and even deferential, from what Leda could see. However, their attitude toward Leda as a genuine specimen of the truly decadent American woman with all of the wild and crazy privileges allowed the species, was rather awestricken. Clearly, as the aunts had seen from their hiding places the night Leda arrived, even her own father approved of her lifestyle and behavior and accompanied her on her adventures, so she was a nice girl, despite her otherwise scandalous behavior. Leda suspected she gave them something to fantasize about. They didn't seem to get out much.

However, when she and Gabriella returned from setting up the beluga to collect her own belongings, a delegation awaited her. The aunts and a couple of female cousins were dressed with their head scarves pinned securely beneath their chins, and each one insisted on carrying some item of Leda's belongings, no matter how small. Then they all piled into the same taxi Gabriella had been using all along, which turned out to belong to Mohammed. A short time later, they exited the cab like a line of graceful and noisy native bearers and wended their way to her new room at the Cecil, where the bed, the chairs, and the television were all duly tested by the family. The aunts liked the room but were chilled by the air-conditioning, which they disdained, chattering among themselves.

Leda felt like she could finally breathe for the first time since she'd arrived, but Gabriella said, "They fear you will catch cold. It is better you should acclimate yourself, they think."

"Tell them I'll turn it off before I get frostbite," Leda said.

This required some explanation from Gabriella, but once the joke was understood, everybody laughed, then departed to leave Leda in peace for her third night in Alexandria.

CHAPTER 7

By the time the first tremor came, Leda felt like the whole operation could use a shaking up. Unwilling to stay cooped up in the windowless lab, however cool, while the science and exploration went on in the harbor bed, Leda set out to charm all and sundry. She introduced herself to Namid and actually apologized for putting him out on the day of her arrival with her inopportune phone call. She used her best phone sex voice and her eyes to full effect. He wasn't as receptive as he would have been if she looked as she had twenty years earlier, but he did make a grab at her ass when she was bent over the scaffolding looking at the carving on a stone emerging from the filth on the harbor floor.

She didn't even break his hand. Duke was impressed, which pleased her. He had been her main tutor when it came to figuring out how to turn on the charm, but she wasn't about to tell him that. "You'd better watch it, Kid, or you'll get the rep for being a team player," he teased her one evening when they were sipping nice *cold* brews on the lanai that was part of her hotel suite. He preferred staying in the barracks with the other unattached men. He could keep an eye on things better from there, he said. She didn't have anything except the equipment to keep an eye on, herself, and he posted a guard on the beluga when she was away, so she didn't worry about it.

"Well, all those years in the Navy teach you nothing if not how to kiss up and worm your way into the good graces of total creeps," she said with a shrug. "Besides, I *am* a team player; we both are. We're just not saying whose team we're on."

She kissed up with a vengeance, begging for the shittiest jobs and pleading her ignorance often, while still performing the hard, dull work she was given with meticulous competence. Meanwhile, she spent a lot of time listening to people young enough to be sure they had all the answers pontificate for hours about the subjects of their theses— usually the diving expeditions conducted in the harbor's waters a couple of decades ago.

It wasn't all bad. After the initial complaints from her arthritic joints, which she medicated and ignored, as usual, she actually began to feel better. Maybe it was because she was doing something that she'd always wanted to do and her mind wasn't taking any crap from her body, so to speak, but she made herself walk as much as the others, back and forth across the miles of scaffolding covering the harbor floor, up and down the ladders reaching to the top of the dam, the island, and the dike supporting the island.

She spent hours bent over the scaffolding, unearthing carved bits of stone from the muck on the harbor bottom. She squatted, sifting dirt. She lifted what felt like tons of soil and stone. She sweated buckets and buckets and felt she was drinking as much, but as the water poured out of her body, it lightened and made the moving quite a lot easier. Also, even though the Cecil had very nice European-style meals, she wasn't there for most of them but snacked on cold food at the site or in the lab.

After awhile, the sweating even lessened her frequent trips to the chemical toilet, which was not in the harbor basin where somebody might pee on an artifact—never mind that the sewage had been dumped all over them for years—but up top.

If the other members of the expedition wondered why Nucore had sent a beluga to house the work of someone who seemed to be doing about the same thing the Egyptian laborers did, they were too busy telling her all about their own ideas and personal problems to ask. All the while, she maintained an internal fantasy of being a modern-day counterpart to her favorite fictional Egyptologist, Amelia Peabody. This helped her listen through the sweat pouring down her face and the throbbing of her joints and muscles.

As she worked, she looked up often to see her old man prowling the dike and the dam, staring into the hole with his eyes shaded like some Indian scout from an old politically incorrect Western. The kind he liked. His eyes were still pretty sharp, though he needed reading glasses, and he could spot her from clear back at the dam. If she happened to catch his eye, she waved, and he returned it. She didn't bother returning to the Cecil in the afternoon but went to the air-conditioned lab. The air-conditioning was a waste of money, when she was spending little time there and had only the specimens she brought with her, but they were precious specimens, obtained through a lot of trouble and at high cost. And she could keep a few beers in the little fridge. Her dad often stopped by and helped her drink them. And sometimes she actually took a siesta, though more often she input data on her computer, keeping track of the work done on the site. Then by around three in the afternoon, it was time to return to the basin and get back to work until dark.

After dark, she returned to the Cecil. If Dad wasn't on duty, he might come by to enjoy the luxury away from the former Egyptian Navy barracks he occupied with the other foreign men who had no families. Once or twice he brought Pete with him. They had really hit it off. She asked Pete why someone in his surely highly paid position didn't indulge in a hotel room, too. He grumbled something about needing to be on the site to keep an eye on the dam.

"That's not it, though," her dad told her later. "You were right about the guy not being any good at marriage, Kid. He keeps marrying women who make less than he does and don't know how to manage money, so he has to pay a lot of alimony and child support and stuff. Keeps the poor devil broke." Leda got a lot of grim satisfaction from that, as her father had known she would. Dad, of course, had always married women who had enough money that they wouldn't miss an extra withdrawal once in awhile when there was a toy her dad wanted or a fishing or hunting trip he wished to take. He worked, of course, but the things he liked to work at didn't quite support him in the style he liked.

One day, as she was returning to the beluga for the noon break, Namid surprised her with company.

Namid was dressed a little more formally than usual, in the togs he wore for conducting TV interviews, looking as dashing in a bush shirt and pith helmet as a short, stocky, barrel-chested man in his sixties could look. He was clean, too, which made him contrast with her and with every other worker on the site. Behind him came three men, an older one she mentally dubbed The Boss and what looked like two young sycophants, The Yes-Men, all in tropical white suits.

The older man wore a snappy yellow shirt.

It went with his decidedly unsnappy jaundiced skin and banana-colored schlera. This was a guy whose internal organs weren't working so hot. And he wasn't used to it, either, you could tell. He was no great beauty, but it was hard to tell his age because his skin had been stretched and cut so often she suspected his nipples might be hiding behind his ears. He had been expensively toned, too, but the muscle had quickly reverted to flabbiness. He hadn't felt well in some time, it was clear.

The Yes-Men were everything he had apparently wanted to be, at least physically: young, handsome, fit, but maybe not as bright as he was. Or at least they hid it well enough to fool The Boss, who probably wouldn't tolerate employees who could outplot him. Their facial expressions were in perfect harmony with his at all times.

"Dr. Hubbard, Mr. Rasmussen and his staff are here to tour the Nucore investments and facilities here in Egypt. Mr. Rasmussen"—and here Namid's tone was rather agitated, indicating that though, perhaps, he had intended to keep this important guest to himself, the man had proved more difficult than anticipated and was now being foisted off on her—"has his doubts about the value of our project to Nucore. Perhaps you can explain it to him from a corporate perspective a poor academic such as myself is at a loss to understand. Once he sees the *vital work* you have been doing here, I hope he will reconsider his opinion. I have contacted Dr. Faruk, with whom you are acquainted, I believe, and she will be here soon to help guide him to the other local sites."

"Why, certainly, Dr. Namid," Leda said, her weariness vanishing with pleasure at the bombastic archaeologist's high color and carefully controlled words.

About that time, Duke moseyed up, looking unflappably pleasant. Leda was relieved. Mr. Rasmussen had no idea how unpleasant Duke could be while looking so amiable.

"Won't you come in, gentlemen?" she asked in the professional guide voice she had cultivated while touring big shots through nuclear subs for the Navy. This was back before she spent her duty hours trying to match dog tags with bits of people in body bags.

Duke entered behind them and closed the door, then

stood at parade rest, looking very official and not at all paternal as she bustled around, finding things for them all to sit on.

"Did Dr. Namid have a chance to show you the site yet, sir?" she asked Rasmussen.

"He tried. Nothing down there but a lot of smelly dirt and rock." He craned his neck and looked all over the interior of the beluga, evidently dissatisfied. "Where do you keep the mummies?"

"What mummies, sir?" she asked. She wanted to tell them she only had a daddy here, no mummies, but didn't figure Rasmussen had much of a sense of humor.

"All of the specimens for future blends, of course!" he said. "Don't be coy with me, young woman. I know what you are doing here." He peered at her closely. "Do you?"

"Yes, sir."

"And that is?"

"Classified, sir." She used her best "name rank and serial number is all you get" stony expression and tone.

"Don't be ridiculous, young woman. I'm a majority stockholder in the corporation. We have wasted a ridiculous amount of money on this outrageous program, holding back the Mediterranean while Namid and his people dig through debris discarded twenty years ago by divers. If there are no mummies, what are we doing here?"

Leda just raised an eyebrow at him.

Duke cleared his throat and asked, "Could I see some ID, gentlemen?"

"What?"

Duke shrugged. "If you'll show me some ID, I'll get on our security computer and find out what you're doing here, if you don't know. Wouldn't want you to think I wasn't doing my job either."

Rasmussen started to sputter, then decided to laugh. "Well, at least there is one competent professional here. Mr. Avaro, if you would show the officer our credentials?"

One of the smooth young men slithered to Duke's side, where the old man was already seated and had logged into the Nucore security system.

Meanwhile, the laughter dropped out of Rasmussen's voice like a large segment of the Pharos Lighthouse plopping into the bay as he said, "I have had your appointment to this position investigated, Dr. Hubbard. I see that you are an old school chum of Doctors Chimera and Wolfe. This looks like another waste of company funds to me."

"You'd have to take that up with them, sir," she said. "My understanding was that I was hired because, in addition to being qualified, I have the trust of my old friends. You can understand why I'm not rushing to prove them wrong the first time someone asks me about my work."

"I am not just *someone,* madame. I have invested a great deal of my fortune in this project, because of Nucore's involvement, and I have every right to know that the funds are being wisely utilized."

The computer was printing out something now, and Duke was using his phone. After a moment, he refolded the phone into the little rectangle that fit into his shirt pocket, picked up the printout, and gave it to her.

"Couldn't do the retinal scan here, Kid, but these people seem to be who they say they are, and they have Class Six clearance. I checked with the boss, and he said you can show them how you use the fingerprinting process to show that two individuals are related." To Rasmussen, Duke added, "He also hopes you gentlemen will remember to protect your investment by keeping Leda's mission here covert, since the Arab holy rollers in charge of the government would shut us down if they knew exactly what we're up to."

He glowered meaningfully at them from under bushy white brows.

Rasmussen looked almost intimidated. He had probably checked out Duke's file as well as hers. Yes, that would be why, because his tone with her dad was much more polite than it had been with her. "That goes without saying. As I was just telling Dr. Hubbard, I have a considerable investment in this project."

She scanned the printout Duke had handed her and the two-buck coin dropped. So that was who Rasmussen was! He was the big shot Chimera had told her about, the one who wanted his own DNA blended into one of his staff members. No doubt the tycoon was trying this little power play to get her to do the first part of the procedure for him, under the guise of testing her. Well, the verbal instructions Duke had passed along gave her an out.

"Okay, Dad, time to make a deposit," she said and took a small cell scraping from inside his cheek while he made "aaah" noises. This she injected into a gel medium in one of the petri dishes she had prepared, just in case.

"Why him?" one of the flunkies asked. "Why not Mr. Rasmussen?"

"Are any of you related to him, or have you brought along a few cells from a close relative?" she asked, hoping they had not. "Even if you had, actually, with two related people here, me and—this is my father by the way, Duke Hubbard—" Duke waved a genial wave at odds with the slitty-eyed regard in which he held all of them. "We can get fresh specimens. I can show you the results more quickly this way."

About that time, there was a knock on the door, and Duke answered it, admitting Gabriella.

Leda placed her dish under the microscope and turned to make introductions. "Mr. Rasmussen, this is Dr. Faruk. You have so much in common. Dr. Faruk's aunt, Contessa Virginie Dumont, is a major stockholder in Nucore, too."

Rasmussen said rudely, "I thought no Egyptians were supposed to know about this."

"I am an exception," Gabriella said. "I am certainly not a Muslim fundamentalist, and I'm only half Egyptian. The other half is Greek and French. Besides, I am familiar with the process, as Dr. Hubbard knows."

"You've had it?" Rasmussen asked with more interest than he had shown in anything so far.

"No, but I have observed it. Are you considering it yourself? Were you hoping perhaps we had found Alexander himself already? I am sorry to disappoint you. His resting place remains a mystery thus far. I will be happy to show you some of the sites where they thought he might be but was not, two of which are now covered by hideously modern municipal buildings."

"Dr. Hubbard was just showing us how to prepare a specimen for the transfer," Rasmussen said.

"Oh, I'm only authorized to show you the DNA fingerprinting part so you'll know how I'll identify the remains of any notables that we might find. Like Alexander's, for instance. If his grave isn't known, his father's is, and we have an ancient specimen from that. These days, we can work with material that at one time wouldn't have been decipherable."

"No, I want you to actually prepare a specimen for transfer. Any technician can do what you're doing now."

Duke cleared his throat. "The authorization doesn't cover that."

Rasmussen said, "Then we'll have it extended."

"Okay," Leda said. "We have plenty of time, though. This part of the process will take a couple of days, and by that time, if I've received the authorization, I can show you the rest when you return."

"We can't wait that long!" Rasmussen said.

She shrugged and cooed, "Oh, I'm *soo* sorry then, gentlemen. Can't rush it, you know. These things must be done delicately. Maybe you can check with me again on your way back from Luxor."

Gabriella winked at her and cajoled Rasmussen into joining her for a tour of the museum and other sites.

Leda sighed. She had no doubt that by pulling enough strings and threatening loudly enough, Rasmussen would get the necessary authorization.

But if he did, she didn't hear about it. Nevertheless, when the two days passed without his return, and the specimen was ready for the next step, she went ahead and processed it.

"What are you doing there, Kid?" Duke asked when he joined her for the noon beer.

"Oh, hi, Daddy. I just prepared your DNA for relative immortality," she said.

"I'm immortal enough, Kid. Give that here. Otherwise no telling what trouble it will get me into." Removing the cell phone from his shirt pocket, he stuck it into his belt, and placed the specimen in the shirt pocket instead, next to his heart.

She laughed and handed him the specimen. Later, she would begin the preparation of her own specimen for show and tell instead.

But the tremor occurred two days later, and with it the discovery that drove every previous concern from Leda's mind.

CHAPTER 8

Funny how easy it was to take even the most alien environment for granted after you'd worked and sweated in it for a few days, Leda thought.

She was walking back to work along the eastern side of the harbor, where the huge stones from the ruins of the palace complex and the Ceasarium were found. Leda weaseled her way into working on this part of the excavation because some authorities believed that this was where the warehouse for Cleopatra's books had been before it was burned.

As she began climbing down the ladder leading from the dike on this side of the harbor to the scaffolding crossing the seabed below, she saw the Mediterranean beyond the cofferdam, in that moment looking calm, placid, benign.

And then, just as she set both feet on the scaffolding, she caught a glimpse of the most western edge of the sea dropping its postcard pose to quiver like a bowl of Jell-O. Before that image had quite registered, her feet vibrated, and then the boards under them gave a little buck and knocked her on her derriere.

This phenomenon also captured the immediate and rapt attention of the diggers, who were suddenly aware that they were not digging under normal circumstances but were, after all, standing in an area to which about five and a half square miles of agitated sea held the mortgage. Foreclosure suddenly became a very real possibility.

The dam was attached to land on each side of the semicircular harbor of the island. On the western side it was moored against the far western side of the island containing Fort Quait Bay. On Leda's side it was connected on the seaward side of the dike that was all that had remained of a little penninsula that had held the palace complex and some other structures.

It was possible that Leda, having just descended the ladder, could make it back up to the top of the dike before the water ruptured the dam, but most of the other people in the basin were too far from the ladders, shallow staircases, and makeshift elevators worked by hand pulleys to make it. Besides, there was bound to be some sloshing. Big sloshing. Anyone on the dam would be knocked off. Probably the same thing would happen to anyone on one of the narrow dykes or at Fort Quait Bay. The ladders didn't matter. If the dam broke, they were all screwed and very very wet.

For a few seconds, no one breathed.

The ground shook. The scaffolding rattled as if attacked by hail. A few boards popped up. The dam groaned. The quivering Jell-O did give a slosh. A slight slosh that spewed three glistening spumes of spray over the dam, wetting the upturned faces of the diggers. Then the shaking subsided. For about fifteen minutes, nobody moved. Nothing happened.

Finally, feeling a little dizzy from the lack of oxygen that came with holding her breath, Leda cautiously exhaled, and as the same exhalation was echoed by all of the other people in the basin, it sounded like a single strong burst of wind. Then everyone began fanning out, checking their work areas for damage.

Before she began inspecting the area around her, she looked up toward the top of the dam. Her father was up there, grinning down at her, and made a gesture of swiping his forehead with his hand as if wiping off sweat.

"Phew, for sure, Daddy." She grinned back and waved.

All around him, the engineering crews swarmed over the dam like monkeys.

Duke turned away to prowl the perimeter with such deliberation that she thought of him as a big cat with a long clubbed tail lashing from side to side. He walked up it and on the way back down, scanned the harbor bed.

She was still standing there, staring around her and waiting for her heart to slow down and the blood to stop roaring in her ears, when he hollered. She looked up again to see him standing with his hands cupped around his mouth. He was close to the eastern edge of the harbor, perhaps half a mile away and seventy feet above her, so she could hear him faintly. Then he pointed. She turned and shielded her eyes, trying to read what he was calling to her attention. Several times she looked up and saw him shake his head. Most of the other crew members were on their bellies already, lying across the scaffolding and crawling awkwardly along, examining the sea floor.

She stepped over three of them and walked down another few yards of scaffolding before he raised his hand three times and pointed definitely at the spot where she stood. Two boards had been dislodged and were sticking up at about a twenty-degree angle from the boardwalk.

She dropped to her knees, then to her belly, and examined the boards and the area around them but couldn't see anything. She glanced up. He was still pointing. She waved her arms in a negative gesture. Damn. Next time she should bring the cell phone. He turned his hand palm up and made a shoving motion. She should look under the scaffolding.

Okay. She did. And she saw it. The old man was amazing. He had great eyes. When she glanced back up to let him know she'd seen it, he dropped his binoculars back to where they hung from his shoulder on the opposite side from his pistol. Old fart. He hadn't wanted her to see the binoculars.

Beneath the scaffolding, silt and trash had shifted, revealing a crack between two pieces of what seemed to be hewn stone. That wasn't unusual, as they were always finding parts of the floor of this or that structure down here. But this time there was something wedged between the stones, revealed by the crack but still half buried in the muck. It was the curved belly of a jar. Where its surface had scraped against the boards, pushing them up as the tremor pushed it to the surface, the muck had been stripped away, leaving a shiny white patch in the middle—the patch that caught Duke's eye. The sheen was distinctive, though Leda had seen very little of this substance outside of museums. It could only be alabaster.

She felt light-headed all of a sudden, and her hands shook as she pulled her gloves from her pants pockets and found that putting them on was like trying to hit two moving targets. It was so inexplicably difficult she would have dispensed with the gloves except *no* one dared dig barehanded in the filth exposed when the sea was pushed back. She wondered if Moses had experienced the same problem, warning the Children of Israel to be sure to don protective galoshes before crossing the part God had provided in the Red Sea. Reed Sea, she corrected herself. The Bible story had been retranslated, and now they knew it was a sea of reeds, but the original version was more poetic, as well as more intriguing.

Her hands protected, she studied the exposed surface of the jar. It could be part of a statue, a vase, or some other item, but somehow she just *knew* it wasn't. She was being unscientific, silly, gullible to think what she was thinking, but in her gut she knew what its true purpose was. And finding it was a miracle, a genuine, certifiable miracle.

From another pocket in her pants, she took a small camera and a tape measure. Laying the tape measure atop the jar, she snapped three shots, two bracketing the first. She looked around like a criminal casing a likely house, but nobody was paying her any attention so far. She turned the tape measure sideways and snapped three more photos, then replaced camera and tape in her pocket.

Just for a moment, suspicion crossed her mind. Had it maybe been salted here for her to find? Were the others playing a trick on the newbie? Or maybe it had been put here to impress Rasmussen so it could be "found" and the project therefore made more worthwhile in the board member's eyes. But nobody else was looking up or paying any attention, and she was sure either she or Duke would catch onto the joke if that's what it was.

Maybe Duke was the one playing a joke on her. If he was, he'd have had to con someone else into planting the jar for him. He almost never came down into the harbor bed. He said it gave him the creeps. After the tremor, she knew just what he meant. But he was pretty tight with most of the Egyptian guards and workers. They liked macho old guys like him: friendly, amiable, good storytellers, dangerous if crossed.

Nah. He wouldn't play that mean a joke on her. He knew what this meant to her. Besides, he knew he would find sugar in the tank of his bike and both tires slashed the next time he tried to ride it if he did such a dastardly deed to his baby. He wasn't the only one who was dangerous if crossed, and he knew it. She glanced back up at the dam again thoughtfully, just for a moment. Pete now, he might do it, for malice, to run her off. But he had become friends with the old man, and surely he was a shrewd enough judge of character to figure out that a trick of such proportions played on her would not endear him to her daddy.

The hell with it. Her gut was jumping around as if she'd swallowed a flea circus. If she was cool about this and called the others over, then she would lose out altogether. Better to extricate the jar and have faith in her own knowledge that she would be able to tell whether or not it was genuine.

But, as she pawed the dirt and muck away from the jar's surface with her gloved hands, a little brush, and a very gently applied pocket knife to loosen the soil around the vessel, she felt as if an elevator inside herself was going all the way to the penthouse.

More of the jar's curve emerged from her patient digging. She kept expecting to find a jagged edge where the vessel had been broken but encountered only the deliberate indentations of its carving on an otherwise smooth and unmarred surface. She was panting and sweating as she worked, trying to keep herself calm and her pace steady. Most of all, she was trying not to hope that this would be what she thought it was. If it was, surely it would be empty after all it had been through. But from the feel of the outside of it, somehow she couldn't believe that. Her hand worked downward and inward, toward the mouth of the jar. Her fingers encountered, instead of space, another shape.

She had her toes hooked over the far edge of the scaffolding, and now she unhooked them and scrabbled forward, so that from the waist down, she was bending over the scaffolding until the topknot of her long brown hair brushed the sea floor. Removing a pen flashlight from another pocket in her cargo pants, she stuck it between her teeth and kept working, though the sweat ran into her eyes and plastered her T-shirt to her.

Alternately brushing and working the object free, she finally made out the shape of the carved lid. It was in the shape of a dog, Duamutef, one of the guardians of the dead, as she had deduced from groping its shape. That made it exactly what she thought it would be, hoped it would be. A canopic jar. Still apparently sealed. Still apparently a very useful as well as a very important find, being the first evidence of human remains in this area. Especially human remains mummified in the ancient Egyptian fashion, which was by no means the preferred funeral style throughout the latter part of Alexandria's history. And a jar of alabaster, of this quality, could only belong to someone of nobility, even royalty.

She had been working with such concentration she hadn't noticed the crowd gathering around her until she pulled the jar free. She would be paying for this heroic straining of her back for years to come with visits to her chiropractor. She hauled the jar up to the scaffolding and had to swat sandals and tennis shoes aside to put it down while she twisted around to a sitting position again.

The excited babble of voices was drowned out by the ringing in her ears.

Dr. Yussuf, the scientist in charge of this particular section of the harbor, leaned forward with hands outstretched for the jar, but she swatted at him with the rubber glove she'd just removed. She had been pleased that he had condescended to allow her to do grunt work on his section of the dig, but now was the time to pull rank, with all of the privileges thereof.

"Ah ah ah," she said. "Off limits! Nucore, meaning me in this instance, gets first crack at any possible human remains and this," she said, patting her find in a proprietary way her father referred to as "putting one paw on it and growling." "This is definitely a canopic jar, and as such it would definitely hold human remains."

"Perhaps," Yussuf said, kneeling to inspect what was visible of the inscription on the jar but keeping out of range of her glove. "But you have not the experience to judge,

Leda. It is most likely a false canopic jar, though of very fine workmanship. It is very close to the surface to be from the more ancient times when such jars were used in the way you're thinking of them. In later periods, the viscera were wrapped and returned to the body cavity and the jars, such as this one may be, were merely carved to resemble those which once held viscera. They were used strictly for ceremonial purposes."

"Ceremonial purposes, for sure. I never thought otherwise. But most of the funerals of the well-to-do were highly ceremonial. And there were always cults of holdout traditionalist priests who liked to do things the old-fashioned way. Maybe some of those guys did the mummification of this person."

"Yes, and maybe it fell off a British ship when our esteemed British colleagues were looting Egypt," said Habib, an Egyptian grad student who thought he was a full tenured professor already. He eyed the jar's rounded middle critically. "That shape was not in use during the reigns of the Ptolemys. Rectangular boxes were more often used."

"It might be one of the finds Goddio made at the end of the twentieth century and returned to the ocean," Solange Cousteau, a descendant of one of Goddio's divers, opined. "Perhaps something collected from upper Egypt and brought here."

"Don't wake Leda from her dream world," Yves Dulac said. "She thinks she has in her canopic jar the womb of Cleopatra."

Leda regarded him with her best imitation of the sphinx. "Could be. If I was dreaming, I would have picked someone from an earlier dynasty than the Ptolemys to make my discovery. But this isn't exactly the Pick your Favorite Pharoah of the Month Club, is it? If you'll all get out of my way now, I'm going to examine my find."

"You don't just pluck something from a site and carry it

off with you! Its location must be documented, it must be photographed and measured, it must—"

"I took its picture with a tape measure," Leda said patiently. "I will measure it better when I get it back to the lab. Meanwhile, there is the hole. Document its location all you want. Knock yourselves out. But remember, these things usually come in sets, and even if you find one, I have dibs on being the first kid on this dig to collect all four."

"There is no need for such haste."

"Actually, there sort of is. Haven't you ever heard of aftershocks? This probably isn't the only tremor we're going to have, and I think this thing was coughed up by a new fissure in a stone floor. If you want any more goodies before another little quake closes it back up again or breaks things, you might want to get right on it."

"We scientists do things in an orderly and methodical fashion. We must examine this artifact and *I* must read the inscription," Yussuf said. "That is what I am here for, after all."

She smiled up at Yussuf, which he must have enjoyed for once. He was about five four, and she was five ten. He was also in his early thirties and she was forty-five. What happened to all of the white-haired old dignified guys she thought all senior archaeologists were? Maybe she just assumed they were mostly old because what they studied was. "I'll be sure to call you if I need any help, but I was reading hieroglyphics while you were still in grade school."

He shrugged. "Your interest does you credit, of course, madame, but you are an armchair archaeologist. That does not make you a reliable field Egyptologist."

"I am a fully qualified forensic anthropologist, actually. Furthermore, I have spent considerable time training in techniques to preserve and restore such finds as this so that they will yield more information than they ever have previously about the lives of their owners. Your conventional methods would ruin what I need to implement my own." She was only lying a little bit, evading one truth by making a sharp left before she got to its core, and exaggerating the dangers of letting the sample out of her control. What would ruin it for her purposes was that she was pretty sure she'd never get it back if she let Yussuf and Namid have it.

"This is what *I* am here for," she told him firmly. She shoved sweaty strings of hair from her forehead, wrapped her arms around her find, and stood. She may not have published in any fancy journals, but she certainly knew her way around dead people. "In exchange for spending heaps and gobs of its shareholders' money on this project, Nucore gets first crack at anything resembling human remains. I'm sure this was explained to all of you during orientation," she said, clucking like an officious file clerk. "I represent Nucore here. If you don't like it, have your company's lawyer call my company's lawyer."

"Me, I am not budging," Habib said. "You will damage the jar, and it will be lost to my people."

"Sorry you feel that way. But you could get damaged yourself if you don't get out of my way. I'm feeling all hot and cranky now. So all of you scoot." They continued to surround her. Hugging the jar closer, she cleared her throat and hollered, *"Dad-deeee!"*

Fortunately, she didn't really have to yell that loudly. Right after he pointed out the jar to her, her father's curiosity had overcome his dislike of the harbor floor so much that he had clamored down one of the ladders. Now he jogged across the scaffolding toward them, the boards bouncing under his feet and then bouncing some more as three of his security crew followed right behind him.

"What's the matter, Kid?" he asked her.

"Take this, will you? It's heavy."

"Officer Hubbard," Yussuf protested, "you must not allow personal considerations to enter into this. Dr. Hubbard is behaving badly."

"Nah, she's doing good," Duke said. "She hasn't stamped her foot yet or held her breath till she turns blue, but I suggest you give her her way. And by the way, this isn't a personal consideration. Helping her retrieve and take care of this stuff is what I was hired to do."

When Duke had the jar clasped firmly to him, Leda stood and looked down on Yussuf. He hated that. As she figured he would, he stormed off, looking for Dr. Namid. Duke and his men momentarily cleared the scaffolding of the rest of the muttering onlookers.

Duke then handed the jar back to Leda and, with him walking point and his posse protecting her flank, Leda abandoned the corpse of the sunken city for the belly of the beluga. As they left the basin, the other diggers, like the Red (or Reed) Sea, reconverged upon the place where they had been and began searching the basin floor with renewed dedication.

↲CHAPTER 9

Of course, Dr. Namid had to tell her what he thought of her conduct.

She tried sweet reason first, using the same argument she had used on Yussuf, but with no more success. "I don't see your problem, here, Dr. Namid. You agreed to this already, and in the end, it can only provide us with more information about this individual and his or her life and times. It can only enhance your own reputation and increase our knowledge about this person, place, and era."

"Bah!" he said. He actually said "Bah." She waited for the "humbug!" but it didn't come. "I did not understand that valuable artifacts would be removed entirely from my own care to be subjected to some experimental hocus voodoo by an amateur. If you truly care about Egyptology as you claim to, you will allow us to record and gather the information we need from this piece before you contaminate it with your untried and unproven tinkerings."

"Which you won't give a chance," she said.

"Which I have never even seen demonstrated!" He

countered. "Which have not been properly published in scientific journals or discussed in scientific circles."

"Well, I'm sorry, but that was the deal. As for contamination, the jar is in the clean room in a special storage cabinet, and I think I can assure you that my work will contaminate it way less than anything you'd do to it. You have a whole empty harbor for your sandbox, Dr. Namid. Why don't you go back to digging and maybe, like I said, you can come up with the other three jars or even a nice mummy?"

He called her a crass American opportunistic degenerate—and those were just the adjectives. The noun was a very rude word in Arabic, which he didn't think she understood.

She'd been called worse. After all, sailors were famous for inventive terms of endearment for those of the—well, it used to be only the fair sex, but since women sailors served aboard ships, now the terms were applied by each sex to the opposite.

She heard him out, maintaining a cheerful smile in the face of his tirade. He was very upset. However, he couldn't flunk her. He couldn't fire her. And he couldn't take the jar away, because Daddy was standing at the door. Ah, it was so good to have backup!

"Dr. Namid, really, this is very unprofessional of you, and you're getting all red in the face for nothing. It doesn't matter to me how loudly you yell, I'm keeping the damn jar," she said when he had sputtered out of breath. "I know you're disappointed not to get to probe and pry into it yet, but just think what Mr. Rasmussen would say if he heard you carry on like this! He already thinks the whole site is a waste of money, and if he could hear your—well, the only word I can think of is *ungrateful*—your ungrateful attitude toward Nucore, when they have been *so* generous letting you have the entire harbor to play in and only wanting this one itty-bitty artifact I found all by myself . . . I just don't think he would understand. He would feel that Nucore shouldn't be letting someone like you run this at all. He might want to replace you."

"If that happened, I would be forced to ask the government why it is that Nucore is interested only in canopic jars," Namid said with cool menace at odds with his ranting of a few moments ago. "Oh yes, Dr. Hubbard, I have learned a few things about the company's activities in other parts of the world, and I would be forced to let the press know that similar abominations are being attempted here. How our past and our dead are being prostituted. Again."

Duke cleared his throat. "I hate to hear you say that, Mahmoud," he said in a man-to-man voice, moving in a bit. "And I'd really advise against it. Because I've done a little checking on Mr. Rasmussen, and from what I can tell, people who tried to make a name for themselves at his expense ended up disappearing so thoroughly nobody can remember their names at all."

"What are you talking about?" Namid demanded.

Duke sighed as if he was trying to be patient with someone who was acting stupid. "Let me put it to you this way. Nucore is a very idealistic outfit, really. They want to do this project of yours in cooperation with the government and not upset anybody. The attitude toward the fundamentalists has been, well, what they don't know won't hurt them. And if you started trouble over this because you got fired, think of the jobs you'd cost your people and the loss to its heritage."

Leda lifted her brows at her father's high-minded arguments.

"But more than that, what I really want you to think about is something Rasmussen told my daughter the doctor while he was here. He said that because of the interest he holds in Nucore, he has a substantial amount of his personal fortune invested in the projects in this country, especially this one. You doing as you say would cause him to lose a lot of money. Now, this is not a nice man, Mahmoud. Made a lot of money in the illegal arms trade. Knows a lot of dangerous people, some of them within range of you, and I mean that literally. Some of these friends of his might take it personally if you cost Mr. Rasmussen a lot of money because you didn't want to keep your agreement with Nucore and let my kid here do her job."

Leda rolled her eyes. Wow. Daddy had been reading way too many Tom Clancy novels and watching too many gangster movies. He was, in her opinion, overdoing it a little. However, he was very good at this sort of thing, and it was one of the longest speeches she had ever heard him make. It was incredibly fatherly and protective of him, a side she had seen only once before, at the used car dealership when the car they'd sold her broke down for the twelfth time in the first three months she had it.

So she said soothingly, "I promise Nucore will share with you the information we glean from this technology *and* let you have all the credit. We just need to make sure what's in there, and if it's what we need, well, we'll need that, too, or most of it, but you can have almost all of the data we gather and all of the glory, and when we're done, you can have the jar, too. But for now, I need you to scat. I have work to do."

He started in again, but then he saw the look that passed between Leda and her father and backed away quietly, compared to how he'd begun the conversation. He didn't even slam the door of the beluga. Before the door had closed, however, Leda's father quietly slipped out behind Namid. No doubt he intended to saunter nonchalantly along behind the good doctor, just to make sure he didn't get into any trouble.

CHAPTER 10

When everyone had gone, Leda measured and cleaned her find carefully, brushing it, wiping it with dry rags. She meticulously collected the dust and dirt samples in a sterile bag. It was always possible there could be some dried skin from the mummy on the outside of the jar, especially inside the carvings where the dirt and stone from the harbor floor wouldn't have contaminated them. Until she knew the condition of the material inside the jar, she needed to protect all possible sources of DNA. If the organs had been sufficiently dried and had withstood the years, it was possible she might find definitive, nuclear DNA within the sample.

So she continued brushing and collecting until the carvings on the surface were all as clean as her brush could make them. She kept catching her breath in little gasps as she cleaned the cartouche, and the evidence of the jar was revealed. At first the very shape of the jar made Leda doubt her hunch about its royal origin.

King Tut's canopic jars had been miniature coffins of the pharaoh. The animal figures were not as distinctive. But here, below the dog's head lid, engraved in the stone and chased with gold, was the written evidence, in words both Egyptian and Greek, spelled out in hieroglyphics that were both pictograph and phonetic representations of letters and ideas.

The queen's cartouche was a long one, full of the royal titles both granted to and arrogated by a powerful woman. Embodiment of Isis and Hathor. Pharaoh of Upper and Lower Egypt. Cleopatra.

Actually, from what Leda had read, the Egyptians wouldn't have been able to pronounce the name Cleopatra correctly, since there was no *l* sound in the Egyptian language. But they approximated it with *r* and *rw* sounds. If Cleopatra didn't herself have a little bit of an Egyptian drawl—and it was well-known that she was a Greek culturally and linguistically, so probably, being an upper-class lady, she didn't have the local accent—she must have felt she was constantly being Elmer Fudded by her kingdom's indigenous people who would have pronounced her name "Krwiwapadra."

As she cleared away more of the dust and encrusted dirt, Leda also uncovered the rest of the queen's credentials.

Lest anyone confuse Cleopatra the Seventh with her ancestresses, siblings, or descendants, besides her royal titles and names cartouche there were two others, the obvious Ptolemy cartouche, of course, which, situated beside Cleopatra's, had helped researchers decipher the code of the Rosetta stone. And her nickname, Philopater, father-lover. Every woman in the Ptolemy family seemed to have been named Cleopatra, Berenice, or Arsinoe, which covered the names of Cleopatra's sisters and herself. There was even another Cleopatra who was her older sister. So the nicknames were essential for keeping people straight.

Leda could see where the main cartouche had actually been lengthened in three separate places, as old boundaries were filed away and new engraving added by a slightly different hand, new titles added, borders and gold reapplied.

Such fine materials and such an awesome object to have such strange imperfections in craftsmanship lending it an almost secondhand air.

Hadn't she read somewhere that Cleopatra had actually surrendered her own tomb with all of her jewels and funerary equipment to Octavius when her threat of burning herself up with it failed? So, what was this then? Cleopatra's death was famous but her resting place unknown. Some histories said she'd been allowed to be buried with Mark Antony, and he had been accorded all of the rites of a pharaoh, but that seemed odd, since he still had a wife and children in Rome. Some authorities believed Octavius had ordered Cleopatra's body burned so that according to her adopted Egyptian religion, she could not have an afterlife.

And yet, here was seeming proof to the contrary.

Only a portion of the cartouche had been visible on the exposed area of the jar, but it was distinctive enough to fuel her hopes, and she knew that she wouldn't be the only one to recognize it. Its presence was the main reason she had been so protective of her find. If Yussuf and the others had seen it, Dad would have needed an army using deadly force to keep them away from the jar.

Once she was sure of what she had and the original sample as well as the decoded replicated strands were safely in Nucore's lab and presumably, in Mrs. Wolfe as well, she would tell Namid and the others what she had found.

Show them even, though without revealing anything about what the information had been used for, of course. Then, if Namid hadn't done so already, he would have his crews conduct a thorough deep excavation of the area and maybe find more of the last pharaoh and her goodies. That would also keep them off Leda's back. So she would let them know. Later.

However, first she had to open the jar and make sure there was enough tissue there to obtain the samples she needed. Besides, it wasn't unknown for one corpse to end up in the funeral equipment of another. Even canopic jars. And she needed positive proof that the tissue belonged to Cleopatra, not just the jar.

She was puzzling over the best method to open the jar without damaging anything when there was a knock on the door. She carefully set the jar on a countertop beside the computer and checked the exterior TV screen her father had installed the day after Rasmussen's visit. Gabriella stood outside, dancing from foot to foot as if she needed to use the bathroom.

Leda separated herself from her friend's find long enough to go to the door and pull back the deadbolt Duke had installed the same day he put in the camera.

Gabriella burst through the door and danced inside before Leda fully opened it. Eyes sparkling, Leda's friend stood looking around the lab as if it had turned into a ballroom.

"Leda! Is it true?" she asked while Leda cautiously rebolted the door. "Namid called and told me you found a canopic jar and had become completely paranoid guarding it from all comers."

"That was thoughtful of him. I was about to call you myself," Leda replied and led her to the jar. Gabriella peered at it cautiously but did not touch it while Leda turned it to show her the cartouche.

Gabriella gasped, a satisfying reaction.

"Have you got anything over at the museum to open this with?" Leda asked. "Like an ancient Egyptian can opener?"

"Oh, Leda, really, this is not something that should be left to one person. This should go back to Nucore's lab on the island or at least to the one in Cairo—a discovery of such magnitude! What were they thinking to put you here alone!"

"That's how they wanted it. Most of the stuff is done on computers, anyway, and it only takes one person to run.

Besides, with fewer people, the security risk is less."

"Well, yes, unless, of course, *you* decided to take advantage of the situation—"

Leda laughed. "They've checked my clearance and also, both Wolfe and Chimera know me pretty well. Otherwise, my computers are linked to their computers. My work is constantly monitored by the lab. If I made a questionable move, I'd hear about it. Besides, no one outside of Nucore has the equipment for transferring the data to the host, and the data is, while not exactly useless, not nearly as valuable without it. So it's safe enough for them to rely on a one-woman, one-security-dad, one-computer team here. In fact, had you not shown up, I could have downloaded information on how to open the jar."

"All of these archaeologists salivating to get their hands on the jar, and you would have used the Internet?"

"Nucore's site. They have experts on tap, too. I guess they'd have their own people here, except that Egypt is so touchy about foreign archaeologists these days. Heaven knows I'm having a hard enough time as it is. So I'm glad you're already here and in the loop. The fewer people who know what we have here, the better, at least for now."

"Are you kidding? This is the find of the millennium! Surely you can't hope to keep it secret?"

"Only for a little while. Until I can test the tissue, do the match, then patch and replicate a complete strand. I send the computerized version to Chimera and return the original material as well, so it can be cross-checked. You may find you've really got your liaison work cut out for you, once news of this gets out, Gabriella. The truth is, whether or not anyone knows about the process, Nucore has the closest and most authoritative facilities for this kind of testing. Even if I weren't here, the samples would probably be sent to them eventually by Namid and the others. But by then, they would have wrecked the tissue for this kind of work."

"So, if that is true, why doesn't Nucore just tell them so and tell them how to prepare it to be sent to the labs? Why *do* they need you here, Leda?"

Leda laughed. "Don't take this wrong, Gabriella, but there's an old saying in the military among the high-clearance spooks. 'If I told you any more, I'd have to kill you.' Actually, you know enough to put two and two together."

"Oh, of course, you must already have a client anxious for this specimen. Naturally. A very important client, I would guess, for Nucore to have you ready with this nice laboratory *in case* of a miracle like the one that just happened—and you found the right specimen."

"Why, Gabriella! I'm sure your aunt could tell you that at Nucore, we consider all of our clients *reeeeally* special," Leda joked, almost giddy. "But seriously, finding an intact jar like this that *seems* to belong to such an important person is a lot more than anyone expected. Especially since anything we find on this site has been underwater. Apparently, this has been in a sealed chamber of some kind for a long time. Well, shall we see what we've got here?"

They very gently removed the golden seal, the resin, the beeswax beneath the resin. Before removing the lid, Leda took the jar back to the clean room, where the fingerprinting and splicing was done with the least contamination. Gabriella followed. The room was actually an indoor tent made of heavy-duty clear plastic and zipped shut when not in use. Most of the very expensive equipment Leda had brought with her was here. Now she unzipped the doorway and she and Gabriella slipped inside. She unwrapped a sterile tray and tongs. Then Gabriella held the jar steady while Leda pulled off the dog-shaped lid and reached with the tongs to pull forth the material inside.

Both women held their breath. Leda supposed that for strictest security, she should ask Gabriella to leave now, but she suspected she'd have to pull a gun on her friend to make her do it. She already knew almost as much as Leda did, anyway, and Leda needed the help.

Pulling forth the ancient papyrus-wrapped bundle, Leda felt a moment of pure awe. This was nothing like dealing with the remnants of more recent bodies. If the canopic jar was to be believed, people all over the world, down through the centuries, knew about the life and death of the woman to whom this little scrap belonged. And maybe, just maybe, they were about to discover some answers to her mysteries.

When the sample was taken and the initial preparation of the sample complete, Leda stored the rest of the tissue before she and Gabriella toasted the grand opening with a couple of Cokes from the fridge in the outer room of the beluga, and Gabriella asked, "How soon will you know?"

"Well, for the PCR—preliminary chain reaction—I can find out right away. I have a sample from Cleopatra's daughter's tomb. So our tissue can be compared to that, and we can find out that the sample is from Cleopatra Selene's mother or maternal line the next generation up. It could be one of Cleopatra the seventh's sisters, of course, but they would have been long dead or out of the country before the queen took on some of the titles mentioned on the jar."

"Yes, well, still, one must be certain. There are surely a great many cells there in that little packet of tissue. Will you need to use all of it?"

"Probably not, but I'll have to find enough intact material to piece together the information I want. Then I make a good new copy of it for our use. I'm not telling you any big secret here. That's how it's always done. But I need to send back some of the original evidence for Nucore's own verification, even though I can upload the part they need for the process."

"I see. So you will really have an unlimited supply of whatever it takes for the transfer?"

"Uh—I have to plead no comment there."

"I understand. But say, if you do have a good supply, will Nucore offer the blending to more than one client?"

"I'm not sure. I asked about that, and from what Chimera said, I doubt it, at least for a while. Besides, we can't be greedy. Most—all, as far as the world knows— will have to be reburied under current Egyptian law. Seems like a waste, doesn't it?"

"It certainly does," Gabriella agreed, her voice even and light. Leda, anxious to return to the machine that would give her the mitochondrial code for her specimen, sucked down her Coke and headed back to the clean room. Gabriella watched her go, but Leda was already thinking ahead to what the machine might show her and didn't see that her friend's fierce expression in no way matched her tone.

CHAPTER 11

Leda deserted her room at the Cecil, except for an occasional shower, and moved her toothbrush and sunscreen into the beluga. Her dad had one of his crew buy a sleeping bag, pillow, and mat for her at the *souq* so she could sleep in the lab when she came to a stopping place in her work.

For almost three weeks she saw little except her computer, the samples and chemicals, and her microscope. The little Ziess electron microscope she had carried in a suitcase from Nucore headquarters was strong but not quite strong enough, so she had to request a booster lens from Nucore and asked Duke to ride out to the airstrip to get it.

He called her on the cell phone from the door so she could unlock the deadbolt. Otherwise, the door stayed locked, and she spent most of her time zipped inside the clean room, her world centering on the DNA fragments she pieced together like a jigsaw puzzle.

Inside the windowless beluga, she was unaware of day and night. Often, when she broke for a breath of the hot, salty air outside, she was surprised to see the site empty and quiet, though not unlit. Huge floodlights illuminated it at all hours, and Duke's guards patrolled the outer perimeter, wary of looters, terrorists, or even overly inquisitive tourists.

In relatively short order, she established that the DNA in the jar's contents belonged to someone the next generation back from Cleopatra Selene, from whose tomb a tooth had been clandestinely removed. The mitochondrial DNA proved that. Also, from what some historians reported, it was possible that had the jar's DNA belonged to one of Cleopatra's sisters, there would have been no match at all. It was widely believed that all three of her sisters had been born to a different mother than the famous queen.

Insubstantial thoughts flitted across the surface of Leda's mind while she searched the field for fragments, for the tiny attachments to the main strands that indicated the additions of data collected during life, not present at birth. These, amazingly enough, were memories, those ephemeral things formerly believed to be housed solely in the brain and now confirmed to lodge in most cells of the body.

The nuclear DNA contained in the lungs was in remarkably good shape, considering its age, but still it required much painstaking work to make the necessary matches, to splice the broken ends. The computer did much of it, of course, but it had to be fed new data from new samples to give it sufficient material to work with.

She had been afraid that the substances used to embalm the organs had damaged the DNA, but somehow the ancients had steered clear of that hazard. The natron they used to preserve the tissues was little more than a highly concentrated saline solution. Had they somehow magically been guided in their choice of substances that would achieve the ultimate goal, preserving the body for immortality? Because Chimera's process was as close to immortality as anybody was likely to come.

Folkloric beliefs always seemed to her to be the smoke hovering over some very hot sparks of truth.

Once she was sure that the material in the canopic jar belonged to Cleopatra, Leda sent her preliminary message to the Nucore home office with the code Chimera had given her. Normally, all results from remote sites went into the banks of Nucore computers at large, but this code would give the transmissions an exclusive rating, allowing the data to be viewed only by Chimera and a few trusted assistants. Chimera would personally notify the client.

She decided against alerting Namid that the remains had indeed been Cleopatra's. He had stayed away so far, and she liked it that way. Besides, he'd want to tell the press, and she really didn't want that until she had finished her work.

Once she had pieced together the strand, the computer replicated it and performed one more task that went beyond identifying a person from her cells and replicating a DNA strand. Now the computer decoded the strand, read and reencoded the material containing memory and personality traits to a form that could be transferred to light frequencies. These patterns were what would be imprinted on the retina of the client.

Leda had to admit she'd had some initial qualms about being in cahoots with Chimera to use Nucore resources to make Gretchen Wolfe's secret wish come true. Saving a marriage was not a real big motive to most executives of multinational corporations, especially when it involved setting aside protocol in such a drastic fashion. But then, when she thought about how the process had come to be created—from the strength of Chime's and Jetsun's bond—she realized that Chimera took marriage much more seriously than almost anyone she knew. Given her own background, as her father's daughter, she found the scientist's (scientists'?) attitude touchingly sweet and naïve. She was all for it.

While the computer was crunching the final bit of data in the report she would add to the original donor sample, Leda stepped outside for what seemed like the first fresh air she'd taken since she found the jar.

The heat hit her like a dragon's belch, but when her eyes stopped swimming, she saw the setting sun splashing the sky with Halloween orange above bright blue waters turning to indigo. Outlined by the sea, the partially lit silhouette of a man strolled across the back of the dam. Her dad on his rounds, his stride at that distance now almost as familiar to her as his face. Now and then he took out binoculars to have a long look at something or other in the hole below, but when he turned the lenses in her direction, she waved.

He waved back. She picked up the cell phone, to call and ask him to come to the beluga. She had already sent a message to Chimera that Dad would be bringing the specimen to Kefalos.

Duke stopped, lifted the phone from his belt, and she heard a few staticky noises. With the scientific approach to technology of men from his generation, he glared at his phone, shook it, held it up to his ear again, and jammed it back into his belt.

Then he waved again and doubled back along the dam in the direction of the fort, beyond which the beluga claimed squatter's rights.

She waited for him.

He joined her with a "Hi, Kid. Damn phone. Batteries are about gone, and I forgot to put any more in my pocket before I left. Hey, don't you have sense enough to go in out of the heat?" The two of them stepped back into the cool white cave as her computer beeped to announce it had finished the crunching. She hit Send for the report and opened the minifridge, extracting a couple of Italian beers for them to celebrate with.

The fridge jittered against the floor, and at first she thought it was making ice cubes. Then she remembered it didn't do that.

And the fridge wasn't the only thing jittering. The earth beneath her feet rolled and bucked like a ship on stormy waters, rattling the machinery on the counters and in the storage cupboards. Her computer's mouse jumped off the desk and tried to escape. The generater bounced against its bolts, and the lights flickered. Then the air conditioner died with a sigh and a thundering silence.

Leda dove under the desk for the errant mouse and hauled it back toward her. "Oh, no, you don't," she said. As she tried to rise again, she saw the computer screen's error message blacken to a blank screen. "Aw, shit," Leda said. But for the moment, the earth stopped moving.

At the first tremor, Duke's eyes had narrowed into the watchful, hawkish expression he assumed when he was in a questionable situation, as he often was.

"What?" he asked, nodding at the dead computer screen. "Did it go through or not?"

Leda sighed with relief and frowned as she rolled up a sheet of paper. "Not, I think, but I got the printout. You can take it along with the specimen."

"Wait a minute, Kid," he said. "I'm not going anywhere right now."

"Daddy, you have to. What if we've had—are having— a major quake?"

"Exactly."

"No, the most important thing is to get this to Chimera. If my data is damaged, it can be reconstructed from this. It's the most important thing in the whole country right now, Daddy. Because this is her. She, I mean. It's she."

Duke had from time to time peered over her shoulder when he came to check on her, but her work didn't mean much to him. The computer screen was always a mess of numbers and letters that looked a lot like algebra, but with brown dashes beside them, zigzag graphs that looked like the ones a heart monitor showed, or little squiggles.

"She who?" he asked. "Oh, her," he said, striking a pose like a dancer on a tomb wall and making chicken-pecking movements with his chin.

"Of course, her!"

"You're sure, are you? I still haven't seen any sign that says 'Julius Caesar *and* Mark Antony slept here.'"

"Silly asp," she said, smacking playfully at his arm. To her surprise, he went sprawling. So did she. Beneath them, the floor shook as if a freight train was rumbling across it.

"Damn, there it goes again," she said, hauling herself up after a few seconds from the still-vibrating floor. She grabbed her specimen and the three-inch-long titanium cylinder that was its transport case.

Her dad had prudently moved himself into the door frame, but she was determined to by God accomplish her damn mission. She hadn't come this far just to let a little hissy fit on nature's part screw things up.

Inside the clean tent, something crashed with an extremely expensive amount of noise. Leda cringed and paused for a moment, willing the building to stop shimmying. There'd been four more minor tremors in the last week, but none of them disturbing enough to mess up the power supply or even distract her from her work. All of them had subsided so quickly that Leda had only realized they'd happened afterward. This one was more tenacious, but she was determined to ignore it if she could.

Her dad was grinning as he assessed the situation. He liked things that bucked and snarled: motorcycles, turbulent air when he was flying, race cars, most of his ex-wives.

They were adrenaline junkies, both of them, father and daughter, though Leda's addiction had a more intellectual bent to it, causing her to get all fluffy about things like the canopic jar and Cleopatra's personal cartouche.

The building lurched and swayed again, and something groaned deeply, while more glass crashed. The ceiling began to bow. Leda finished preparing her precious specimen for its trip and stuck it in its special container. About then, the floor jerked out from under her, and she landed on her butt.

"You okay, Kid?" her father asked, taking one hand from the door frame.

"Sure. Who knows? If the last quake brought us Cleopatra, we might get Alexander the Great with the next one. It could happen." She rose to all fours and crawled toward him, the specimen tube inhibiting use of her left hand. "But you need to get this to the airstrip pronto."

"I need to ride herd on what's happening here, Kid," he told her. "My job, remember."

"Delegate it," she said, and it was the first and last time she would ever give her father an order. "This is way more important."

"Hey, you could get hurt here."

"So could you. Do it, Daddy, please?"

He grunted and reluctantly accepted the tube.

"Don't forget your phone batteries," she called after him. "I want you to call from the airstrip."

He made an impatient slapping gesture back over his shoulder but jogged toward Fort Quait Bay. He paused near the control center, and in a moment the lights filling the bowl of sea floor below the dam blinked out. When they came back on again, he was running from the barracks where he and the other single men slept. A squad of other men, some in uniform, some in street clothes, some in night clothes, were right behind him. One of them—Pete maybe?—stopped for a second and exchanged a few shouted words with Duke.

Dad retraced his steps to where he had parked his bike, jerked something from his saddlebags, shoved something else in, and secured the bag again before jumping on his bike. Then, without so much as a "Hiyo, Silver!" he was away.

The shaking began again.

About to bolt for the beach, Leda suddenly remembered her data and the canopic jar with what remained of the original specimen in the clean room. She sprinted for that instead. Unzipping the outer flap, she stepped over the wreckage of the PCR machine and popped a minidisk from the computer hooked up to the electron microscope. With this, she had the data she'd duplicated from the patched strand. As long as she was safe, so was Cleo.

She reached for the canopic jar, deciding that now would be a good time to take it to Namid's office and tell him whose DNA it contained, before it got broken.

But before she could lay hands on the jar, the ground shook like a wet dog, a boom and roar filled Leda's ears, and beneath the plastic ground cloth zipped to the walls of the clean room, a wide trench began opening in the floor.

"Oooooooh, shit!" she said and bolted for the doorway, which was crumpling toward her. She'd be smothered *and* crushed if she didn't get it open. The zipper jammed, and she had to lay down the jar and use both hands to yank at it, with the floor tilting under her and the refrigerator toppling forward along with the computer and other equipment.

The room went dark suddenly as the generator gave up the ghost. Well, at least she wouldn't be electrocuted as well as smothered and crushed.

She unzipped the door just enough for her to stick her hand out before the damn thing stuck again. All the while, the ground did the bunny hop under her sandals. Her toes cringed under the sandal straps as glass from the screens of the ruined machinery tinkled. Meanwhile, the plastic underfoot drained like water into the trench the quake made in the floor.

She groped around on the floor until her hand closed on a long sliver of the glass. Wrapping the tail of her T-shirt around it to protect her hand, she stabbed at the plastic. It was tough plastic, but the broken glass pierced it and with a log tug she opened a rent, then sawed at it until it looked big enough for her. She turned to pick up the canopic jar, but it rolled toward the trench. She lunged for it, but her feet flew out from under her, and only her grip on the doorway kept her from following the jar down the hole. But the tent was rapidly collapsing. If she didn't get her ass through the hole now, she would become a plastic-wrapped mummy, entombed in the hole under the ruins of the beluga.

She forced her arms and upper torso through the slit in the tent.

The slab on which the building sat, made of a quick drying ready-mix plastic composition material, cracked in another place, and she lost her footing again. Her arms flailed at the floor outside the tent while she kicked wildly, trying to free her feet and legs from the plastic.

The price of being an isolationist: She'd sent her only ally away, and now she would die alone in this damned thing if she didn't get out. She looked up as the supporting rods on the beluga's ceiling bowed inward, and the ceiling's belly ballooned toward her.

One more kick, a twist to free her foot, and she half crawled, half ran for the door, praying it hadn't jammed shut.

CHAPTER 12

Despite the roar and vibrations from the souped-up old Sopwith between his legs, Duke definitely felt the causeway lurch under his tires as he sped toward the mainland.

He gunned the motor, congratulating himself on the modifications that allowed him to treat the relic with such disregard for its venerable age. He was pretty sure he could make it fly if he had to.

The Nucore-sponsored airstrip lay in a field west of the city. Theoretically, it serviced Nucore-sponsored excavations throughout Egypt, but in reality, most of the traffic it received was small fixed-wing and helicopter shuttle flights from Cairo. Otherwise, occasional private or courier flights arrived from Kefalos or Rome, the staging city for the Egyptian digs.

One of the fixed-wings was there for Duke's use. He could drive almost anything with a motor. Planes, boats, even minisubmarines, bikes, cars, trucks, you name it, if he hadn't already logged in plenty of miles in a vehicle, give him a few minutes, and he'd figure it out. He was also a former Navy deep-sea diver, sky-diver, para-glider, jet-skier, snow-skier, snowboarder, and ex–hockey champ. There were probably a few athletic skills he hadn't mastered, but hell, he was only seventy-two. He figured there was plenty of time. He had to practice his marksmanship and get married some of the time, so that slowed him down a little. His kids said that no matter how old Daddy got, he was always looking for new ways to die young. Or, as Leda liked to say, "Daddy has a Swiss Army life."

For a few moments, the tremors seemed to quiet. Duke risked his life, not to mention a traffic ticket, weaving through the confusion on the Corniche. The joint was jumpin', literally, and not in a good way. Flimsy buildings crashed all the way down the beachfront as if they were made of toothpicks. Fires were breaking out, sirens wailing, people screaming and darting into traffic.

He veered southeast off the Corniche down the Ras at-Tin and roared along the edge of the inner harbor, parallel to the tram line.

The tracks were all over the place, stuck up in the air, jutting across the road, halfway into the water.

Over the growl of his bike he heard the squeal of rubber, metal grinding against metal, and the crash of smashing glass right behind him.

In his rearview mirror he saw cars accordioned into one another all the way back up Ibrahim-al Auwal. What looked like a small mountain erupted into the middle of the street about 300 feet back from the turnoff. He headed due west through El Wardyan, which was more or less the local ghetto. Just to the east of the cutoff and along the shores of Lake Mariout was the street with Gabriella's villa. He wondered briefly if the poor kid was okay. He'd have to check on her on the way back.

For Leda to put delivering this doohickey he carried above her own safety and the safety of everybody else on the site, it had to have top priority. He was glad nobody had any animals there, no pets or donkeys or anything. The people could get themselves out for all he cared, but animals were different. He suddenly missed Leroy, his cat, back in McMinnville with his current wife.

The road shuddered again, and a chasm opened up a hundred yards or so from his front tire. Now was the time to see if the Sopwith could fly.

Reflexes taking over, he slid to the rear of the seat, shifting his weight to the back wheel. At the same time he jerked the bars up and gunned the motor.

Yep. It could. It flew across the mother of all potholes as pretty as his Indian did after the races in Portland, when the first biker to lay down the front wheel had to buy the next round of beer.

Another turn toward the west through a crowd of people running in every direction. Fellahin, Egyptian peasants. A couple of the boys on his staff came from this district. They were Egyptian salt-of-the-earth types who usually lived in housing so poor it didn't take much to bring it crashing down around their ears, the way it was doing now. Damn.

He kept wanting to turn back, to see what was going on, to help people instead of protecting this damned piece of some long-dead gal, no matter how famous she was. Was the Kid okay? Would she have sense enough to get out of that flimsy death trap? And how sturdy was Pete's dam, anyway? The only thing that stopped him from turning back was Leda. She knew him, she knew what he would be inclined to do, and she insisted that the tube was the most important thing. Nothing for it but to get to the plane, ferry the thing over to Rome, and fly back as soon as possible. Shouldn't take all that long.

He slowed the bike and looked back across the city in his rearview mirror. The spire on a mosque broke like a pencil while he watched, its dome toppling to the street soundless in the greater roar of the catastrophe. The town was still rocking, even after the worst of the shock passed.

Some of the taller office buildings, the ones that were built along quake-proof recommendations, would be okay, but even as he watched, others crumpled to pieces as if Godzilla stomped them. The city's lights suddenly extinguished as if Godzilla had blown them out after stomping the buildings.

Duke turned on the siren he had installed on the Sopwith and roared through the mass of fleeing people. Suddenly he was far from them and their houses and tearing along the Desert Highway toward the city's most remote outskirts. He turned off the siren and sped ahead. The quake didn't seem as bad out this way, he was thinking.

Then came a huge, loud, wet, roaring sound as if Godzilla had flushed his Godzilla-sized toilet. He wished he could stop thinking of everything in terms of Godzilla. That was the Kid's fault. Her and her collections.

But he knew what the sound was. The dam had broken. He shook his head, as if to dislodge the idea of any imaginary good he might have done if he'd stayed there.

Nucore should have sprung for that extra layer of fortification, the one where they froze the floor of the sea where the sheet metal pilings were driven in. He hoped the Kid was okay. He couldn't help her now. He still had to take this metal doohickey where it was wanted with what was left of Cleopatra. He imagined the old girl as resembling his favorite schlocky version of the story, the one with Elizabeth Taylor back in the days when she was a babe.

The road ran along beside the airfield for a mile or two before the gate. The runway was eerily unlit except for starlight. Why the hell hadn't the guy in the shed started setting out flares, anyway? Emergency supplies would begin arriving from Nucore before long. He could see the outlines of two planes, which appeared undisturbed by the quakes. The runway didn't have any obvious damage he could make out in the poor light, either.

He was at full throttle when he turned toward the gate.

Suddenly, the headlamp on his bike picked up a taxi-van. The vehicle was kitty-corner across the gate, blocking it. The driver-side door was open, and the torso of the driver hung down over the seat and half out the door. *What the hell had happened here?* he was wondering, when a familiar figure crossed in front of the van and began limping toward the bike, waving her arms.

"Duke!" he heard her cry. It was Gabriella Faruk.

He skidded the bike in a semicircle to avoid colliding with her or the cab, so that his front tire was headed back the way he'd come. At which point he collided instead with the nose of a jeep roaring up onto the road from the desert side.

To minimize the impact, Duke leaned to the right and laid the bike down, smacking his helmet against the road as he did.

He heard Gabriella yell something in Arabic ladies weren't supposed to know how to say. The last thing he was aware of was two or three guys grabbing at him and hauling him toward the Jeep while all the time Gabriella, closer now, bawled them out.

CHAPTER 13

"You didn't have to kill him," Gabriella told her idiot cousin. "He could have been a lot of help to us, he and Leda."

"He's not dead yet," Mo said. "Do you want what's left of him?"

"Of course. Bring him with us. Has he got the specimen?"

"Here it is," Mo said, reaching into Duke's shirt and pulling out the little titanium cylinder.

"Excellent. Very well, then, into the plane, quickly. The airfield will be crawling with rescue missions soon. The rest of you, return to the villa and check on your mothers. Send me a radio message at Ginia's. Coded, please."

Mo flew the plane while Gabriella played paramedic to Leda's father. Duke's rasping breathing reassured her that he still lived. She liked the crusty old devil, for although he was in some ways all of the things she despised about men, he was evidently not as bad as he appeared, having raised a daughter as independent and capable as Leda. He was also funny, and that went a long way with her, and he was genuinely brave, from what Leda had told her.

Gabriella had never intended that he be harmed, which was why she had set up the diversion herself. Damn Mohammed's careless driving, but she supposed he was rattled, as they all were, by the quake. He was a good pilot and the best hacker in Egypt, but as a terrorist, he made a better computer programmer.

The access she'd gained to the computer during her visits to the beluga had enabled him to hack in and monitor Leda's transmissions from his own machine back at the villa. He had intercepted all but that last message, the crucial one. It had been interrupted by the quake. But before that, they received and decoded Leda's E-mail to Chimera saying that Duke was bringing the specimen back to Nucore for Chimera, who would then use it on the client who had claimed Cleopatra. It was not a very subtle code. Leda had decided that most Egyptians wouldn't be able to understand pig Latin, but in fact, it had amused Gabriella back in her college days, and she was easily able to translate the message.

By now, Gabriella knew the Hubbard family well enough to know that if Leda's message said Duke would be flying from the airstrip in the next hour with the specimen, that was exactly what would happen. A mere earthquake was unlikely to stop either of them. But it did throw off the plans Gabriella had formed to meet Duke and the specimen and possibly persuade him to take her with him back to Kefalos.

At some point she could then have injected him with a fast-acting sedative and relieved him of the sample. Afterward, she had intended to leave him somewhere safe to sleep it off. Even now, she hoped he could still be saved. After all, nothing really incriminating had happened while he was conscious, and if he lived and they could be persuaded, he and Leda could be real assets to the movement.

Now movement of another kind entirely made the city below her resemble Tokyo after her favorite movie monster had made a recent appearance. Whole flattened areas were lit only by the fires in other areas.

As she flew out across the coast and over the Mediterranean, she saw that the largest archaeological dig of all time was now once more simply a harbor filled with water, the debris of buildings far more modern than the Pharos Lighthouse bobbing on its still-turbulent surface.

She owed Leda a lot for rescuing the precious remains of the great queen before this happened. She desperately hoped her friend had survived the collapse of the dam and would become part of her plans for a new Egypt, influenced by the wisdom and insight of its last, best, and truest pharaoh.

As they approached the airstrip at Mykonos, she had Mo put in a call to Dr. Nessa Benoit, Ginia's personal physician, and ask her to meet them. Nessa was loyal, and her clinic on Mykonos was totally funded by Ginia.

Nessa wanted the patient to be brought to the clinic, but Gabriella needed to avoid the possibility that Duke would ask awkward questions in public when he woke up. So she flew Nessa and Duke across in her little Glinda the Good Witch of the North bubble of a helicopter, which was blessedly not pink.

She hadn't seen much of Ginia since immediately after her blending.

When they met this time, it seemed to Gabriella that although her own greeting was as warm and enthusiastic as ever, Ginia's was somewhat reserved. She turned her head, in fact, so that Gabriella's kiss landed on her cheek. Gabriella supposed it was natural. Half of Ginia didn't actually know Gabriella all that well since the blending.

They had discussed this sort of possibility before Ginia underwent the procedure, but it didn't help. Gabriella tried to ignore the sense of abandonment that swept over her with the coolness of her best, and at times only, friend.

She tried instead to focus on anticipating her own blending, but for a change, that didn't help. How much more would it complicate her already interdepedent relationship with Ginia when each of them carried the memories and personalities of another woman as well as her own? At least Cleopatra was known to have had only two lovers. Pandora Blades supposedly had many, of both sexes, to ease her pain over her long-standing passion for her estranged husband, Theo.

Nessa and some of the servants were carrying Duke into the house on a makeshift stretcher.

"How is he?" Ginia asked.

"Not doing very well. I think if I can relieve the pressure from the skull fracture, however, he may improve. Where may I use as a surgery?"

"Show Dr. Benoit and her patient to the folding room in the laundry," Ginia instructed the servants. "There is water, clean cloths. Do you require anything else?" she asked Nessa.

"It will be an awkward surgery to perform alone," the doctor replied.

"I'll assist," Gabriella said. "I have had some practice opening people, after all, even if they have been dead for thousands of years. Meanwhile, Madelaine can check this and make sure it's ready for transfer." She pulled out the titanium canister. Ginia took it from her and, without another word, headed for her assistant's office. Her new assistant had been recruited from the Nucore laboratory staff. She hadn't been hired to plan parties and cancel charity luncheons but because of her knowledge of the blending procedure. Gabriella, through Mo, had been transmitting Leda's decoded messages to Madelaine for clarification since Leda found the canopic jar.

Brain surgery on a living person was quite different in

some ways. For some reason, she had forgotten about how much flowing blood was involved with the live ones. She didn't consider herself squeamish, but the room, mainly the province of servants, was not air-conditioned or even particularly well ventilated. The smell of hot bone as the saw went through it was nauseating, the spurt of bright blood that when mopped away revealed old dark blood that had pooled, putting pressure on the brain, left Gabriella feeling dizzy, as well as queasy.

It occurred to her that if she was going to have to kill anyone, perhaps she should do it with a very long-range firearm. Or better yet, drop bombs on them from a high-altitude airplane. This was altogether too personal.

But then, so, too, had the death of her mother been personal. How had he stood it, her stepfather, killing someone with whom he had eaten and slept?

She felt better once Nessa had closed the wound and they had mopped away the worst of the blood. The servants finished cleaning Duke and wrapped him in fresh sheets before taking him to the room Ginia had designated. It was between her office and the room she and Gabriella usually shared.

As they passed the office, Madelaine came out, wearing a puzzled expression.

"Whose donation is this supposed to be?" she asked Gabriella, indicating the little tube.

"You know very well," Gabriella said, suddenly exhausted from her exertions of the night. "Cleopatra's."

Madelaine shook her head. "Impossible. This is much too new and much too old, and the wrong sex besides. Instead of being from a young woman of ancient times, this sample belongs to an elderly man of present times. In fact, it might be a very good match to that sick fellow next door."

Gabriella buried her face in her hands and groaned. Of course it wouldn't be this easy. She should have known. Leda and Duke were both very clever. They had tricked her.

A thorough search of Duke's clothing revealed no other specimen, and it occurred to her that perhaps the specimen had been on his bike rather than on his person. She must get on the radio at once and tell the boys to return for the bike. She couldn't blame them any more than she blamed herself, of course. Having found the first specimen in his shirt, none of them thought to look any further.

"I take it we won't be using this one then," Madelaine said, nodding toward the office and presumably, the donor sample.

The original plan was to verify the specimen, then, under the guise of delivering it to Chimera, persuade, bribe, or force the scientist to blend the queen's DNA with Gabriella instead of the client he had in mind. Madelaine only knew about part of the scheme. There was no need for her to know too much.

"No, of course not—oh, wait!" Gabriella said, when a sudden delicious thought hit her that caused her to grin mischievously. "Dr. Chimera will still be expecting a prepared donor specimen for use on a special client who claimed Cleopatra's DNA before anyone else knew the material was available. It seems only right that we provide one."

CHAPTER 14

Chimera received Leda's message with an ambivalence stronger than usual, even for someone who was, by choice, of two minds.

On the one hand, the feminine side of Chimera was pleased that their friend Leda had succeeded, that the queen of the Nile had been found. That soon Cleopatra's thought patterns, memories, attitudes, personality traits, and much of what had been her character would once more be known. Perhaps many great mysteries would be solved and great discoveries made possible because of the queen's knowledge.

On the other hand, the part of Chimera who was such a loving husband that he could not stand to allow his wife the ultimate change from life to death without needing to keep a part of who she had been alive within him felt that he was helping abet a great mistake. Preoccupied Wilhelm Wolfe might be, but Chimera's masculine side felt sure his friend and ally, the CEO of Nucore, loved his wife as she was. He felt deeply that Gretchen Wolfe would regret her blending.

The questions this brought to Chimera sent the scientist back to the laboratory, where the experiments kept being interrupted by nagging spiritual questions applying to all Nucore clients.

So it was with a degree of both relief and dismay that Chimera received Leda's message that she was sending her father with the properly prepared DNA specimen.

Neither relief nor dismay gained ascendancy in Chimera's blended mind when the Nucore-uniformed pilot handed over the titanium metal transport tube. Chimera merely expressed surprise that Duke had not personally delivered the specimen, as Leda had specified.

"Oh, he was on his way when the earthquake began," said the pilot, who seemed to be Egyptian.

"Was that what interrupted the electronic transmission of the prepared specimen?" Chimera asked.

Chimera thought the pilot looked puzzled, but of course, he would. He had no way of knowing about the computer failure.

"Certainly it must have been," the pilot said. "But all the same, Duke entrusted me with this and said it is all ready and I should bring it straight to you. If you will excuse me now, Doctor, I must pick up emergency supplies and return to Alexandria."

"Of course," Chimera said. There was just enough time to fetch the portable unit from the laboratory before the motor launch sailed for the mainland, where Chimera caught a ride on another Nucore plane heading for Austria to pick up supplies. Having already received the scientist's message that the desired material had been obtained and was en route, Gretchen Wolfe sent a car to the airstrip.

Chimera had hoped to be able to spend time with Gretchen, to remain with her until she awakened from the blending. However, an emergency message from Kefalos about the dual catastrophes of earthquake and flood in Alexandria required the scientist's immediate return.

Once the process was complete, Chimera left Gretchen sleeping, under the watchful eyes of her servants, with a message to notify the scientist by phone when Gretchen awoke. All the way to back to Kefalos, Chimera had the feeling that something was very wrong. Was it just that it seemed a shame that Gretchen, of all people, required another personality? What would the blending with sensuous and devious Cleopatra do to the straightforward, compassionate Gretchen? Would she even be someone Wolfe still liked? Chimera didn't care to think about it and felt once more that this might be a terrible mistake. It had been wrong to do this important blending secretly.

However innocently, Chimera had colluded with Gretchen to deceive Wolfe, to go behind his back in a matter that intimately concerned him. More importantly, however, it had been performed without the lengthy, soul-searching interview Chimera and Wolfe normally conducted. Gretchen was a friend, and such an interview, for some reason, had seemed more intrusive than the process of adding Cleopatra's personality to hers.

Chimera felt uneasily that it was more urgent than ever to find a safe and predictable way to reverse the blending.

Dr. Gretchen Wolfe, for her part, had submitted to the blending with no second thoughts, no qualms or reservations, once she decided to go through with it. That had been back when she confided in Chimera that she feared she was losing Wilhelm, and the only thing that could help her, as she saw it, was a charisma transplant. She had narrowed it down to that.

She already had undergone surgeries to correct her largish nose, her weakish chin, her sagging eyelids, and thinning mouth. She had had her thighs liposuctioned and her tummy tucked. Her skin had been abraded and lasered of all correctable defects, and her hair professionally returned to the golden glory of her youth. She finally admitted that she needed makeup and had allowed herself to buy expensive but becoming clothing, after years of preferring to shop frugally and give generously to charities.

She feared she had even neglected her patients in her quest to perfect her appearance, and still Wilhelm didn't seem to notice that a basically reconstructed woman was at his side every time she joined him. When she finally resorted to the asinine "Do you notice anything different about me, darling?" game, he had replied, as he always did, "You are perfection itself, *liebchen*. You must never change anything. I love you as you are."

Hah! And yet, did he ever come to her at their home now? Always he was busy in deep consultation with the international jet-setting beauties, billionairesses, actresses, divas, that sort of woman, who came to him to make themselves interesting inside as well as outside. It was all for the blendings, *ja,* she knew. But she also knew that a man was a man, and these women, they were very beautiful to begin with and unscrupulous about married men even before they blended with the greatest courtesans, temptresses, or heroines of history. Gretchen knew that in some ways she was simple. She was a doctor. She was a wife. She did not understand politics—not even hospital politics. This caused her much trouble sometimes. She did not understand sexual politics. She felt sometimes that Wilhelm had chosen her simply to have a wife to be a shield against all of the women who wanted him, and she had been so willing to please him, to do things his way, how much trouble could she be? But now, that was not enough. She needed to understand these things, or she felt she would lose him.

After considerable thinking, Gretchen finally knew who she had to have to give her not only the ability to understand complex personal and sexual matters but also the extra dimension of sensuality and intriguing mystery she needed to hold her husband against such odds. She must have Cleopatra.

Truthfully, she didn't really need *all* of Cleopatra, but there was no choice in that. She reasoned that the personalities that eventually emerged after the process were always a blend of the two, with the stronger being perhaps more dominant. It would be terrible if she turned into a full-time seductress. The idea horrified her.

She wanted only to keep her own husband. She wouldn't know what to do with other men. She didn't want to find out.

Their marriage had been sound when last they were together, she was sure. And she understood that her husband must put himself into his very important work. She herself had done the same thing in her practice as a pediatrician. At one time, it had been Wilhelm who complained of her long hours in the clinic and hospital, hours that had become longer once they discovered they could have no children of their own bodies. Before they had come to a conclusion on what to do about that exactly, Chimera discovered the process, and its development had consumed so much of Wilhelm's time that he spent virtually all of his nights and days in quarters at one of Nucore's facilities or another. He was closer to Chimera than he was to her, and had she not remembered Chimera as Chime and Tsering from their college days, the sweet couple whose love was so much like she wanted her own to be, she might have felt jealousy. Chimera had understood her at once and had promised to help without reservation. Whether two people or one, Chimera was her friend, too.

She had tried at first to go to Wilhelm, had many times observed the procedure, conversed with Nucore scientists, even made a few modest suggestions. She had considered returning to university for an advanced degree in genetics. But no, it would only put more distance between them and make her unavailable for those rare times when Wilhelm could be with her. Besides, she liked working with the little children. She was good with them, yes. So sad that she and Wilhelm could not have their own, but years had passed since they last spoke of the matter. Now she, ten years older than Wilhelm, was well past safe childbearing age, even if she could become pregnant.

Cleopatra had had many children. Perhaps her memories of her children would be of some comfort to Gretchen. She had died so young, the queen, that perhaps she would be disgusted to wake up in an aging body? But no. She knew pain, the poor girl. Her death was by her own hand, no less. Of course, there were extenuating circumstances. It was not as if antidepressants would have changed things for a queen whose husband was supposedly dead and whose country was being conquered, herself to be paraded in chains through the streets of Rome. These things were personal catastrophes, and although Gretchen felt that the queen had somehow given up on life too soon, she could understand a little. Even so, snakes! Gretchen shuddered, thinking about it. She would have to be very firm with the former queen of Egypt about that, too. Under no circumstances would snakes in the vicinity of her bosom be tolerated.

CHAPTER 15

"Lady, does the phrase 'head for the hills, the dam's breaking' ring any bells for you at all?" Pete Welsh yelled over the din of traffic and the groaning of the dam as he pulled Leda from the ruin of the beluga. He had reached her by chopping down the door in a properly testosterone-enabled fashion, rather like a bald Paul Bunyan with an ax that had fortunately and magically materialized from someplace.

She was delighted that he had chosen to use his muscles on her behalf at that moment. Otherwise, she would have been smothered by beluga wreckage as she was almost smothered by clean-room plastic a few moments before. But he didn't have to be so snarly about it. He was just in a bad mood because the dam really was breaking from the pressures of the sea outside it and the ocean floor cracking up somewhere out there. The dig actually looked quite stable—no cracks that she could see offhand but—

"Move it!" Pete barked.

"Okay, okay, but I can't head for the hills. There aren't any." She realized he was perfectly right to try to spur her to action. Oxygen deprivation was making her a little drifty at the moment, not quite ready to heed the call to action.

"Head for the sand dunes then. This whole area has to be evacuated. We still might have a tsunami: and are bound to have at the least a pseudo tsunami if the dam doesn't hold."

He turned his red and sweating face away from her and jogged up toward a freshly arrived gaggle of tourists, yelling, "Run!"

That got her attention. It dawned on her suddenly, as she stared at what was left of the lab, that while a tsunami, real or pseudo, would be very scary, it was nothing compared to Namid once he found out the canopic jar was lost in the quake. And Daddy was gone. The most prudent thing would be to go to the airfield and wait for him and have him take her straight back to Nucore, the salvaged mini-disk tucked safely in the front of her bra.

She wasn't an awfully good runner, but she seemed to teleport to the road. Although power failures had plunged the rest of the city into darkness, the thoroughfare was ablaze and ablare with the lights and horns of vehicles that were going nowhere.

"Taxi, madame?" An unmarked elderly Buick in front of her sprouted a head and torso from the driver's-side window.

She felt like laughing and at first was glad her sense of humor hadn't deserted her, then realized it was probably hysteria. The guy was enterprising, if unrealistic.

"You think I want to hire you to let me sit in your car while the sea breaks over the dam and drowns us?" she asked, even as she spoke figuring he probably didn't speak enough English to understand. "Or were you planning to carry me piggyback?"

He ignored that last remark. "Where do you wish to go?" His English was actually very good.

"You know the Nucore airstrip west of town?"

"Oh yes."

"There. And I'd say step on it, except all that would do right now is end up crunching your front end."

"Madame is very wise and uncommonly understanding of the situation. It is an emergency?"

"Yes," she said as the ground shook again and another clash of metal screeched a few car lengths ahead. "For both of us."

"Yes," he said, following her gaze to the dam, over which the Mediterranean was impatiently sloshing. "Come."

He slammed the driver's-side door into the vehicle beside his and jumped out, ran around the cab, popped the trunk, and lifted out a bicycle built for two. He displayed this with the same dramatic flare merchants at the market used to present "an ancient necklace from the tomb of Nefertiti, oh yes, the one she is supposed to have been given on her wedding day."

"Gosh," Leda said, slithering out of and around the cab to join the driver and his emergency backup measure. "Is this the very same bike ridden by Cleopatra and Julius Caesar? The one they took with them on the barge so when they wanted to go ashore she could show him the real Egypt?"

"Ha ha. Madame is joking. That will be twenty dollars, American, please."

"Should be ten if I do half the pedaling."

"Oh, no, madame. If I did all of the work, it would cost you nothing because I would leave you here and save myself. However, madame did say she needed to reach the airstrip on a matter most urgent?"

"Okay, okay, you got me."

They hopped on and pedaled for all they were worth. Usually, they could find a path between cars, but at a couple of points, they had to dismount and portage the bike over jammed cars until they reached the turnoff for the Desert Highway. After a few hundred feet, Hassan braked the bike so hard it toppled sideways and only the foot of Leda's long leg stopped them from falling over. "What is it?" she asked.

"Your American Grand Canyon, madame. We must go around now, I think."

Leaning out to see beyond him, she beheld a deeper shadow in the night-shrouded road. A very much deeper shadow, about two feet wide. "Okay," she said.

They detoured through the deserted lot of a deserted office complex and continued at a more cautious pace. There were three more serious breaks in the road, but Leda and her "driver" were able to walk the bike across two of them, although the pavement crumbled under their heels in an alarming fashion. Once the road and surrounding structures piled up in a mountainous heap in the middle and it was just after they detoured around it that they heard a sound like—well, all Leda could think of was Godzilla rising from the bay in Tokyo. Then she realized what it had to be. "Shit," she said.

"Excuse me, madame?" the driver asked.

"The dam broke."

"In that case, I think perhaps we must pedal more quickly, madame," he replied.

Ahead, the air was thick with smoke. Heading into the district occupied by many of the poor fellahin, Leda saw much of the district was on fire, the flames leaping from hovel to hovel, more stalled cars, trucks, carts, food squashed, skinny chickens squawking and flapping in panic, people rushing to and fro like souls on first arrival in hell, before they received their assignments.

Leda pulled up her T-shirt tail and covered her mouth and nose against the smoke and kept pedaling.

The driver was beginning to exude an unpleasant smell from his manful efforts on the front of the bike, a goaty pong not particularly improved by its overlay of Old Spice.

At last they neared the airstrip.

The treacherous moon was still shining overhead as if all was right with the world below. Its rays brightened a long, placid strip of runway, miraculously unperturbed by the quake. And unoccupied by any kind of aircraft.

"Shit," Leda said.

"We have missed your flight?" the driver asked.

"Bingo," she said.

"So where do you wish to go now?" he asked.

She was about to say they should return to the harbor— a harbor no longer dry, she felt sure, but once more filled with the Mediterranean, which had probably taken as interest the excavation's headquarters, part of the beach, perhaps some of the highway and Fort Quait Bay. That much damage was to be expected from the crashing of the sea back into its natural bed. Had there been a tsunami, she and the driver and most of Alexandria would have drowned by now.

As they turned, a glint of light caught her eye. Moonbeams winked from a small metal heap on the side of the road ahead. "No, wait, let's see what that is," she said. But she recognized it already. Her dad's bike.

"Step on it," she told the driver and pedaled harder.

She wanted to think that in his enthusiasm to get her specimen to Chimera, in perhaps his eagerness to run his errand and return to the earthquake, Dad had ditched the bike and sprinted to the runway, tube in hand, hopped aboard the plane, traded motorcycle helmet for leather aviator's helmet, tossed his figurative aviator's neck scarf back over his shoulder with a cry of "Curse you, Red Baron!" and flown away.

Fun to think that, yeah. Because Dad was the kind of guy who be anxious to *return* to the disaster to do what he could about saving lives, keeping the peace, getting the injured to medical care, and protecting property in his copious leisure time.

But not this time. That was his bike. And just a few

yards beyond it was his helmet. 'Old Mothah Hubbard' was blazoned across the back in silver letters. A long crack ran between the last two words and up to the crown. The inside was wet when Leda touched it, and her fingertips came away with dark stains.

Setting her jaw so tightly she could hear her orthodontist screaming, she walked back to where Dad's prized Sopwith lay, not wrecked but just lying there. Nevertheless, the road was also covered with a wet, dark stain that wasn't gas or oil, and when Leda held her fingers up to the moonlight, the light dyed them red.

The driver stared down at her and fidgeted.

"It's perfectly obvious to the trained eye what happened here," Leda said. "There was a tremor, the bike went down with Dad, he hit his head, and trying to see how badly he was hurt, he took off the helmet and threw it over there. He probably dragged himself over to the control shed to call for help. Maybe he's passed out in there now."

"Yes," the driver said. "And my twenty dollars?"

Ignoring him for a moment, she picked up the Sopwith. She tapped the tank to see if there was still fuel in it. She didn't smell any on the road, so she wasn't surprised to hear a slosh. She checked the wires and the gear lever, but Dad had been true to his usual form. The bike was fine. All she really had to do was start it. She hung the broken helmet over the handlebar, slung her leg over the bike, and grabbed for the clutch—and got the brake. "Shit, it's a Brit!" Of course it was. Everything was on the wrong side. The driver was pulling at her sleeve.

She swore again, dug inside her pants pocket for the twenty bucks, and handed it to him. He pedaled off back down the road again.

Switching hands this time to accommodate for British bikes having their controls on the opposite sides from American ones, Leda pulled the clutch in, goosed the gas with a twist of her thumb and forefinger, stomped down with her right foot on the kick lever to start it, then jerked her leg the hell out of the way so when the lever sprang back it didn't add to the collection of bruises she was already sporting. The bike gave a little cough and caught, roaring and popping before settling down to the thrum of a powerful beast eager to run and play. As she increased the gas, it jumped a little, but she eased down on the seat and rode slowly up to the Quonset hut.

All the way she searched by the light of the headlamp, looking for drag marks, more bloodstains, any evidence of what had happened to her dad.

No light shone from under the Quonset hut's firmly closed door, but then the power was out all over the city now. Or maybe the dimwit who worked there was getting more beauty sleep. She checked the back, where he had been sleeping before. No one was there. The rat had abandoned the sinking ship. Maybe he had friends or relatives he wanted to take care of during the emergency, but it was going to cost him what was probably one of the best jobs in Egypt. Or maybe—wonderful thought—maybe the runway guy had heard the crash and took Dad to the hospital in his own vehicle.

Leda called, "Anybody here? Runway guy? Dad? You in there? You okay?" But neither word nor grunt answered. She shoved open the door and walked in. Moonlight followed her inside.

She plucked her little penlight from a pocket and shoned it around the room until it found an oil lamp, which she lit.

She sighed and perched on the edge of the desk, trying to think what to do next. Her knees felt like cooked noodles from the pedaling, and she was still a little light-headed. She hoped Dad hadn't tried to fly away with a head injury like the one he must have sustained to crack the helmet the way it was. She didn't see how he could still be conscious, but if he was, she wouldn't put it past him to try.

Her cell phone was in another pocket of her pants—

handy things, these cargo pants, not flattering but very practical. She didn't really expect to get him, but she dialed his number anyway.

His phone rang a few feet away from her, from the Sopwith.

"Omigod, the saddlebags. It's in the saddlebags," she said, and pulled them off and with trembling hands pawed through filthy cleaning rags and underwear. Something hard was inside the first roll, but it wasn't the cell phone. That fell to the ground, unheeded, with another clump of dirty laundry, while she stared at the little round titanium tube she'd unwrapped.

Where the hell was he? If he flew off, it wasn't to finish his mission, because here was the sample.

CHAPTER 16

Leda made herself useful as long as she was there. With the runway manager missing, someone needed to take up the slack, and she'd been around enough airstrips and aircraft carriers that she knew the drill. She got her exercise by setting out flares along the runway, glad of Dad's bike so she didn't have to walk the whole distance. Then she started the emergency generator running, which turned on the low-intensity overheads. She called Nucore on Dad's cell phone, after inserting the new battery he had jammed in the bags with it at the last minute, to apprise them of the situation and ask what airborne assistance they could expect within the next few hours. She also informed them they were going to need a relief runway manager.

After that, she answered the phone a lot. Nucore was fast; she had to give them that. Within about two hours, the planes and copters began landing, and she was so busy she couldn't think straight. Pete and a number of the men from his crews arrived in the most rattletrap collection of trucks, cabs, donkey carts, and motor bikes Leda had ever seen to take delivery of equipment and supplies.

Leda ran out to meet him.

He looked up from hefting a box of supplies and grunted.

"Pete, have you heard anything from or about Dad?"

"No, but I've been a little busy since you left," he said. "The dam broke."

"I heard. I bet they heard it in Cairo. How is . . . everybody?"

"Everybody with sense enough to get the hell out of the way as fast and as far as they could is pretty much fine, I guess. Those who didn't aren't so lucky. There is going to be a lot of cleanup to do. My replacement will repair the dam and pump out the harbor again so work can continue. Now, if you'll excuse me, I'm a little busy."

"Oh, sorry," she said. Then asked, "Your replacement?"

"I got fired. They had to blame somebody, didn't they?"

"Shit, sorry," she said.

He put his load down again and turned to face her. Her uncharacteristically contrite tone alarmed him. "Why? Didn't Duke make it here?"

"Yeah, but it looks like he crashed the bike and busted his head open."

"Just his head huh? He's probably okay then."

"I hope so," she said but couldn't manage a smile. "Can I help?"

"Sure, start lugging stuff to the trucks."

That kept her occupied for several more hours. But then, finally, she had to think about where to go and what to do with herself. And how to go about finding Dad.

Belatedly, she remembered the specimen. How in the hell had she ever thought getting to Kefalos was the most important thing in the world? She'd forgotten about it so utterly she hadn't hitched a ride on the last plane going back for more supplies. Well, she'd catch the one after.

The relief runway manager finally arrived, and she showed him what she'd logged.

"I don't know where the other guy went," she said.

"His family was visiting downtown someplace," the relief guy said. "But look, you've done enough. You're exhausted. Go in the back and lie down."

"I need transport out of the country ASAP," she said. "Back to Kefalos."

"I'll let you know when the next plane in gets ready to leave," he promised. No further urging was necessary. She hit the cot and dropped into a deep hole of sleep.

Gabriella, having made a brief foray to Mykonos to give Mo the specimen to deliver to Chimera, flew back to Ginia's villa. The helipad was located atop the flat roof of the east wing, and a strange copter was sitting there when Gabriella arrived.

Madelaine and Nessa Benoit, medical bag in hand, came out to meet her. "Can we hitch a ride back to Mykonos before you shut down?" Nessa shouted over the copter blades.

"How is he?" Gabriella countered.

Nessa shook her head and said in a tired, almost mechanical voice, "Gone. I left him for a few moments to go to the bathroom, and when I returned, he had stopped breathing. We tried resuscitation, but we couldn't save him."

Gabriella could have mistaken the weariness in the doctor's voice for professional disappointment except for the quick glances Madelaine kept darting first to her, then to Nessa. The girl looked as if she desperately wished to chain-smoke. Gabriella said casually, "It's too bad. We did what we could."

"Yes," Nessa said shortly and turned her head away, starting to climb into the copter. "What we could. Under the circumstances. Oh, I have a message for you," she said, again in that mechanical voice. "Ginia said to tell you that although she's sure you will be wanting to return to Egypt right away, you must come back here when you've delivered us to Mykonos. There's an important guest you are to help her entertain. She says to dress for dinner."

Madelaine took the opportunity to scramble aboard, but Gabriella could have sworn she saw the girl's shoulder blades contract when Nessa mentioned the dinner guest.

"Merde!" Gabriella said, feeling as weary as the doctor sounded. Nothing was further from Gabriella's desires than to entertain, but Ginia would have known that. Mo hadn't been able to reach anyone at home to tell them to return for the bike, and so they had no idea if the brothers had made it back safely or if the villa and its occupants had survived the flooding of the harbor.

Nevertheless, she dropped Madelaine and Nessa off and returned to Dilos around eight. She hadn't slept in almost twenty-four hours. The last thing on her mind was primping. She pulled a black silk tunic and trousers from the closet, though she never ordinarily wore black and had bought the outfit to set off an Egyptian collar Ginia had purchased for her from an antiquities dealer. Not the sort of thing she could wear in Egypt, the collar, but she'd worn it here. She didn't bother with it now. A pair of hammered silver earrings, a little touch of makeup on her tired, red-lidded eyes with liner, shadow, and mascara, some lipstick and a silver scarab ring. She scooped her hair into a twist on top of her head and pinned it, shoved her feet into silver sandals, and dragged herself to the formal dining room.

The glass doors to the terrace were open, and the red-tiled outdoor room glowed with candlelight from hundreds of candles set along the walls and stairways. The place looked like a church, Gabriella thought with distaste. One of the servants would catch her skirt on fire. Over the strains of a viola solo, Ginia's husky laughter poured, warm and intimate. Her head was inclined toward the dinner partner sitting next to her at the table. Wine was poured in three glasses. Ginia was wearing a turquoise long sleeved shirtwaist gown, the one with the flowing skirt that she wore with the American Indian silver and turquoise belt and earrings Gabriella had given her when she returned from Berkeley. Except tonight she wasn't wearing the belt or earrings. Gemstone drops sparkled against her hair.

The man's voice was amused and intimate, too. Gabriella had heard it recently.

"Gaby, my dear, there you are. Mr. Rasmussen has come to see us. Isn't that lovely? He told me you two had met in Egypt, and when he heard you were here, he wished particularly to see you, so of course I invited him to stay."

Rasmussen inclined his head and fixed Gabriella with eyes that were more appreciative than her appearance warranted, she was sure. "You are looking rather . . . subdued, Dr. Faruk," he said.

"I was informed by the doctor that a friend of mine has just died," she replied. "And I am very tired. The crisis in Alexandria, I'm sure you're aware of."

"I certainly am. It's cost me millions. I've had the fellow who built that flimsy dam fired, of course."

She nodded absently. "Ginia, may I speak to you privately for a moment, please?"

"Can it wait, Gaby dear? The first course is on its way, and Cesare was just telling me the most amusing story."

"I'm afraid not," Gabriella said, her patience ebbing rapidly.

Ginia fluttered to her feet—actually fluttered—laid her hand on "Cesare's" shoulder, whispered something in his ear, and joined Gabriella, who pulled her off into the deserted dining room. Ginia's face was flushed with wine, and her eyes very bright.

"What's he doing here?" Gabriella demanded.

"As I told you, he wanted to see you. He is very interested in the process, you know, the blending, and when I

told him you were acquiring Cleopatra, he seemed fascinated. He asked me to let him know when you arrived, so I
contacted him."

"Without saying anything to me?"

"Don't be so touchy, darling girl! I'm saying something
now, am I not?"

"He is a slimy man," Gabriella said.

"He is a powerful man," Ginia defended him, "with far
more wealth and resources than I have. You're fortunate
he's taken an interest in us. Even when I told him that your
plan had backfired and all you had was the DNA of that
coarse little policeman you brought home to die, he was
not put off but found it hilarious. He seemed charmed by
your wit. He wishes to back your 'movement.' You should
be glad. That movement of yours has not been moving
much of anywhere for some time now."

"It will once I have Cleopatra. Surely you can see that I
must return to Egypt immediately. The sample must be on
Duke's motorbike. Failing that, I must see what Leda was
able to salvage."

"Delegate, darling. I never ask you for anything, but
you must catch Cesare up on your progress."

"It sounds to me like you've been doing a very good job
of that already. Is that awful little man the one Pandora has
selected as your first mutual lover and mentor?"

"Can't I have friends, too? You have that dreadful
American woman. As if she wasn't bad enough, you had to
drag her father here to bleed all over my laundry room. Really, Gaby, what if he'd lived? I have no idea what laws
you've broken already, but you might have been more
thoughtful of my position."

It occurred to Gabriella then that Ginia had killed Duke,
or had him killed, simply because he was an inconvenience—or because Rasmussen convinced her that he was.
Ginia's voice had gone high and brittle, and she avoided
Gabriella's eyes, as Nessa had done.

"Oh, no, Ginia . . ."

"Just this once, try to please me instead of yourself for a few moments longer, will you? It's true that Cesare and I are attracted to each other, but that changes very little between you and me. I am still the one who rescued you from my brother-in-law when you ran from him to the streets. You'd be selling yourself to tourists or dead—stoned to death by now—if it wasn't for me. I took you in, let you choose your own schools, helped your father's sisters after their husband died, used my influence to get you the museum job. I have even financed this so-called movement of yours, and I've asked you for nothing in return until now."

"Yes, and you've never tried to make me feel guilty about it before, either, Ginia. What sort of a spell has this man cast over you, anyway?"

"No spell. We simply enjoy each other's company. And he is very impressed with how much information you've been able to gather regarding the Chimera process. Just give him a few moments, darling, then you can return to Egypt. In fact, I think he'll insist upon it."

Gabriella felt as if she had stepped through the wrong door and come to a place where a Ginia impostor had taken the place of her longtime friend, supporter, and protector.

She returned to the table, following the drift of turquoise skirts, and sat facing Rasmussen, whose expression was hatefully smug.

"I understand it has been a busy and exhausting time for you, my dear Dr. Faruk," he said. "But I believe we can work together. Ginia tells me you have many important projects you had hoped to assist by acquiring the Cleopatra material. I myself am not interested in Cleopatra specifically, but I am most interested in acquiring a complete knowledge of the Chimera process to use at my own discretion. You have already made strides in that direction. I think we can help each other. I like you, Gabriella—I hope I may call you Gabriella, such a lovely name. And our dear

Ginia likes you, too, of course. She tells me your rescue efforts on behalf of abused Muslim women needs more funding, more backing, which I can certainly provide. She also tells me that ultimately you hope to replace the current fundamentalist Islamic government with a more secular one. That would also be a project to which I could lend support. Never fear, my dear, once you join in the alliance Ginia and I are forging, all of this will work out for the best, you'll see."

"I appreciate your interest, of course, Mr. Rasmussen," she said carefully. He did not say to call him Cesare, even though he had used her first name. "And on Ginia's recommendation, I will certainly carefully consider your offer. However, as you say, it has been a busy time for me, and I find I have no appetite. I hope you will both excuse me if I return now to Alex. I have no idea how my aunts and cousins are faring."

He nodded graciously. Ginia simpered. Gabriella longed to throw the table into both of their laps but settled for making a hasty departure instead.

Working "with" someone like Rasmussen was not possible. He would always be in charge. He was the same species as her stepfather, only even more dangerous because he was wealthier and had more power. Why couldn't Ginia see that? Also, Gabriella knew for certain that Duke Hubbard had not simply died, nor had Ginia stooped so low as to kill him. It had to be Rasmussen who had finished him off, and both Nessa and Madelaine knew it.

"Dr. Wolfe, I don't know if you remember me or not but I am Gabriella Faruk, the niece of Contessa—"

"Of course, I remember you, Dr. Frauk," came the deep, smooth, masculine voice, only faintly roughened by Wolfe's German accent. "What can I do for you? It's a bit harried here at the moment, due to the earthquake in Alexandria. We're mounting a relief effort from here."

"Of course you are! I knew you would, and that is why I am calling. I was visiting my aunt when the quake occurred, and there is no public transportation available back to Alex because of the quake. Aunt Ginia sent her pilot to volunteer to trasnsport Red Cross supplies, and I am stranded here, frantic to know how my family is doing and if my work survived, but I am unable to return. Do you suppose, if I could get a launch to Kefalos, I could ride home on one of your aircraft?"

"I don't see why not. As a matter of fact, I was going myself to assess the damage and speak with some of the government officials about Nucore's role in the rehabilitation of the city. Perhaps we could even enlist your services as a translator?"

"I'd be happy to assist however I can," she said.

"Where are you now?"

"Mykonos."

"Don't bother with the launch. I'll be leaving in a few minutes. I'll just have the pilot swing by and pick you up."

"Thanks," Gabriella said and hung up with an extremely self-satisfied smile on her face. At least some things were going well. Mo had remained on Kefalos only long enough to refuel the Nucore plane and was no doubt already back in Alex.

Gabriella, who felt she was now very much on her own, wished to stick very close to Nucore, so accompanying Wolfe to Alex was preferable to any alternative except accompanying Chimera to Alex.

CHAPTER 17

Duke regained awareness with the distinct feeling that something was missing. It was as if he had opened an elevator door and found that the first step was a lulu.

The last thing he remembered was making his donation for the kid to show Rasmussen how to match up relatives using DNA fingerprinting. And then . . . and then he was wherever he was now. In bed apparently. But how had he got there? He didn't even remember taking a drink, much less getting so blotto he had a blackout. Had Rasmussen slipped him a Mickey for some reason? If so, had he slipped Leda one, too? Was the Kid okay? For that matter, was *he* okay?

Geez, the things he let that kid talk him into. Why was she so damned interested in this line of work anyhow? After all, they let women onto police forces now. Why hadn't she done something sensible like that after the Navy instead of going into this weird occupation that involved digging up dead people? He knew he shouldn't have taken her to see all those Indiana Jones movies when she was going through that tender, impressionable age girls did at thirty-one or so.

But this Nucore gig of hers was something else. Chimera and Wolfe were okay, he supposed, good friends to Leda and all that. But this work of theirs! He'd hired on to protect it, and he would, but he just didn't get it, this two folks/one body thing.

The last he had heard, doctors usually tried to cure people of having split personalities, not cause the split. Times had sure changed. Now it looked like even human nature might be changing as well, what with the scientists dicking around with it. Maybe he was getting old. Nah. He felt fine. Just a little confused.

But fine, otherwise, actually, really warm and happy and cozy. None of his old injuries ached for a change, and something about him felt kind of young and bubbly. Like he was falling in love again but he couldn't remember anyone who might be responsible.

Still, the mystery would probably solve itself, and meanwhile, it was great feeling this way: sensual, flexible, kinda luxurious. He stretched his arms, catlike, and flexed the pink-tipped ends of his fingers. Whoa—nail polish? Shocking pink? What the hell!

Pardon me, gracious queen. I was in such a hurry I forgot about the manicure. This is just our modern-day equivalent of henna, which is what you would have used to beautify your nails.

"The hell I would!" Duke answered the feminine voice in his head. Or was *his* the voice in her head? Whatever! He threw the light sheet aside and was amazed to discover he was in drag.

"*Nein,* Frau Wolfe!" Six big blonds in pink scrub suits ran to his bedside.

"Wolfe?" he asked, but his voice came out in a soprano squeak. It was a good thing he was lying down, because what he was beginning to realize was enough to make a strong man faint. He wasn't him anymore. He was—had to be—the sample Leda had just—in his memory—processed. And he had been incorporated into someone else. A woman someone else. "I'm . . . uh . . . What's the term? Blended? With Mrs. Wolfe?"

Although she had just awakened, the lady was so excited, she was missing a few little clues that something might be slightly amiss.

Yes, gracious queen, she thought to him. *How brilliant of you to already grasp the essence of my husband's work. I hope you will find me a worthy vessel for your exalted presence. I also hope you will be smart enough to realize that this is a second chance I give you to live through me, so you will not be running always after Italian government officials, like you did in old times. I have a very good husband. It is about him I have you here. I want to keep him, ja? You will help me do this, teaching me feminine wiles, and you and me, we will get along fine.*

With all this babble happening inside the head that seemed to be his own, Duke was momentarily baffled about how to stop it, and the good frau continued.

I am trying to hang onto my husband, you see, even as you once clung to Caesar and later to Mark Antony. I know it all ended tragically for you back then, but mein *Wilhelm is not at war with anybody, and neither am I. We have a good life and are very well-off, but I have never learned how to fascinate men and now, with his new prominence, Wilhelm meets so many attractive women. . . .*

Uh-huh, Duke interupted as if he were in a conversation he didn't want to have. He had frequently left women who didn't know how to fascinate him when he met those who did. He felt like he was on the wrong side of this discussion. *I hate to tell you, ma'am, but I ain't a queen, even if, being joined with you, I might appear to be one. You've been robbed, and I've been shanghaied. My daughter told me that if they found Cleopatra, you would be the one to—*

uh—benefit. But apparently, someone pulled a fast one on you and transferred my DNA into you instead of Cleopatra's.

Shock and disbelief filled him—them—her, really. Hell, he knew what he was saying already, so it didn't shock *him.* How did any of these people stand this process without going totally nuts from bewilderment? Of all the crazy mixed-up—

But—but that is impossible. Nucore alone possesses the secret to preparing the codes for transmission from the cells to the new host! A trusted friend of Dr. Chimera's personally prepared Cleopatra's DNA from a tested specimen for me. It was a secret.

Don't go blaming the Kid, now, lady. I mean, Leda, Chimera's friend, she's my daughter. She knows her stuff about getting the specimens ready. See—I'm here, aren't I? And I'm still me—well, mostly. But—look, you're going to have to pay close attention here, because it's confusing, and I don't really understand it myself. But what you got here is just that little bit of me from a cell, and the rest of me is out there somewhere, maybe still alive and kicking, but probably not, if somebody got their hands on the specimen. I mean, that part of me that's here—and got me—it— in here with you. Obviously, I'm going to need your cooperation to find out just what's happened to me.

To you! I went through this procedure to be more alluring to my husband, and instead of the queen of the Nile, I get a man who talks like an American, what is the term, gumshoe? Private dick?

Policeman. Detective Sergeant Duke Hubbard, or what's left of him, he told her.

I thought we were supposed to be blended, Dectective Sergeant Hubbard, she said.

I think we're going to get real tired of standing on formality, ma'am, us occupying the same body and all. I'll try to think of you as my new feminine side I'm getting in touch with, and you can think of me as your inner Duke, if you want.

Ja, *that is very amusing, Duke. But what am I to do? What are we to do? This is a big mess we have here,* ja?

As we say where I come from in the Pacific Northwest part of the United States of America, ja *shore you betcha,* he told her.

I think first what I must do is call Chimera and have the process reversed. I am told this can be done if done quickly. And we two—why, we are not a blend! We are two distinct people inside of me only, and I am still me and you, are still you, although I slept the required length of time, I am sure. The blending part has failed entirely, do you not think so? So it should be only a matter of removing you, and I will be again me.

Glad to hear you sounding so happy about it, Duke said. *Nothing like a little disaster to give a person a sense of perspective.*

What do you mean?

Well, apparently this marital problem you've been having that drove you to this desperate act and so to this mess we find ourselves in—

It was not a marital problem! she said. *I am trying to prevent one, only!*

I understand that, but it was enough of a problem for you to risk all the stuff that could happen when you go through this kind of thing—like ending up with me instead of Cleopatra, for instance, though that's probably not in the handout they give at Nucore on what to expect when you go through the process.

It was a worry, ja, *but before it becomes a problem, I am trying to correct what is wrong.*

A preemptive strike, huh? Against . . . what exactly? Yourself?

Against my own limitations. My husband is a brilliant

*man. I wish not to be left behind. So now I call Chimera,
and you go your way, I go mine to begin again.*

Okay, but first, can I ask you a favor?

I suppose so.

*Can you tell me what you know about that Cleopatra
material you should have received? I seem to be missing
some time here, because the last thing I remember, nobody
had found anything of Cleopatra's. In fact, this character
named Rasmussen and some of his buddies were on the site
in Alexandria harassing people about it. Mr. Rasmussen
was afraid he was losing money on the deal. So, could you
kind of fill me in on what you know that happened after
that?*

*Yes, certainly. I wish you no harm, you understand. But
I did not . . . invite . . . you.* She was feeling, as the rape
victims and even robbery victims would say, *violated.*

Duke said softly, *I think I understand pretty much how
you feel. Believe me, and you ought to be able to do that
now, since I don't know that I have any way to deceive you;
I didn't ask for this, either. I didn't want it. I had no idea it
was going to happen.*

Yes, she said, and he felt her heart open a little toward
him. Silently, he urged her to continue and tell him something that would help him find his bearings.

*Chimera called me three weeks ago to tell me Dr. Hub-
bard, his friend at the Alexandria dig on behalf of Nucore
and—and me—had found something. There was, you understand, a small earthquake, much smaller than the one
last night.*

Last night?

*Oh, yes, a very big one last night. But that I will tell you
of in its own time. This small earthquake from the harbor
floor extruded a canopic jar. Dr. Hubbard is believing from
its markings this jar is belonging to Cleopatra. Inside of it
are a lady's lungs. Immediately, Dr. Hubbard is establish-
ing that the remains belong to the mother or aunt of*

Cleopatra's daughter, from whom there is a sample, you see? The day of the disaster in Alexandria, she is sending a message to Chimera that her father—this is you, ja?

Yes, ma'am.

That her father is bringing the patched DNA along with the specimen ready for upload to me. She is also sending to Chimera the code for uploading by computer, but before it is received, the big earthquake is happening, and Chimera does not receive the second message. So it is necessary to wait until the specimen arrives. Yes, now I am thinking of it, Chimera expressed to me concern that the specimen was brought by a person not—ah, not yourself. So you were injured in the earthquake maybe, ja?

Maybe. But that doesn't explain how my specimen . . . Well, let me see, here, a little induction. What would I do if I were me? When Leda took this specimen from me and got it all ready so if somebody wanted to they could actually load it into somebody else, I know me well enough to know I wouldn't think much of the idea. I don't think I'd let something like that out of my sight, to be mistaken for something that—well—this should happen to. So something must have happened to me, and then someone found my specimen and thought it was Cleopatra's and delivered it to Chimera by accident. But they didn't say something had happened to me?

Chimera did not say so, no.

Guess we both need to talk to the doc then, and I sure would like to talk to Leda, too. She's probably with the rest of me right now. He laughed. *I really need to pull myself together!*

It is a problem, that. So. Now I will call Chimera.

Good idea.

But they couldn't get through. The lines were tied up, and when Gretchen called the operator, pleading an emergency, she was told that the earthquake in Alexandria was also an emergency. The operator sternly told her the best thing to do was to clear the lines and pay attention to the news, when a central emergency number would be broadcast. Neither Wolfe's nor Chimera's cell phone numbers worked, either.

I guess we'll have to take two aspirin and call back in the morning, Duke said.

I myself am a doctor. I find that joke rather old, Gretchen informed him.

It's the only one I could think of. But you know, it might be a good thing. This is all a little fishy. Could be we shouldn't be discussing it on the phone lines. I don't think much of the security system they have on Kefalos, to tell you the truth. Maybe we should just go pay the island a visit. Leda might be back there by now, too. If not, I need to get to Egypt and let her know what's going on. The Kid could be in trouble, especially if she has any more of that Cleopatra DNA. If someone ambushed me to get their hands on it, they might go after her, too.

Such an imagination you have put into my head! I cannot be leaving on a whim. I have here a practice, a household to run.

Well, I can understand the inconvenience, Duke said, *but I don't see how I'm going to go without you. And come on, if I had been Cleopatra, you'd have taken some time off anyway, wouldn't you? You girls would have wanted to go shopping at least, and I'll bet she would have wanted to see her old stomping grounds again, too.*

That well may be, but you are not Cleopatra.

That's true. But I am a cop, and it seems to me you can use one if you're going to find the real Cleo.

My husband's company has investigators for such things.

I know, Duke said patiently. *I'm one of them. The one in charge of the site where you say Leda found the jar. I'm the guy who would normally be doing this. Besides, I thought*

*this business was hush-hush. Just you and Chimera and
Leda knew about it?*

Well . . . it was.

Who better than me then? I'm already in the loop.

Knowing that his argument was unbeatable, even by
this stubborn Teutonic female, Duke relaxed a little and
pursued a more interesting line of thought. All he could do
till he could convince her to cooperate was think, after all,
and all she could do was think back at him. Maybe this was
where the blending took place? Lord, if the boys back at
the precinct could see him now!

*You know, there's no reason we can't work together on
all of our problems while we're at it. I mean, I could help
you in ways Cleopatra wouldn't have a clue about. You just
sort of wanted a marriage counselor and sex therapist,
didn't you? Well, I've been married more times than she
was and probably am a lot more expert on how to really
please a man.*

*Perhaps. But it seems to me if you have been married so
many times you are no expert on how to hold on to a husband, except perhaps as an example of what does not
work.*

*Okay, I admit I deserved that. But I doubt very much the
queen has any tricks up her flimsy pleated kilt that haven't
been tried on me at one time or another. And you know,
where I am at the moment—I mean, with us blended—
though I agree it seems more like oil and water or the mak-
ings for a Molotov cocktail, I could not just advise you, I
could actually make the right moves, say the right things,
with your body and in your voice. Besides, when we've ac-
complished what we both need to do and get the process reversed, if you listen to me, you'll have learned a couple of
things about men and have your husband back for yourself.*

Maybe this is so.

You bet. Whereas, say you do get blended with Cleo and

he falls in love with you all over again. Aren't you going to wonder, just a little, if he only wants you for the Cleo inside of you?

You are a very—how do you Americans put it?—cagey man, Mr. Hubbard. You are thinking if you sell yourself to me as an expert on men, I will keep you.

Duke chuckled to—themselves. *You're on to me, but can you blame me? I may be just a set of light frequencies based on a sample of spit and cheek cells, but I'm all I've got, as far as I know. I'll never know, though, will I, until we figure out what happened? We may find Cleo in the process, and then you can trade me in on her. But I'm just saying that personally, I'm pretty sure you'd be getting the short end of the stick in that deal. I'm told I grow on people. You'll probably miss me.*

I should like very much the opportunity to find out, Gretchen grumbled, but he felt her being charmed nevertheless, though she added quickly, *Not so cocky, please.*

Up until recently, I had a lot to be cocky about, he said. *Do we have a deal? You help me find who done it, and I'll play Dear Abby with you for your husband. When it's over, I go.*

Even if you—the rest of you, that is—isn't still alive?

You drive a hard bargain, but okay. I wouldn't stay where I'm not wanted.

Very well, then. But you will be a gentleman, ja? *No dirty talk or thoughts.*

I thought you wanted to get your husband back, Duke said.

CHAPTER 18

If Leda had hoped that she would awaken to find it had all been a terrible nightmare, she was disappointed. Her bruises, scrapes, aches, and pains gave her an immediate reality check on the situation.

She yawned, groaned, sat up, poked her feet into her sandals, then shuffled out into the main part of the Quonset hut.

"I think I have a ride for you," the new runway manager said. Unlike his predecessor, he actually seemed to be working, typing things into the computer. "There's a plane from headquarters due in about fifteen minutes."

"Great," she said and wandered outside. For now, the planes and copters, trucks and piles of supplies were all gone. Something else was gone, too.

"Hey, did anybody move the motorcycle that was parked out here?" she asked the relief guy.

"Not that I saw. But I got pretty busy, and there were a lot of people coming and going. Have you checked out back? Maybe it was in someone's way."

She checked. No bike. Then she had a happy thought.

Maybe Dad himself came back while she was asleep, saw the bike against the wall, and rode it away. Naaaah. For one thing, from the damage to the helmet, he had a hellacious head injury. For another thing, he would have checked the pockets for the specimen and the phone and found them missing and asked around. Besides, someone would have seen him and told her. Surely they would have. Maybe he sent somebody to pick it up?

No, all that sleep had turned her into Little Mary Sunshine. She knew in her gut nothing that good had happened. Dad was down for the count, at least. Maybe he was still in a hospital or one of the emergency facilities here in Alex. Maybe someone had taken him back to Nucore. The latter wasn't very plausible, because everybody there knew he was her dad; the facility wasn't a large one, and the old man had a way of getting around and gabbing with people. Someone would have called her or gotten word to her, even in this mess. It had been almost twenty-four hours now.

The bike probably had been stolen in the confusion of all of the aircraft landing and taking off again. It was the most likely thing in the world, and she kicked herself for not thinking to bring it inside. The old man was going to kill her when he got back. If he got back. Where the hell was he, anyway?

CHAPTER 19

Where do you usually find an airborne messenger, other than crapping on granite war heroes and national monuments?

Duke asked his feminine side, then answered his own question. *The airport, that's where. My guess is that somewhere along the way, there's a mole in Nucore working for whoever hit me.*

As soon as he is reaching Egypt, we must warn Wilhelm.

You got it. But with no phone service, we gotta do it in person. So let's get dressed.

He was going to leave that part to her but couldn't stand to do it. Her closet was a mess of outfits totally useless for the purpose he had in mind. Her hands surged through blouses with pussycat bows and Peter Pan collars. Even her underwear drawer was boring: white and pastel cotton, unadorned and practical.

He shook their head when she held out a pair of trousers for scrutiny. They'd be fine for a PTA meeting in the suburbs of a particularly dull Midwestern town. *Nope*, he said firmly. *You got anything in leather?*

She pulled out a long leather skirt with fringes that looked like a thrift shop find from someone else's hippie days. Without even asking, she frowned and hung it back up.

Ah! Wilhelm's lederhosen! she said hopefully.

Not unless you can yodel. I can't.

She was kinda pathetic. Not even her boots were made for walking.

Exasperated, Duke said, *Okay, lady, pack up your portable phone and your money. We're going to do what my kid calls a little shopper-gatherer activity,* he said.

I do not like to shop, Gretchen said.

Me neither, though I have picked out some pretty snazzy outfits for my girls from time to time, but we aren't looking for Sunday school dresses this time. Help me find a place that sells biker's leathers in the phone book, okay? Last time I checked, I didn't read German.

She had a chauffeur, no less. Very tony and maybe a little safer for the wife of a rich man than driving herself around in some fancy car, but personally, he liked to be in the driver's seat himself.

Europeans didn't have a legacy of Jimmy Dean and *Easy Rider,* so they didn't know what bikers were supposed to look like. Their leathers came in a wild assortment of colors. Gretchen was like a kid in a candy store with these and immediately chose a fuchsia and purple outfit that would have put any self-respecting cow to shame and made him feel like a cross between a court jester and a wind sock.

He steered her toward basic black. *Always appropriate, easily accessorized, and, here's the best part, fairly inconspicuous,* he said. *After all, we may have to go undercover.*

He also insisted on the German-style jacket, a little longer, laced on the sides, rather than the shorter kidney-chilling bomber style.

They compromised on leopard print lining for it and a

waterproof leopard lap robe for riding in rainy weather. *We should get you some undies to match,* he suggested.

She reacted with stiff indignation.

Just an idea, he said. *I have undies to match. You know—and I think I can say with confidence that Cleopatra herself would tell you this, too—you might want to rethink your wardrobe strategy a little if you want to woo your husband back again.*

I have bought new clothes. Nice clothes. I cannot help that you did not like them. And those lacy panties that are nylon, they give you the vaginal infections and the brassieres can cause the allergies of the breast skin, she told him.

Well, now, I think that's more than I wanted to know, he said.

But he could tell she was thinking over what he said. She was a little shy.

However, when they surveyed her image in the mirror, he had to admit s/he was now one hot babe. Legs a little short but good boobs, trim waist and hips, all slicked down black and shining. He noticed that her body felt tight, and not in a good way. It hurt in several areas. *My cosmetic surgery,* she told him. *One must suffer for beauty.*

Geez, I had no idea. Most of the time, I've been the one suffering for beauties.

They got good sturdy boots with reinforced arches for her dainty feet and sleek gloves for her little hands.

He was afraid Gretchen would balk at wearing a helmet and messing up her blond mane of hair. Normally, he would have suggested, in his role as marriage counselor, that she change to a red shade, but this lady was a natural towhead, a happy condition that was not broke and he would not even think about attempting to fix. As it turned out, she was also a sensible woman, and as a doctor, inclinded to be safety conscious.

But what is this you are having painted on it? she asked. *Old Mothah Hubbard? This means—what?*

This means, for any sonovabitch who's paying attention, that I may be down but not out. Now then, I don't suppose you have a bike in the garage already?

Ja, *I am riding it to work at the hospital every day,* she said. *You joke with me.*

Nope. Dead serious. That's a joke, hon.

Very amusing. But she ordered the driver to find a bike shop. They tried Harleys but the truth was, Harleys weren't what they used to be. If Duke had time, he'd soup up an older one, get it purring like he had his Sopwith. Gretchen kept going for little toys in colors that would make them stand out like a sore thumb. They compromised by getting the lean mean running machine he wanted, again in basic black, and a second one to match her fuchsia outfit. *But we're dealing with killers here, lady, so we want to be as low-profile as we can be considering that we look like a very foxy blond in tight black leathers on a machine like this. You can be fashionably color coordinated when I'm outta here.*

You are a most bossy guest, she told him.

Standing in the display window of the motorcycle shop, Gretchen saw her reflection reach up to scratch her chin with thumb and forefinger, Duke was surprised to find the chin soft and silky instead of bristling as his usually was two hours after a shave. The salesman returned with the title to the bike and temporary license.

We go now where? Gretchen wondered.

Well, Kefalos I guess, and maybe Egypt.

Ah, if Egypt, we must stop then at a dress shop.

Why?

Because there they are not liking women on the streets in pants. As Wilhelm's wife, I must conform myself to local customs and avoid offense.

We should have brought the leather hippie job from your closet.

But within the same block as the bike shop, in a little secondhand shop, she found what Leda called a broomstick skirt: lightweight, also black, with full, tiered pleats, and ankle length so the biker boots wouldn't look funny with it and she could carry it in her saddlebags.

Gretchen dismissed the driver, and hopped on the new bike. *The airstrip then,* they agreed. Gretchen was pleased that her new inner voice was in accord with her on this matter. Duke expertly showed her small hands and feet how to operate the bike.

I don't know anybody at this strip, Duke said, as they dismounted and parked the bike near the airstrip's central hangar and business office.

It matters not, Gretchen told him, and marched into the office, straight to the big guy with the white-blond crew cut at the desk and said, "I am Frau Doktor Gretchen Wolfe, wife of Wilhelm Wolfe, and my . . . motorcycle and I are going to Kefalos to see my husband. You will find us a suitable aircraft, and we will fly there now, *ja?*" Anyhow, that was the gist of it. She was speaking German, of course, but Duke was understanding more the longer he was with her. He guessed Chimera's process came with its own universal translator that was more direct than anything science fiction could dream up.

Money, Gretchen thought in reply, *This is another good universal that all understand. And power.* She was right. The guy at the desk was busily tapping his key.

Ja, Frau Wolfe, he told her. The small Piper nine-seater is available.

We'll fly it ourselves, Duke told her. *I'm a pilot, and I'm qualified on that one.*

"I personally will be flying this aircraft," she told the fellow.

"You will?" the man asked.

"I have said so, *ja*?"

"Your pilot's license, ma'am?"

"Is on file," she said airily.

Duke cheered her silently.

The guy shrugged. Go figure rich bitches.

That was all there was to it. One word from the lady, and she/Duke and the bike were loaded aboard. *Hey, all right,* Duke said as they climbed into the pilot's seat. Gretchen felt a little skeptical, a little scared, but also thrilled. First a motorcycle and now an airplane!

By the time they landed on Kefalos, she was full of internal giggles of pride. *I am feeling just like Mrs. Emma Peel from the* Avengers *stories of the television,* ja?

The Kefalos airstrip was all but deserted, and Gretchen made the landing without much nervousness.

Well, now for the moment of truth, Duke said. *Cross your fingers that Chimera's here. Probably is. I mean, what's he going to do in the middle of a disaster in Egypt? Bandage knees?*

Chimera—or half of Chimera—was once a very fine surgeon of the eyes. No doubt there are many eyes injured in such a catastrophe.

No doubt. But we'll have to hope the doc didn't decide to jump in and be helpful just yet.

Duke was frustrated that Gretchen needed extra muscle to unload the bike from the plane.

I am not a weakling, she protested. *It is a large machine, and I am a small woman. I have been working out regularly.*

Sorry, I'm just not used to having a different body.

And I am not used to having a mind that thinks I should be able to do such things, she replied tartly.

They checked in with the Greek air traffic manager at the strip, who looked a little shocked but very appreciative at Mrs. Wolfe's new image. He told them that Mr. Wolfe had departed some time ago for Alexandria with several of the senior management executives and had arranged to pick up Dr. Faruk on Mykonos en route. Dr. Chimera was not among them and was still on the island, according to the log.

They rode down the winding road, past the white-washed buildings that terraced the mountainside, their red roofs and brightly painted doors faded by the moonlight gilding the sea. The ride down to the beach didn't take long, and it was there they found Chimera, deep in conversation with a young girl who seemed to be crying.

Duke recognized her. *That's Maddy, one of the lab techs. What's eating her, do you suppose?*

The headlamp of the bike caught the gleam of the tears on her face before Gretchen doused the light and walked it over to where Chimera and the girl sat on a low wall.

"Gretchen!" Chimera said, sounding both surprised and relieved to see her.

Maddy's eyes grew wide and scared.

"What's the matter, honey?" Duke asked without waiting for Gretchen to translate it into her own speech patterns.

Chimera suddenly became very still and looked up expectantly.

"Who are you?" Maddy asked.

"This is Mr. Wolfe's wife, Gretchen, Madelaine," Chimera said.

"No," the girl said, her voice so high and tight that it hurt to hear it. "I know that. I've seen Mrs. Wolfe. Who else are you?"

Chimera regarded her uneasily, "You know of the blending?"

"That's what I was trying to tell you. I monitored the whole thing."

"Then you know that Mrs. Wolfe is blended with Queen Cleopatra?"

"Uh . . . there was a little hitch there, Doc," Duke said again.

"Oh, *no,*" Madelaine said. "Oh, Duke, I am so sorry. If I had known what he was going to do, I would have tried to stop him!"

"What who was going to do, Maddy?" Duke asked. Gretchen was fuming inside her own body, but he reminded her that he was the one skilled in interrogation of suspects, and Maddy was looking more suspicious by the minute.

Gretchen put in her own question, nevertheless. "You mean that you knew the donor code Dr. Chimera blended with me was not Cleopatra's, but this—this Old Frau Hubbard's?" she asked.

"No. Yes. I mean, yes, I knew that, but not at once. I had no idea what they meant to do. The contessa told me only that she wanted to privately monitor the scientific information regarding the Cleopatra specimen passing between Dr. Chimera and Dr. Hubbard. She said she was protecting her investment and that she and Dr. Faruk—Gabriella—had a much better use for the specimen than to indulge the fantasy of some rich housefrau. Gabriella has been trying to rouse the women of Egypt to be more autonomous and has been rescuing and providing a safe house for other Middle Eastern women seeking to escape oppressive conditions among their own families in their own homelands. She even provided the weapon Malik Massad's sister Farida hid beneath her abaya when she assassinated her brother for ordering the murder of her husband. Meanwhile, Dr. Faruk hid Farida's children and had them sent to the contessa, who sent them on to relatives in the west, though of course they couldn't save Farida."

"What?" Chimera and Gretchen/Duke asked at once.

But Madelaine was continuing, "So I thought it was all right. Gabriella said that if she could also become Cleopatra and gain the queen's knowledge of what lay beneath Alexandria, she would have some leverage with the government for restoring its wealth. She thought she could probably even get herself put into some high office and make real changes. But I never knew she and the contessa were going to hurt anybody. Honestly."

"They hurt someone, the contessa and Dr. Faruk?"

"Yes, Dr. Faruk said Duke was carrying the specimen, and there was an accident. Oh, she acted very sorry and brought the contessa's doctor from Mykonos, but he had a terrible head injury and should have been taken to a hospital. Instead, the doctor and Dr. Faruk operated on him there. I didn't realize who it was until they had finished and I had checked the donor sample. I went to tell Dr. Faruk that it was the wrong one, and that's when I realized it belonged to Duke. I didn't reveal that I knew you, Duke, because I realized the plotting was deeper than I had known. Dr. Faruk was mad, I think, that she hadn't gotten Cleopatra's donation after all, and she decided to play a trick on you, Dr. Chimera, by sending Duke's DNA—"

"A trick on Chimera?" Gretchen fumed in high Teutonic indignation. "What about me?"

"Yeah," Duke said. "Not to mention me!" Then he realized the girl had stopped only because they had interrupted. Her face was still quivering with anxiety and guilt. He felt something inside his own little corner of Gretchen being try to crawl off into a corner and hide, then he told it to get its ass out there and face the music. "There's something else though, isn't there, Maddy?"

"Yes. I'm sorry. I would have tried to stop him if I knew, but while Dr. Faruk was taking the specimen to Mykonos to be brought to Dr. Chimera, Dr. Benoit had to go to the lavatory. Another guest had come—that horrible Mr. Rasmussen. I'm afraid of him. So is Nessa, Dr. Benoit. I think she's going to leave Mykonos . . ."

Duke knew she was getting off track and nodded encouragingly. "Why?"

"Well, the door to my office was open, and I saw his reflection, Mr. Rasmussen's I mean, on my computer screen as he walked past the doorway toward the room where Duke was. And then, in a few moments, I heard the doctor come back and groan and say something like, 'Oh, no.' When I went to see what was the matter, she told me. Duke was—is—you are, I mean . . ."

"Dead," he said, Gretchen's voice giving the word a flat, hard intonation that sounded even more final in German. "I guess rumors of my recovery were highly exaggerated, huh?"

He turned off then, as if being told of his death had killed something in him—in the part of him that still existed inside Gretchen. Distantly, he heard her speaking with Chimera and Maddy: Chimera asking did she want to reverse the process and Gretchen mumbling something noncommittal but negative, Maddy whining and crying some more. What finally broke through to him was when Chimera said, "Very well, as you wish. You go to Alexandria, tell Wilhelm what happened, and let Leda know about . . . what happened, at the same time obtaining the other specimen from her. In the meantime, Maddy," and it was this last part that really cut through to Duke as if he had suddenly been switched back on again, "what did they do with Duke's body?"

CHAPTER 20

Ducking to avoid the wing, Leda waddled toward the little plane as the passengers were disembarking. There was Wolfie—good old Wolfie—and right behind him the other person she most wanted to see, Gabriella!

Before they could exchange greetings, however, the runway manager grabbed her arm from behind and handed her a cordless phone. "For you, Dr. Hubbard. It's Dr. Welsh from the site."

Leda's heart leapt. *Pete had found Dad! What a relief! What a blessing! Thank you, Bast!*

"Punkin, you'd better hightail it out of Egypt fast if you don't want to spend the rest of your days in a really wet jail cell. Namid has called out the gendarmes, and they're after you for violating the antiquities act."

"Huh? How did you find out?"

"Never mind, just move it. I'll call Nucore HQ on Kefalos if I hear anything about Duke."

Gosh, he was cooperative. Perhaps he was trying to get rid of her? But no, there was a vehicle outside on the road now.

Wolfe and Gabriella were within earshot, and she pulled his ear to her mouth and said, "Dr. Namid, the inspector of antiquities, is trying to have me arrested because he thinks I took an artifact I was examining. The truth is, it's still in Egypt. It's in the hole that swallowed the beluga. But I don't have time to explain that."

"Don't worry," Wolfe said, patting her shoulder. "It is good you're leaving. I'll straighten it out. Namid has been difficult to deal with all along. I will need to speak to his superiors again. I'll notify you on Kefalos when it's safe for you to return."

"Leda, you're leaving?" Gabriella shouted. She looked like hell. Even in the darkness, Leda could see the deep shadows under her eyes and the way the curl in her hair had flattened. "I wanted so much to talk to you!" Gabriella enveloped her in a big enthusiastic hug that Leda pulled away from just as the headlights of the probable police vehicle swung through the gate.

"Later!" she shouted, and climbed aboard. With the pilot's help, she pulled the ramp up after her. Wolfe gave the pilot a frantic signal, and she started the engines again and began to taxi down the runway. The vehicle tried to catch up and block the plane's takeoff, but Wolfe blocked the vehicle. This wasn't exactly the way to endear himself to Namid for a cozy chat about why the antiquities inspector was being unfair, but then, Wolfe had said he didn't intend to talk with the unreasonable Namid anyway.

Leda didn't stay awake long enough to see the quake damage from the air. She slept all the way to Kefalos. Once there, she didn't bother trying to phone but stumbled down the hill to Chimera's villa and knocked on the door. The night was balmy and calm, and her friend took a long time to answer, though lights were visible in the lab area. She napped briefly against the red door while waiting.

Had she been more alert, she would have seen the troubled expression on Chimera's face.

"Come in, Leda. One of your beers remains in the fridge."

"No, I just need some sleep," she said.

"Of course. But first we have something to tell you."

"It can't wait?"

"It could, yes. It concerns your father."

"What about him? Do you know where he is? Is he okay?"

"You should sit down."

"Okay, but really, how is he?"

"He's not himself at all," Chimera said.

"In what way?" she asked, fearing what was coming even without having any idea what to expect.

"He is blended into Gretchen Wolfe," Chimera said in a quiet, guilt-ridden voice. Leda's reaction was unexpected.

"Dad?" she asked and laughed. At first it was just a snort of laughter and then another, and finally she was laughing so hard she had tears running down her face and was gasping for breath and still she couldn't stop laughing.

When she could speak again she giggled, "I'm sorry— it's just so funny—he must be in hog heaven! Dad inside the body of a much younger woman wealthy enough to buy any toy he wants. Hoo boy!"

"They did not seem to find it as amusing as you do, Leda. Once his DNA was transferred, your father was apparently murdered."

"What?" she asked sharply.

"We did not mean for it to come out so harshly, Leda, but you must know. Gretchen, with your father, came to see us just as one of the employees at this facility was admitting to having assisted with the interception of your communications with us regarding Cleopatra's material."

Chimera explained what the girl, Madelaine, had told them. "We will go in the morning to the contessa and ask her to give us the body of your father."

"Not by yourself, you won't," Leda said. "That bitch

and her snake of a niece owe me big time, but for all we know, the contessa could have you killed, too."

Chimera waved away her objection. "Not so. We are necessary to her plans and those of her confederates, according to Madelaine. We will take some of the security force with us. And of course, you are welcome to come if you wish but—"

"Wild horses couldn't keep me away," Leda said.

"But please, we would prefer to do this in as peaceful and nonaggressive way as possible. Not only are we more assured of gaining the contessa's cooperation with such means, but we also place ourselves in a less dangerous position."

"You are not the one who should be worried about a dangerous position," Leda snapped. "I should have known that damned Gabriella was up to something! She was just tooooo helpful with everything and always going on and on about how much she admires Cleopatra. Hah! She'll never get that specimen now."

"It still exists?" Chimera asked.

"It does." Leda reached into the front of her shirt and with great relief extracted the two hard and lumpy items putting grooves in her boobs. She handed them to him, the specimen case with the original, repaired DNA and the disk containing the data for its duplicates. "Dad was bringing this one to you just before everything went down the drain at the beluga, and this I rescued from the computer before it got eaten by the quake."

"Excellent, Leda. Mrs. Wolfe will be very pleased."

Leda felt an unexpected bolt of anger lancing through her when Chimera said that. Mrs. Wolfe had Dad. She could even afford him, something none of his wives had actually been able to do. Why the hell did she need Cleopatra, too, when she didn't even care about what the queen knew that couldn't be found in the pages of racy women's magazines, which could probably teach Cleopatra herself a few tricks?

"Peachy. Meanwhile, have you told Wolfe about Gabriella? Because the two of them arrived in Alexandria on the same plane."

"We have not been able to get a call through, but Gretchen and your father left only a short time ago. They will warn him if we cannot reach him any other way."

"I suppose that will have to do. I'll try again pretty soon."

"Yes, we must find your father's body as quickly as we can and take fresh tissue samples before the DNA has had a chance to deteriorate. Gretchen will want the process reversed as soon as Duke's inquiries into his murder have reached their conclusion. The donor material does not survive the reversal process. When we are acquiring samples for clients, we make sure we have plenty of the original DNA to replicate, but in your father's case, that is unavailable. If we have a good fresh sample, we may be able to find a suitable host and—"

"Bring him back to life?" Leda considered this. It was an abstract idea at the moment, almost a funny one. Dad couldn't be dead. He wasn't the type. "Hmm. I don't know. I guess you'll have to see when the time comes what he thinks of the idea. Maybe Mrs. Wolfe will want to keep him. He has been known to have that effect on quite a few women. Maybe since he's part of her, he'll be able to make her understand, in a way that none of his wives have, just how many cars, motorcycles, and boats he really needs. Or needed." The last word caught in her throat. She didn't like the way it sounded. It was as if she was giving up too easily. It seemed disloyal to count him out before she knew. Maybe Chimera was right about finding the body, if for a different reason than getting a tissue sample. She was not going to believe this until she saw. Dad always turned up okay, somehow.

Chimera smiled a bit sadly. "Maybe so, but it is doubtful such charm would work on Wilhelm as well as it may on Gretchen."

Leda shrank from the gloomier aspects of the situation and decided that until she had more proof, she'd just carry on as if Duke was up to his usual tricks. Playing it that way would help her continue to be useful, whereas the alternative . . . Nope. It wasn't getting brain space right now. "Well, if Gretchen kicks him out, it will be a little like one of the divorces, I guess, and Dad has always been one for . . . er . . . remounting right away. Just so we take enough security personnel with us."

They tried again to reach Wolfe without success, then Leda called Agelakos, the security chief, and told him that she and Dr. Chimera would require a helicopter to Dilos in the morning to recover her father's body. She also told him they'd need enough armed security guards to protect them against those responsible for the crime, since calling local authorities or Interpol could be a bit tricky under the circumstances.

Agelakos was not as cooperative as she might have hoped.

"We are spread pretty thin now. There's a situation developing in Egypt. Rumors being spread about Nucore are causing riots in some areas. Much of our Kefalos security staff has had to relieve the Egyptian guards, who cannot be trusted in the present climate. Relief personnel have been made available to us, however."

"Just so they're large and have really big guns," Leda said. Agelakos rang off.

Leda held onto the phone for several seconds after it went dead, thinking what an odd choice of words Agelakos had used: *"Made available to us."* But then she decided almost everything seemed odd, if not downright surreal. For instance, Daddy was dead/Daddy was running around Egypt somewhere looking like Wolfie's blond wife and riding an uncustomized new bike. The ideas were equally preposterous, and she just really couldn't take it all in. She needed to sleep again so very badly.

Dimly, in one of her mixed-up dreams, she heard a phone ring, but she thought it might be Wolfe. She tried to rouse enough to ask Chimera but couldn't make herself wake up. Every time she thought she was awake, she opened her eyes just long enough to see that she was still in bed and hadn't moved.

Later, she awoke to voices in the living room, which was beneath the room where she slept. A woman's voice, low, tearful, whispery, and urgent.

"Dr. Chimera, you must help me. You must remove her from me. That man-crazy hag has caused me to violate every principle I hold dear, to betray the people I most care about. My doctor, Nessa, is murdered; one of her patients murdered in my own house; and my dear Gaby is in terrible danger. Please, you must help me so that I can help her. Remove that woman so that I can no longer be swayed by her. I admired her so much! I had no idea she was like a bitch perpetually in heat. Oh, tell me you can help me, please!"

"We think we can, yes. But first you must do something for us. Duke Hubbard, the security guard, was killed in your house."

"Yes, yes, he was the patient of Nessa's I told you about. She did her best for the poor man, and Gabriella was most upset about it. It was an accident, you know. No one meant for him to die. No one except *him*."

"We need to find his body, Contessa."

"I cannot help you there. Rasmussen took it when he left, and I'm not sure where he went except that I know he caused Nessa's death. I came also to warn that young woman, Madelaine. But first, dear Dr. Chimera, I cannot promise to be your true ally until you reverse the process."

Leda smelled a rat big enough to swallow Athens. If the imported personality was so dominant as the contessa said, where was she now? Why was she allowing the contessa to petition for separation? Without turning on the light, Leda tiptoed to the window that looked down the hill to the little harbor. A large yacht was anchored just offshore. There were people on the road, too. Not milling around type people, either. These looked like guards, though the security force did not normally park themselves at the entrances of the executives' villas. If Agelakos was short of his own staff, Nucore security had been more than adequately beefed up by whoever sent the replacements. Who might that be, anyway?

She heard footsteps below her again and soon saw the contessa and Chimera riding up the road to headquarters. Two pairs of guards closed in behind them. Leda did not like the way that looked. She did not trust the contessa, and she really didn't think Chimera trusted her, either, not after what the techie, Madelaine, had said about the contessa.

Was the yacht the contessa's? It could be.

But Leda's guess was—not.

She hurried as quickly and quietly as she possibly could downstairs and picked up the phone to call security. This time, there was no answer at all on the other end. That alone confirmed her suspicions. Someone should have been there manning the desk at all times. She hung up and hurried on to the lab. The portable transfer unit was lying there on the table where Chimera had been working with it when she first arrived. So were the Cleopatra disk and specimen case, as if she and her dad hadn't been guarding them with their lives.

But the machine was what the contessa was really after. Chimera didn't trust the contessa any more than she did, Leda was sure. Like a mother bird leading intruders away from the young in her nest, the scientist was leading the woman and her accomplices away from the latest innovation, the one that was most potentially harmful to the most people in the wrong hands. The transfer units at the main lab were larger, hooked into the central Nucore computer, and would be unwieldy to try to use elsewhere.

That meant Leda had a certain amount of time to think

how to hide or remove or use the portable unit to best advantage. First she snatched up the specimens she'd so diligently delivered. She was damned if Gabriella was going to get her hands on them. She'd destroy them first.

And then she realized that maybe the way to use the portable unit to best advantage didn't involve removing or concealing it at all. It looked complete, as if Chimera had either finished the repairs or hadn't yet begun them. She carried it to Chimera's desk, set it up, unscrewed the lid from the cylinder she'd brought with her, and pulled out the printout. Then she stuck the Cleopatra DNA sample, unlabeled, in a tray with other samples, and set it in the back of the refrigerator. She pulled out another sample and ground it onto the floor. For a moment, she studied the disk she had rescued from the computer during the earthquake. Taking a deep breath, she stuck the disk into Chimera's computer. Hooking the portable unit to it, she uploaded and converted the codes as she'd been taught. Carefully placing the printout on the desk in front of her, she pulled the goggle-style eyepieces of the unit onto her face.

CHAPTER 21

The contessa might not be entirely sincere about her motives, Chimera thought, but she was certainly upset and anxious about something. She chattered nonstop about matters so personal that Chimera wondered if she only confided them because she thought the person listening would not be around to repeat the details later. Chimera hoped some of the remorse she seemed to feel was genuine; some small part of it must be. The contessa's reputation had been one of charity and kindness: the sort of woman who took in stray animals, gave lavishly to many causes, sent money to support children orphaned by war.

Even her motive for wishing to blend with Pandora Blades had been altruistic. It was a shame she hadn't been better informed, but then, the process was not exact and the interactions of the personalities involved unpredictable.

The contessa was obsessing now about Gabriella Faruk.

"We had such a fight, said terrible things to each other, Gaby and I," the contessa said as they rode up the hill in the little three-wheeled cart. "I fear she may never come back. Rasmussen frightens her. She had such a hard time as

a little girl, poor thing. Her stepfather drowned her
mother—quite legally mind you—in their swimming pool,
in front of her and other witnesses, accusing the woman of
infidelity. And he had his mother and sisters circumcise
Gabriella . . ."

"They circumcised a little girl?" Chimera asked. "But
there is no foreskin!"

"That doesn't stop them from removing what they feel
might make the girl 'unclean.' It often includes removal of
the clitoris and all of the sensitive tissue around it and the
sewing shut of the vagina, to make sure a girl is "pure" until her wedding day. As why shouldn't she be, since conventional sex will never be pleasurable for her, and in fact,
will only bring pain?"

"And this is permitted in Egypt? Is the religion practiced there so brutal?"

"Her family lived in Upper Egypt at the time, near the
Sudan, and the brand of Islam practiced there is quite fa-
natical, as it is in parts of Africa. Gaby ran away, disguised
as a boy, and for a time lived on the streets like a little rat.
Fortunately, she was old enough to have remembered her
life with her mother and real father, my brother, and me.
One night she was able to steal into a closed shop and call
me. I came to Egypt and collected her. This may shock
you, Doctor, but when I saw what he had done to my poor
little niece, I hired some people to see to her stepfather so
that he wouldn't trouble her again."

She sighed. Her story would have been very touching
except that Chimera felt it was a smoke screen of chatter to
prevent questions or comment on her motives. "She was
never entirely happy in Europe. She felt such a kinship
with the ancient Egyptians, you know, and perhaps, given
her mixed heritage, more kinship still with the Ptolemys.
And now that awful man has come between us and sees her
as a 'useful conquest.' That is what he told me. I feel so

helpless, Doctor. All of the good I have managed to do with my life that poisonous poet has undone."

"Excuse me, sir, may I see some ID?" Two armed figures stepped forward, flanking Chimera and the contessa as they left the cart. Chimera was startled. Challenges were not routine on Kefalos. Most of the security was electronic.

Chimera showed them the required badge, and they seemed to accept it. "We have a procedure to perform on this lady tonight," Chimera told the guards. "We will call our technician to assist, so please allow her to pass as well."

"Just checking, Doctor. We're relief staff and don't know all of you."

"Perfectly understandable. But now, excuse us, please." With that, Chimera stood in front of the sensor, which performed a retinal scan, and the door opened. The guards came in after them.

"We'll escort you into the building, Doctor, in case there are other intruders."

"That is not necessary," Chimera said.

"We have our orders, Doctor."

"Allow me to phone my assistant, please," Chimera said. Picking up the phone in the reception area, Chimera punched in the numbers of the villa, but Leda did not answer. Either she was still asleep or she shared the suspicions that were plaguing Chimera even more deeply with the arrival of the strange guards.

"She does not seem to be where she is supposed to be, Contessa. We're sorry. Let us go up and ready the room, however. Perhaps she was only in the lavatory or out for a walk. There seems to be a lot of activity on the roads tonight."

The building lights preceded them like a ghost carrying a candelabra as they walked down the corridors.

Once they were in the transfer suite, the contessa said,

"Ah, I remember this. Although, Mr. Wolfe, your friend, and Gabriella were here when I had my blending, Doctor, I don't recall you having an assistant."

"The reversal process is a bit more complicated," Chimera said with a small, apologetic smile. The longer these people waited, the better the chance that Leda would be awake, the real security staff would be alert, or somehow something might intervene to interrupt whatever it was that was happening. However, there was no harm, meanwhile, and perhaps considerable good, in honoring the contessa's wishes and removing Pandora Blades. "We can cope, however, so if you will be kind enough to be seated on the bed, Contessa—"

"I don't have to sleep again for the removal, do I?"

"Oh yes. Otherwise you may find yourself quite disoriented."

"I prefer the disorientation."

"But it could seriously destabilize your emotional health."

"The previous procedure has taken care of that already, thank you. In fact, I don't think I have time to do this now, after all. However, I understand that you have a smaller version of your invention, a portable version, one that we could take with us."

"Us, Contessa? Or is it Madame Blades who is now speaking?"

She gave a short laugh, harsh and a bit coarse, unlike the contessa's usual one. "It's all the same, Doctor, thanks to you."

"That machine is not available at the present time. We . . . disassembled it to try to make the reversal process quicker and more certain."

"If you disassembled it, you can reassmble it," a new voice said from the doorway. Rasmussen stood there, flanked by several uniformed men. "I believe we will find the device in the laboratory in the doctor's home, my friends. Shall we stop wasting time and go there now, be-fore we have to kill the entire staff of this facility as they arrive for work in the morning?"

Leda pulled away from the goggles, ejected the disk, and shoved it in with other apparently blank disks, all unla-beled and freshly freed from their packaging.

Then she settled back in the armchair. She might not be able to solve anything or ride in on a gleaming motorcycle to save the day, but she thought she had done enough un-predictable shit to throw a spanner into at least some of the plans Gabriella and company had been hatching. There wasn't a lot else she could do, and besides, she needed more sleep. Blended people always needed to sleep, she thought, and felt herself falling down the rabbit hole of un-consciousness as visions of slave-powered sailing ships and white columns danced in her head.

CHAPTER 22

On the two-hour flight from Kefalos to Alex, Gretchen began to regret turning down Chimera's offer to remove Duke from her life. *I am not unsympathetic to your predicament, Duke, but Wilhelm will be in Alexandria. What if we are . . . reunited?*

Never had a ménage à trois before? Duke asked and immediately regretted it. *Sorry,* liebchen, *just kidding. There'd still only be two bodies: yours and his. I'd just be on the sidelines, sort of cheering you on.*

Cheering is not what I am appreciating at such times, she said and her jaw tightened.

Maybe not; maybe that's what's wrong now. Maybe more cheering should be happening.

Privacy. It was a demand.

You drive a hard bargain, lady. But since this is apparently the only me there is anymore, I guess I'd better mind my p's and q's.

I am sorry, Duke, that they've killed you. But they did it, not me. Me, I am still trying to save my marriage.

He didn't argue with her. She held all the cards. He tried not to think about it. Tried not to think what was going to happen after. He'd faced death a lot of times. He'd just never been actually dead at the time he was facing it. It was an unusual kind of deal, and there were no instruction manuals about it, even if he ever bothered to read instruction manuals.

Holeeee, will you look at that? he asked as they approached over the harbor, now flooded so full that most of Pharos Island and the dike were covered, with water sloshing across the Heptastadion and onto the Corniche.

The moon was well up when they landed on the deserted airstrip. They were pulling the bike out of the plane when the runway manager and Pete Welsh, dragging a duffel bag, approached. Pete hastily threw down his duffel and inserted his body between Gretchen's and the bike. "Here, little lady, let me help you with that."

"*Danke,*" Gretchen said.

"Piss off, Pete," Duke added. "This is no ordinary buff blond chopper chick you're dealing with here. This is the boss's wife, Mrs. Wolfe herself."

Pete took three giant steps backward. It was worth making Gretchen sore and adding another sixteen levels to the general confusion just to see his face. "What the hell?"

"Watch your mouth, buddy, you're in the presence of a lady."

"Ma'am, are you nuts or what?"

Duke, behave yourself, Gretchen said. To Pete she added, "*Danke,* I would like it if you would bring from the plane the motorcycle, please."

The runway manager hadn't heard most of this because he was very intelligently wearing earphones to muffle the noise of the aircraft. Not that there was much noise now. The guy had probably just neglected to take them off.

Pete accomodated Gretchen, looking as if he was afraid

something would pop out of her like a stripper from a stag party cake.

"Where's the pilot?" the runway manager asked. "Dr. Welsh needs a ride out of the country."

"*I* am the pilot," Gretchen said proudly. "I am flying this airplane myself here. My husband has also come here, *ja*?"

"Yes, ma'am. He and Dr. Faruk arrived earlier this evening."

"He and who?" Gretchen asked.

"Dr. Faruk. Pretty young lady, only half Egyptian, I think, works at the museum and has a lot to do with the site, from what I gather."

Gretchen was not amused.

"Good thing she was with him, too," the runway manager, seeing the unhappy expression on the face of the boss's wife, continued. "He got arrested as soon as he set foot in the country."

"What?"

"Yes, ma'am. That Dr. Namid just had to blame somebody for what the earthquake did to the archaeology site. Some people are like that. You know how it is."

Pete very diffidently set the bike down on the runway and dusted off the seat, then thought he might venture one more remark to this lady who seemed to be more than a little strange. "Yeah, well, actually, he was after Punkin. I mean, Leda Hubbard. I called to warn her, though, and she got away in the plane your husband and Gabriella came in just before Namid and the cops—that is, the Egyptian authorities—arrived."

Duke cut in, "The Kid's not here then? Shit, Pete, where'd she go? I thought I asked you to look after her."

Pete took two steps toward them, coming closer to Gretchen probably than he would have ever come face-to-face with Duke unless he was trying to start a fight. "Excuse me, lady," he mumbled, then asked, staring into

Gretchen's eyes so hard it was as if he were trying to X-ray her skull, "*Duke?* Buddy, I like this new look you've got, but you really ought to notify your friends before you have such a drastic makeover."

"It's a long story, Pete. Do you know, your breath smells like you haven't been brushing your teeth real regular. I don't think Mrs. Wolfe appreciates it. Why don't you take a big step backward and explain to us about what happened to make the police come after Leda and Wolfe?"

"Yes, and what is my husband doing with that Faruk woman also," Gretchen added in her own German-accented English.

"As to your question, ma'am, I couldn't really say, except right now, I guess they're probably getting booked into adjoining rooms at the local jail."

"They have arrested Wilhelm? Incredible! I will see that he is released at once, though of course, the woman is another matter."

She mounted the bike and put her hands on the controls, then seemed at a loss for what to do next. Duke said, "Pete, if you're in no immediate danger of arrest, I'd appreciate it if you'd stick around for awhile. For one thing, you don't have a pilot for that bird, and we may need it for a fast getaway once we've sprung Dr. Wolfe from the hoosegow. I need you to try to get ahold of Leda and explain to her, if you can, what's going on here. Otherwise, she's going to have Laney and all of my ex-wives over here looking for me, and I wouldn't wish that on anybody. Also, we may need some backup."

"Are you kidding? I'm not sure what's going on here, but I sure don't want to miss one exciting episode," Pete said.

"You can use the Sopwith," Duke said magnanimously.

"Sure. Where is it?"

"Oh, damn. Probably got lost in the flood, didn't it?"

"Nope, but the last time I saw it, you were riding this way on it."

The runway manager looked puzzled, but he put in, "I think it got stolen. Dr. Hubbard said something about that before she left. She had parked it by the control hut, and while we were busy with coordinating the relief efforts from Nucore, the bike disappeared. Thieves, she figured."

"Maybe," Duke said.

"We go *now*," Gretchen insisted, but she still couldn't get her hands and feet coordinated to start the bike. Duke had basically acted for her previously, and now he was disinclined to do so until he was good and ready.

"Well, hop on then," Duke told Pete. "But don't get fresh with Mrs. Wolfe here."

"I meet a beautiful blond biker, and just my luck she has a cop for an internal baby-sitter," Pete grumbled.

Gretchen was trying to make the bike go zoom, but Duke rode it slowly as far as the control hut.

What looked like the top of a broken egg was lying just outside the shadow cast by the amber emergency light over the doorway.

Duke shut down the bike, much to Gretchen's consternation, and bent over to pick up the object. "Old Mothah Hubbard."

Gretchen, seeing the crack up the back of the helmet with the identical legend to the one she was wearing, winced. "So. This is a massive head injury you are having." The blood still rubbed off sticky brown on her fingers, which were not yet gloved.

"Yeah," he said. He'd been hurt before, but if the helmet was cracked like this, his head must have just about been pulped, too. Maybe Rasmussen did him a favor, killing him.

"Do not be giving that man so much credit," Gretchen said. She was starting to read him now, even when he wasn't trying to talk to her. "If you had surgery, as the girl said, very probably you had only a depressed skull fracture from which you might recover no more cracked than you must have been most of the time."

Duke didn't respond. He handed the damaged helmet to Pete, who hooked it onto the saddlebags by stringing the strap through the buckle of the bag.

He was so quiet that it made Gretchen fidget, but this time, when she tried the bike's controls, her fingers and feet expertly performed all of the proper motions to send them roaring off.

With the hot wind in Gretchen's teeth, Duke guided them back over the route he had taken the night he was hijacked.

The road leading from the airstrip was under repair, probably because Nucore was footing the bill. The main highway was an unlit obstacle course of contruction signs, detours, and witches' hats. By the side of the road, pretzeled power poles and light poles remained as casualties of the quake.

Most dramatic of all, however, was the harbor. Though the pumps were chugging away so loudly that they drowned out traffic noise, filling the night like thousands of giant bullfrogs in heat, the harbor shone with the sea as it had before the cofferdam was built.

This is where the ancient city was being raised? Gretchen asked.

Yeah, and that over there is what's left of the dam. That was Pete's baby. He can tell you about that.

Wilhelm called to tell me when the dam broke. The engineer—this man with his hands on my middle?—was telling him then that he thought the dam was repairable, that only a few cells had been broken. I did not know that dams had cells.

Yeah, well, they're constructed in sections they call cells. They can stand independently, so some of them could give way without necessarily harming the others. Across the littered waters, the long necks of tall cranes, like robot giraffes, stood out against the softer darkness of the night.

They turned off the highway onto the access road leading to Pharos Island and the fort. Water licked the hem of the island again, and as they rounded another bend, Duke looked for the beluga but didn't see it. Then he realized that where it should be there were instead two new hills with a deep gully in the middle and scraps of white fluttering around the site. "Holy shit," he said.

Your daughter? Gretchen held her/their breath.

Yeah, it's a wonder she got out of that, but she is *my kid, after all.*

Pete said, as if reading their minds, "Good thing you gave me a heads-up about Punk—Leda. She almost got trapped in that thing. I broke in the door and pulled her out."

Having viewed the damage, they veered back onto the remaining lane of the Corniche. Many cars had been hauled up onto the sides of the road, blocking pedestrian paths.

"Where's the local cop shop?" Duke hollered back to Pete, his words emerging from Gretchen's mouth oddly accented, in a husky contralto with a little lisp.

Gretchen said, before Pete could answer, "The police are not our first line of inquiry. First we go to the German consulate. My husband's status is such that he should have diplomatic immunity. Never should he have been arrested, and if he was, the consul should have been notified. *Nein,* he should have been present and prevented such an outrage."

"You go, girl," Duke said, mimicking something he heard teenage girls say to encourage their peers. "But isn't the consul going to be off duty, asleep?"

"Any consul worth his title will be awakened for such a crisis as this and for such a person as Wilhelm. If Wilhelm is in jail and the consul is sleeping, he is not doing his job."

The only problem with her argument was that the consulate was one of the buildings that hadn't survived the quake. A hand-lettered sign in German and Arabic said that any tourists wishing assistance should seek it at the consulate in Cairo.

"So!" Gretchen said. Duke knew that she meant, *That didn't work out, time for plan B.* He knew this both because he was sharing brain space with her but also because he counted among his extremely varied ancestors some hardheaded German women. None of them wasted much time, either, when there was something they thought needed doing. "We are dismounting now. The police station is in the middle of the next block. We must look to them respectable. Dr. Welsh must drive the motorcycle as if it is his. I will wear my skirt. You, Duke, will be silent, *ja*? The police will be more cooperative if I speak through Dr. Welsh."

"You mean because of the fundamentalist Islamic thing?" Duke asked, somewhat astonished. None of the women he knew well would have catered to those attitudes.

"Here they are not attitudes, Duke. They are part of the law. As a foreigner, I am excused more than local women, but I wish not to incur scorn and disrespect from the police. So. The charade."

The charade was short-lived and for the most part unnecessary, however.

The policeman on duty was unshaven and looked as if he had not slept in several days. But he was no ruffian. The tourist police were a special branch who had to be well-educated, multilingual, with good people skills. This one was fresh out of the last item. He listened dazedly to Pete's explanation, as fed to him by Gretchen, but simply flipped through his log book and said, "No one named either Wolfe or Faruk has been arrested."

"Uh . . . you'd remember him," Pete said upon prompting. "He's a VIP. His company was in charge of building the dam that broke."

"Is it?" the policeman asked without interest. "That hardly makes him a criminal. Earthquakes destroyed the ancient lighthouse, the palaces, all of the structures the university and museum people have been trying to dig up. A dam would be no better able to stand against it. It is the will of Allah."

"Is the officer who was in charge when Mr. Wolfe and Dr. Faruk were arrested still here? It was only a short time ago."

"That would be me. Oh, yes, I know who you mean now. At the insistence of one of the archaeologists, we sent a car after them, but as soon as they came to the station, it was plain to see the charges were nothing but petty politics. In case you haven't noticed, we have a disaster on our hands. We are still trying to dig out people who were buried in collapsed buildings. Just an hour ago, a wing of the women's and children's hospital collapsed, and because the other hospitals also were damaged, there is nowhere to put the patients. People are homeless and without food. We are using the jail cells to house some of them. There was no room here tonight for the petty quarrels of wealthy men."

"Either that is an unusually sensible and sensitive officer of the law, or Wolfe got a lot of baksheesh passed around real quick," Pete remarked privately to Gretchen/Duke.

The policeman had no idea, and no interest in the itineraries of any of the parties involved when they left his desk.

"I know where we can check on Gabriella, anyhow," Duke said.

"I don't care about *her*," Gretchen said stubbornly.

"Even if your hubby is with her?" Duke asked wickedly.

"Where do we go then?" Gretchen asked.

Duke decided to try to find a back route to Gabriella's villa rather than braving the ruin of the Corniche again. Besides, by the back route, they would pass the museum where the woman worked. Not that she was likely to be there this late.

That assumption was incorrect. The facade of the museum building was striped and strobed with the revolving multicolored lights of police cars, ambulances, and fire department vehicles. From the interior, it was lit by the glow of amber emergency lights from its in-house generator. Police directed traffic, which consisted of a stream of ambulances, donkey carts, taxis, trucks, and vans. These paused at the entrance long enough to disgorge patients who were carried inside on litters, gurneys, or, if small enough, in someone else's arms. Some limped in with assistance.

Gretchen could not keep her eyes on the road. Duke felt her pull toward the hospital. "I should help," she said. "They cannot possibly have enough doctors."

Duke had to admit that except for maybe his own murder, which could probably wait a little while, since he was apparently already as dead as he was going to get, nothing they were doing was as important as lending a hand here.

Gretchen said, "Pete, you will take the motorbike and give transport to anyone strong enough to ride, *ja?*"

"Ma'am, yes, ma'am," Pete said, saluting. Duke smiled. When Gretchen got all dominatrix like that, it was all either one of the guys could do to keep from making very bad Nazi jokes.

Gretchen was no Nazi. She waded into the hospital, took stock of what was happening and who was in charge, walked up, said she was a doctor, a pediatric surgeon, and asked where she was needed. The other docs were all women, too. Men doctors didn't work on women in these countries. Though the wounds looked pretty terrible to Duke, most of them were trauma, bones and flesh that needed cleaning, setting, sewing. The anesthetic had to be saved for the worst cases, and there were few painkillers. Lucky kids had their moms there to comfort them. The others screamed in Gretchen's ears, and in between her commands for instruments, water, and bandages, she kept up a stream of baby talk in German and snatches of little songs to try to lull the children or distract them.

Kids with cuts and crushing injuries to arms and legs, their faces dirty from debris and their noses snotty, looked up at her with dark and frightened eyes. She smiled as if they were in a playground in the park, cuddled them and sang to them, and asked, "What's that over there?" very suddenly. While they looked away, she did the part that hurt before they noticed.

CHAPTER 23

Chimera groaned to see Leda seated at the laboratory desk, the portable unit beside her. She hadn't taken it away then. Why not?

Rasmussen, three of the guards, and the contessa entered the lab at the same time as Chimera.

"*Not* someone else to dispose of," Rasmussen complained, then nodded to the guards. "Very well, shoot her."

Chimera evaded them and crossed swiftly to the chair, placing his body between the guards and Leda. "If you kill her, you will get no cooperation from us, no matter what."

Leda showed no gratitude for this brave gesture. She said nothing, she moved nothing, just sat sprawled in her relaxed position, her back to them, her head to one side. Then, suddenly, she snorted and let out a long snore.

Almost apologetically, Chimera said, "she was exhausted when she arrived. She is not even a witness, so you can take the unit, kidnap us, and leave her alone. You have murdered her father. There is no need to do her further harm."

"None except that the ridiculous woman and her secrecy cost me the only significant find of that whole expensive debacle in Alexandria."

Chimera moved slightly to make sure more of Leda was covered. Doing so jostled the office chair, and her hand slid against a piece of paper, which fell onto the floor. It looked like a computer printout of some sort. And then Chimera saw the mess from the broken sample vial.

"Ahhh," the scientist said.

"Ahhh *what*?" Rasmussen demanded.

"She is sleeping the postblending sleep," Chimera said and stooped to retrieve the fallen paper.

"What's that?" Rasmussen asked.

"Oh, some data she had printed out for me before the earthquake, judging from the date."

"Data about Cleopatra?"

"Yes. She brought me the tube Duke was carrying when he was injured. Leda must have been very annoyed with you and your friends, Mr. Rasmussen. She took material intended for another and transferred it into herself."

"She *did*?" Rasmussen waved at the guards to lower their weapons. "Well, I had not realized she was so highly trained, Doctor. We hardly need you at all, do we? She can conduct the entire transfer herself and besides, she now seems to possess the *ba* of Cleopatra."

"The *ba*?"

"That is the name the ancient Egyptians gave the personality and memories of an individual spirit. I'm surprised you weren't aware of it before. It is the stuff you trade in with this process of yours."

"How enlightening," Chimera said with an ironic little nod.

"You will bring the machine with you, Doctor. You three, carry her down to the yacht."

* * *

In the blended sleep, Cleopatra was the first to make contact, to find the similarities that would lead to a blend. *We are both Philopater,* she said. *Both of us loved our fathers a great deal.*

And both of our fathers were murdered, Leda added.

And once more, we are surrounded by assassins, Cleopatra continued.

Someone said, "The more things change, the more they stay the same."

Did they? Socrates perhaps? Or Aristotle?

I was guessing Will Rogers, myself, Leda admitted.

But in spite of the thoughts flickering back and forth between the two personalities, the blending sleep was lovely and soft, a cocoon of luxury in which she had been borne onto a ship very like her barge and then propelled at the speed of a leopard over the waters. She did not physically see this, but she felt the change in the air currents, smelled the sea, the freshness on her skin, the soft pallet beneath her body when she was deposited on the ship. As she slept, the common memories flowed into and with each other as one channel of the Nile merged with another.

And elsewhere aboard the yacht, as they slept, the strain of trying to appear forty years younger than his eighty-five years caused Cesare Rasmussen a twinge of the pain that he knew would someday herald his death.

Gabriella Faruk was a far different woman than the fey and erudite creature Wilhelm Wolfe had entertained on Kefalos. Though her tone on the phone had been anxious and concerned, she still sounded bright and upbeat. However, the sprightly curl of her hair was now a straggling tangle in need of shampoo, her skin looked dull, and her eyes bore deep shadows beneath them. She was tense, and each movement appeared to require great effort.

She told Wolfe she had not slept since leaving Alexandria two days before. She answered briefly and noncom-mittally when Wolfe inquired about her aunt's well-being since the blending. And though she might have slept on the plane on the way to Alexandria, she appeared to be too ag-itated to do so.

Wolfe realized he should have waited until morning to make this trip, but he wished to arrive, spend the night in Alexandria, and after a brief tour, continue on in the morn-ing to other urgent appointments, two of which were scheduled before noon in Cairo.

Because of the earthquake, Wolfe could hardly avoid in-cluding Alexandria in his itinerary; however, his primary concern was public relations for the Nucore investments in Cairo, Luxor, and other sites along the Nile. The truth was, much of what Nucore funded in Egypt was pure research. The DNA taken from mummies found these days was for discovering commonalities and differences among the var-ious people being exhumed. Most of the truly famous mummies were either in the Cairo Museum or in the British Museum, and the DNA from those had required no large outlay of funds to obtain.

For the most part, however, Nucore was not offering these notables for blending. Too little was known about their actual lives and personalities, even the details of their reigns. As rampant as incest had been among the pharaohs, so, too, could be the aberrations and anomalies resulting from such misbegotten unions, whatever the cultural belief about it might be.

So he was surprised that the secrecy surrounding the blending process had been breached. Protesters barricaded some of the sites and were said to be picketing the entrance to the Cairo Museum. Archaeologists had had their hotel rooms vandalized and had been pelted with rocks in the streets. Nucore property was stolen or destroyed.

All of this he explained to Gabriella Faruk on their way

to Alexandria. The answer to where the security leak origi-
nated was immediately apparent when the police cars, their
amber and blue lights swirling, met the plane at the Nucore
strip and Mahmoud Namid and the police attempted to arrest Leda Hubbard before she could leave the country. The
airstrip, by trade agreement, was actually beyond the jurisdiction of the Egyptian police, but they were in such an angry mood that Gabriella cautioned Wolfe against saying so.
Failing to apprehend Leda, Namid had the audacity to tell
the police to arrest Wolfe himself and Gabriella.

It seemed that the real problem had been that Leda,
upon personally discovering a canopic jar believed to have
contained remains of no less a personage than the great
Queen Cleopatra, had declined to share her discovery with
other members of the team investigating the harbor site.
When the earthquake destroyed the Nucore laboratory
housing Leda's work, the canopic jar and Leda both disappeared in the flood. Namid, it seemed, would have been
happier if Leda had drowned in the subsequent flooding resulting from the rupture of the dam.

And Namid therefore decided that information he had
obtained about Nucore's blending activities should be
made known to the Egyptian people.

Gabriella explained some of this in a low murmur as she
translated; the rest Wolfe was able to glean from Namid's
own accusations.

Fortunately, the police did not share Namid's indignation and were quite receptive to Gabriella's protest that
Mr. Wolfe had come to Alex to aid in the relief effort. He
was here, she said, to take inventory personally of the
needs of the city's residents in order to determine what
supplies and personnel might be sent next to ease the city's
suffering.

Part of easing that suffering would naturally fall to the
police force, and for that, Mr. Wolfe could see that while

they made a valiant effort to cover the city, here they were, still working by candlelight and kerosene lantern. When the power grid went down, shouldn't the police be among the first to have their electricity restored? But they were understaffed, overworked, and lacking in much of the equipment and many of the vehicles they should have to enable them to perform their duties. Mr. Wolfe would personally see to it that these lacks were redressed.

The young woman had risen from her stupor to meet the occasion. She handled the police magnificently: sincere, concerned, charming but not flirtatious, diffident but distant, striking just the right note with the weary officer on duty. The candlelit police desk smoothed the shadows from her face but cast those from her movements dramatically against the wall, a silhouette puppet play enhancing her arguments and lending her gestures extra emphasis and grace. In the end, the charges were deemed unworthy of police attention in a time of such crisis. The officer in charge sternly warned Namid to refrain from causing more trouble than already afflicted the city.

The officer even apologized for not having a car available to deliver Mr. Wolfe to his flat. Gabriella once more came through, however, punching in a number, and after a brief conversation, turning to him, smiling. "My cousin Mohammed drives a taxi. He will come for us."

"Excellent," Wolfe agreed. The taxi was there a short time later, and they stepped from the police station entrance into the cab. Wolfe caught only a glimpse of the homeless roaming the streets, the small cooking fires set up on sidewalks for an evening meal. In the next block, outlined against the sea, he saw the moonlit outlines of people wandering through the ruins of buildings, looting or perhaps looking for lost belongings—or lost relatives—in the rubble.

Mohammed and Gabriella cried out with relief to see

each other and spoke excitedly in Arabic for a few moments before Gabriella said, "But we are being very rude. Excuse my cousin and me, please, Mr. Wolfe. Where is it you wish to go?"

"I have a flat at the Cecil," he told them, thinking happily of his airy room with the large tub and the full business capability, which of course wouldn't be available now, with the power out.

Neither, it seemed, was the room.

"I am so sorry, sir, but the Cecil was much damaged by the quake and the flooding. It is closed."

"Oh," Wolfe said. "Well, then, can you recommend a good hotel that escaped damage?"

"Alas, sir, no. They are all on the water, you see, and that is where the worst damage occurred."

"You must come back to the villa and be our guest, Mr. Wolfe," Gabriella said. "Our place is on the lakeshore rather than the seashore, and Mohammed just told me that except for the collapse of one exterior wall, which unfortunately has injured one of my aunts, it has sustained little damage. My aunts are rather traditional and completely capable of running a comfortable household without power, are excellent cooks, and we have extra rooms for the fluctuating number of guests we entertain. Do say you will stay with us. It would be such an honor. And Mohammed could drive you around while you are here or take you to the airstrip when you wish to leave."

"I have two appointments in Cairo in the morning," Wolfe said.

"No bother, sir, I will help you meet them," Mohammed said.

"And I, too, will help however I can," Gabriella said sweetly. "Only first I must check on my aunt and see what must be done to repair the villa."

"You've been great help already, Dr. Faruk," Wolfe said,

"But if you'll pardon me for saying so, you appear exhausted. I would not like to bother you for anything further until you have had sufficient rest."

She gave him a weary smile. "You are too kind," she said.

Mohammed carried Wolfe's bag inside the villa, which was indeed well-ordered and pleasant, with a fine breeze in the courtyard and a faint scent of sandalwood and patchouli wafting through the halls. Wolfe smiled. In his university days, he would have believed the incense was there to cover up the smell of marijuana-smoking, but the scents were not unusual ones here to cover a variety of other common and less inviting odors.

Gabriella greeted some veiled women with hugs and much chattering, and a short time later, a small meal of couscous and fish was provided, with fruit for afters. Gabriella looked as if she were about to fall into her food, and Wolfe ate quickly and said that he, too, was tired and wished to sleep.

His room was dark and cool with a veil of fine white mosquito netting over the bed, a chair and a table where Mohammed set the candle he carried to light their way. "Sleep well, sir, and tomorrow you can be useful," he said. Was it the candle that gave his smile a sinister cast? For some reason, Wolfe half expected to hear a key turn in the lock when the man closed the door behind him. What he heard instead was a light knock a few moments later and a soft, "Mr. Wolfe? Are you still awake?"

"Yes," he said and at first thought to invite her in, then remembered that this was a Muslim household and to do so would compromise his hostess. He walked to the door and opened it.

"We have learned that the hospital where my aunt was taken had a section collapse and is being evacuated. I thought if you wished to follow through on the promises I made on your behalf for Alex, you might like to come and see the damage."

"An excellent idea," he said. "Although you yourself look very tired."

"I am, but we will just see how she is doing and perhaps we may be able to bring her back here. In the meantime, you may be able to assess what Nucore can do to assist."

CHAPTER 24

You are to be my afterlife, Cleopatra said.

It doesn't really work that way, Leda told her. *We have to share me. And I, Leda, have first dibs. You do realize I didn't do this because I was impressed by your celebrity or title.*

You are thwarting enemies. I understand that very well. Therefore, quiet yourself and listen.

It doesn't work that way, either. We're asleep. We should be melding our personalities and memories to some extent.

This we assuredly must do, but for now, vigilance will save us. I represent the ba *of she who was Cleopatra, but you, Leda, possess a* ba *you may send abroad to listen to those who plot against us.*

I'm not sure I can do that.

I was the embodiment of Isis, and as such, I learned a trick or two that allowed me to foil the plots of my enemies. Allow me guide us both, the voice in her mind said, and her spirit seemed to slip from her body with the ease of her body slipping from between satin sheets.

The body was lying on top of satin sheets, actually, red

ones, on Rasmussen's own large bed, in a racquetball-court-sized stateroom. The bed featured sleek electronic controls for raising and lowering head and feet, like a hospital bed, if hospital beds were created by Italian interior designers. Behind it stood a hollow marble column, inside of which was an oxygen tank.

Set in an island of red, blue, and turquoise tiles Leda was pretty sure had once adorned an ancient mosque, was a sunken black marble Jacuzzi tub the size of her entire bathroom. Jets studded the surface of the tub at all levels and angles like miniportholes. Another remote control similar to the one for the bed lay atop a pile of towels that were red plush, monogrammed with *CR* and voluminous enough to make a sarong for a hippopotamus. Tiered steps led down to the tub's center, which featured a mosaic of water sprites.

A private ampitheatre! Cleopatra exclaimed.

More like a royal bath, Leda corrected. Otherwise, there was a vast closet, and adjacent to the tub, a more conventional bathroom with one surprising feature, which was a connecting door.

From the other side of it came voices. The *ba* followed the sound into a compact but well-equipped laboratory/clinic.

Respirator—one of the new kind that allows the patient to stay awake and talk while it's in use—defibrillator, monitor . . . Leda noted the items in the room with extra emphasis and a mental picture of their function.

The contessa; Rasmussen; the three flunkies Rasmussen had brought with him to Alex, now clad in Nucore security uniforms; and another man faced Chimera. A girl with a blond ponytail and glasses tried to look as inconspicuous as possible, and Leda thought this must be Madelaine.

"Dr. Chimera, this is my personal physician, Dr. Abdel Singer. During our voyage, you will instruct Dr. Singer on your process, or rather, on the variation of it I wish performed."

"You still wish to have your own pattern blended with that of other living persons?" Chimera asked. "We recall that this was the desire you stated when you were interviewed for the blending. At that time, you said it was to ensure that someone who would carry out your wishes for its use would inherit your empire. You have decided on a recipient?"

"Why limit myself to one? There's plenty of me to go around, after all! I have several initial candidates in mind. One of whom is the contessa's niece. I adore spirited women, don't I, my dear?"

Oh, Lord, the *ba* said. *Who's been watching too many old macho movies? That is such a corny line.*

"One would think that if you wish to make sure your will is done, you would choose someone compliant," Chimera remarked.

"I prefer to see just how compliant I can render those who present more of a challenge, even a battle. Bending a will to my own in the most profound possible sense seems to me to be a better, nobler goal even than making sure my fortune is spent as I wish."

The valiant little figure of Chimera shook a head of straight black hair and tried to explain once more that a blending was not a contest of wills; one personality should complement the other.

"Those, my friend, are your rules and your ideas. I shall use my own. There will be no adjustments made to allow the weaker or conquered personality to protest, to back out."

"You may find you are literally driving yourself crazy," Chimera cautioned. "Most people, when they wish to have an heir, have a child. A child with your own genetic material would probably be as certain to carry out your wishes as another strong-willed individual reluctantly carrying your personality. After all, a child carries the imprint of the parent, too."

"Many would say I am crazy now," Rasmussen replied. "I tried having children, but it did not work out. None of my women could bear me a son. You will take the sample now."

"Surely your own physician knows how to do that?" Chimera asked. "Gathering a sample is an elementary procedure."

"Indulge me," Rasmussen said.

The contessa twittered nervously at his side, her expression a cross between adoration and anguished loathing. So she had been at least partially telling Chimera the truth. She had just neglected to mention the part where the blended personality—that of Pandora Blades—had conquered, as Rasmussen would say, the contessa's own less passionate and more compassionate leanings.

"Very well, open your mouth," Chimera said, and took a sample from the inside of Rasmussen's cheek.

"We brought the equipment acquired for the contessa's pet technician, this girl here," he waved a deprecatory hand toward Madelaine, who pretended to be huddling over her computer instead of cowering over it, "to prepare the sample for the blending," Rasmussen said. "You will please do that at once."

Chimera studied the equipment and said, "This is not adequate. We'll need equipment from our own laboratory."

"Don't play games with me, Doctor," Rasmussen commanded. "I need your skill now, but when the woman in the other room has awakened from her sleep, I can use her instead. And in order to gain Cleopatra's knowledge from her, I need not leave her body in good working order. Shall I maim her and kill you, or do it in the reverse order?" The man's voice had been controlled and level to begin with but now rose, as did his color.

"Calm yourself," Chimera said, but Rasmussen suddenly staggered. "My nitro, quickly," he commanded. One of the guards, apparently keeper of the pills so Rasmussen didn't have to ruin the line of his custom-made clothes, produced a bottle, opened the cap, and shook out a pill. Rasmussen slipped it under his tongue, but the pain continued to be so severe that his knees buckled, and he had to be supported by his henchmen and the doctor.

They eased him into a wheelchair and it, followed by the monitor, the defibrillator, the respirator, and a trolley full of medicines, were wheeled into his room. He was rolled into bed beside Leda's still-sleeping body.

Eewww! Leda and Cleopatra were well blended on their emphatic if silent response to this.

"Remove her," the doctor said, pointing to Leda's body.

Rasmussen, with a ghastly smile, shook his head and rasped. "Cle-patra," he said, reaching one clawed blue and white hand over to stroke her arm.

Oh, God, he just got us, and he likes us so much he has to sleep with us like we were his first BB gun or something! Leda said.

Rasmussen continued with a cough and a laugh that sounded like plastic wrap being crushed into a ball. "Nothing . . . wrong . . . with her my . . . surgeons . . . can't fix."

The doctor and a henchman removed Rasmussen's shirt and revealed that he had an intravenous catheter already inserted his arm. Into this, the doctor plunged a needle from a syringe prefilled with some mysterious medication or the other.

"Now," Rasmussen gasped to Chimera, standing at a distance. "You will do as I say *now.*" His color was ghastly, bluish around the lips and fingertips. His breath came with heavy huffs of exertion. The seams from his various plastic surgeries stood out like the ones on the Frankenstein monster, spoiling the illusion of youthful vigor and virility he had tried to preserve.

Chimera looked more exasperated than frightened, as if an attempt to caution a child against doing something foolish had failed. Leda's friend lingered near the doorway until the rapid erratic zigzags of the heart monitor showed a relatively normal rhythm again, and Rasmussen grumbled something as he was hooked up to IV fluids. Only then did Chimera return to the laboratory.

The *ba* hovered, while Rasmussen's breathing slowed.

Damn, Leda said. *I hate it when only the bad guys can afford good health care.*

But the Cleopatra *ba* was focused on Leda's body and seemed filled with dismay at what she perceived. *I see we have aged and have no beauty to aid us in this life.*

Hey, I was cute once. You never got to be forty. What do you know about cellulite and gravity?

True, and the body is warm and lives. Better than a mummy. Living flesh is moldable. When we have the measure of our foes, we may finish our mutual task and awaken, and there will be time to work with the body. Ointments and unguents, perfumes and oils, healthful foods and exercise . . .

Oh great. An internal personal trainer. Better than being sliced and diced by Rasmussen's plastic surgery team, I suppose. Come on. Let's nail the bastards who killed Daddy.

The *ba* surveyed the remainder of the yacht. It was more the size of a cruise ship, to Leda's mind, though a cruise ship outfitted with only the finest of materials: teak decks, a heavy engine, state-of-the-art navigational equipment, and a large crew.

When Cleopatra wondered why she couldn't see the oars, the *ba* examined the gleaming engine room, where Leda explained in some detail how modern ships operated.

In addition to the rooms they'd seen, there was a small apartment for each of the crew members in the fo'c'sle. A fully equipped kitchen and dining hall for the crew, with a private dining room attached to Rasmussen's suite, an Olympic-sized pool, and other recreational facilities (though no shuffleboard, Leda was amused to note), with guest quarters nearly as luxurious as Rasmussen's own.

The contessa had a suite to herself, and when Rasmussen slept again, she returned to it. She was attired now in designer jeans and a long black sweater. Her ravaged face was framed by large gold-coin earrings. In her suite, she flung herself onto her sapphire-colored couch and looked as if she wished to cry. Instead, after a few tortured moments, she arose and went to a desk, where she opened a gold-engraved notebook and began to write furiously.

The ship, meanwhile, continued cruising toward Egypt.

When Gabriella and Wolfe arrived at the hospital, they were told that it had been evacuated to the lobbies of various public buildings, principally the library and the museum, which had the most room. Gabriella quickly changed course for the museum. There, the crowds of sick and injured were being admitted and treated, while anxious family members camped in the gardens and courtyards. The quake-damaged roads were clotted with vehicles transporting patients and supplies.

Gabriella strode up to a harassed looking woman with a clipboard, who greeted her gratefully, "Ah, Dr. Faruk, as you see, we have a terrible calamity on our hands."

"We are here to help, Selima. You see, I have brought along Dr. Wolfe, an important businessman and a friend to the people of Egypt. He wishes to learn what will be needed to help these patients and to restore the hospital. I know you are terribly busy, and I must find my Aunt Naima, who I am told was injured during the quake."

"I believe she is over by the entrance to the ancient

scrolls section, Dr. Faruk, but although I try to assign spaces methodically, we are more crowded than I imagined possible. Right now, our greatest need is food for these people and their families."

Wolfe punched a number on his cell phone, waking up one of his brokers, and after giving the man instructions, handed the phone to Selima, telling her to apprise the man of the hospital's food requirements, which would be supplied from grocery wholesalers in Rome. Shipments of drugs had already been sent to the hospital.

While Selima spoke, Wolfe began wandering through the wounded, trying to form his own assessment of what was needed.

The smell of unwashed bodies, blood, putrescence, and excrement was strong, along with the heavy yeasty female smell that vaguely embarrassed him. Some of the patients tried to conceal their faces as he passed, and he pretended not to notice them. Women in labor, women with tumors, women with dreadful injuries, the ones who must have been in the collapse of the extra wing.

A great long line wound around one wall, and he wondered what it was for, until he saw that most of the people going in were, after a time, returning looking relieved. Sanitary facilities! Retrieving his phone from Selima, by now busy again with new admissions and her clipboard, he punched in more numbers and ordered portable toilets flown in from the Nucore supplier in Rome. Then he ordered Nucore's own chief dispensary executive and her staff to come to Alexandria at once. He felt ill equipped to identify all of the needs these people must have by himself.

He spotted a familiar blond head bent over an injured child, familiar hands expertly exploring the small body. He stood beside her for several moments before she looked up and saw him.

"Wilhelm!" she cried and then, in a much different tone than he had ever heard from her, said in their native tongue,

"Good to see you, big boy, pull up a hemostat or a syringe or something, and make yourself useful."

You're not going to go all stupid on me just because your hubby's here, are you? Duke asked as Gretchen tied off the last of nine stitches in a child's lacerated wrist.

You have your concerns. I have mine, the doctor told him stiffly, but aloud she asked, although she knew the answer already, "You are here long, *liebchen*?"

"A few hours only. Dr. Faruk and I had some unpleasantness with the police when we first arrived. How did you come to be here? Did your hospital send a delegation?"

"No. But I knew the dam was one of your projects and I wanted to help," Gretchen said simply, then changed the subject. "This Dr. Faruk, she is a lady, *ja*?" Duke scrutinized Wolfe's handsome features for some sign of evasion or duplicity but saw none. He looked a little tired and as if he was trying not to show it. He seemed unruffled by the tragedy around him, but his jaw was set in a determined line, and his eyes continued to roam the room as they spoke. Duke didn't think Wolfe missed much.

"*Ja.* An excellent woman. You will like her, I think. Have you tried to check into our flat at the Cecil yet? It is not available. Gabriella has graciously extended to me the hospitality of her home."

Duke spoke up, in Gretchen's voice, "And you think this is a good idea?"

Gabriella had apparently been standing off to one side for a second or two because she said, "Mr. Wolfe, we are in desperate need of more intravenous fluids. Also blood."

"Very well," he said, but before he made a note of it, he said, "Liebchen, this is Dr. Faruk; Gabriella, my wife, Dr. Gretchen Wolfe."

Gabriella looked genuinely delighted to meet Wolfe's wife, which puzzled both Duke and Gretchen. "How wonderful that you have come to help, Doctor," she said. "Please, your husband has already accepted the hospitality of my home in Alexandria. It would be perfect if you would stay with us, too. My auntie Yasmin studied medicine in Germany. She is over there, by the fiction hall, you see? My cousins tell me she has been volunteering at the women's hospital since before the wing collapsed. You must meet her, really. It would be a great joy for her to speak with you."

You gotta hand it to that Gabriella. She is smooth, Duke said as Gretchen looked over at the woman bending over a figure concealed behind a screen. *And she has more aunts and cousins than anyone I ever met. Do you think these could be some of the women she's hiding? The ones on the run from their own countries?*

It is possible, Gretchen said. *I must tell you, Duke, that I also am hearing of these outrages against women, and I am more inclined to wish to help this girl than to bring her to what passes for justice in such matters.*

Why, Frau Wolfe, I didn't know you had terrorist tendencies!

Gretchen moved on to another patient, Gabriella and Wolfe following her.

These atrocities they encourage under the name of Allah, Gretchen said. *They are acts abhorrent to the good God, not how things should be done.*

Well, I'd be the last one to want to do away with so-called immoral women, Duke said, *Even if some of their crimes don't sound to me like anything to get excited about. But this particular lady terrorist got me killed, if you'll remember right, and sent what was left of me to you instead of Cleopatra. You're still mad about that, right?*

Gretchen's concentration was on her patient by then, a small boy with a gash running from the roots of his dusty black hair to his eyebrow. Her leather jacket was gone, wrapped around a woman who had been going into shock, and was replaced with a white coat. Despite all the things the makeshift hospital was missing, a good supply of white coats had come over from the laundry.

Much later, the patients with superficial injuries and homes to go to had been released, while those who had been treated but had no homes were sent to a public shelter Wolfe organized in a disused theater building. The patients who needed more intensive treatment had been transferred to Cairo or Rome by Nucore copters flown in from that city.

Gabriella worked tirelessly, organizing, reassuring, escorting, chaperoning, even assisting with medical chores when necessary. Many of the women seemed to know and trust her more than the medical staff.

Someone mentioned that it was Dr. Faruk's investment of both money and influence that had caused the women's hospital to be built in the first place and had kept it going since.

Finally, other hospital staff members arrived to relieve them of the care of the few patients left at the museum. At Gabriella's urging, Wolfe and Gretchen wearily agreed to return with her to the villa.

"Your aunt?" Wolfe asked.

"How kind of you to remember," Gabriella said. "She was transferred for further treatment to Rome. I fear her right side may take considerable time to heal."

Gretchen rode beside her husband in the back of the van. His arm went around her, and she snuggled under it.

He actually looked down. At her. "That's an unusual costume you're wearing, my dear," he said. Having lost the white jacket as well as the leather jacket, she was clad in the skirt over her leather pants and a rather revealing laced-up leather vest, most immodest in a Muslim country.

"You are liking, Wilhelm, *ja*? It gives me, I think, a dark gypsy biker babe look, do you not think?" And as she said this, she had an uncharacteristic twinkle in her eye and her hand, so skillful at healing, edged over the top of his thigh and rested there playfully.

"*Ja.* Before we met, I drove a motorcycle, you know."

CHAPTER 25

Rasmussen slept deeply for several hours. Then, as if even in his drugged sleep he kept a navigational chart on the insides of his eyelids, he awakened. The yacht was approaching the waters of Alexandria's western harbor.

The contessa vacillated between hanging over Chimera and Madelaine, apologizing and giving false reassurances about their safety, and holding Rasmussen's hands in hers.

Probably trying to make sure he doesn't cop a feel of us, Leda said. *Not that we would like that any more than she would.*

Suddenly, Rasmussen roused, his eyes flying open. He struggled to sit. When the contessa tried to press him back down again, he called out. The doctor, who had been in the lab with Chimera, and all three flunkies came running.

"Launch the boats. Bring Faruk to me. She," his eyes indicated the contessa, "will show you where."

"And if there are witnesses?"

He shrugged, which the *ba* interpreted to mean *kill them.*

The contessa interjected, "Gabriella's household in

Alex is composed of some of the women she harbors from punishment by influential families in Egypt and other Islamic countries. She often brings them along on her trips to see me, and I smuggle them for her farther into Europe, with new identities. They could be valuable—or useful, at least—in controlling Gaby."

"Bring them, then," Rasmussen said indifferently. "She will tell you." He had raised himself a little as he said this, despite the contessa's efforts, but now he subsided onto the bed again with a sigh like a bellows collapsing.

Mo parked the van, and Gabriella climbed out and stretched her legs. In the back, Gretchen nudged Wolfe awake, and the two of them climbed out as well.

The villa was silent. All of the "aunties" remaining would be asleep now. Mo said good night and disappeared around the moon-shadowed corner of the main building to his own quarters within the "family" compound.

As they entered the front of the house, Gretchen said suddenly, "*Gott!* Pete! We forgot about Pete and the bike."

"Who is this Pete?" Wolfe asked, as they stepped through the entrance hallway and into the courtyard.

"He is . . ." and her voice died away. As they stepped into the courtyard, they saw two women bound and gagged, kneeling at the feet of men in the uniforms of Nucore security. Gretchen began to back up, but something hard and cold prodded the middle of her back.

Steady, Duke advised. *I'll show you what to do when the time comes. Just look all scared and girlish for now.*

This is not very hard, I think, she replied.

The black and white night shadows that had been so sharp a moment ago suddenly melted to gray. A flotilla of clouds covered the moon. The fronds of the palms and the branches of the other trees sheltering the courtyard rustled fitfully. A brief flash lit the sky as thunder grumbled in the distance.

The lightning showed for a split second a woman's form in the doorway, and Gabriella gave a sharp cry, as if in pain. "Ginia! What have you done?"

The contessa stepped into the courtyard, her tiny, crooked form flanked by a pair of guards standing over the bound and gagged women.

"Gabriella, it is the only way. I didn't know you had company, dear. Why! It's Mr. Wolfe! Cesare will be very happy to see you, I'm sure. You can cheer him up. He is having some health problems. That's the reason for all of this haste and rudeness, Gaby, dear."

Wolfe spoke up, "Contessa, I don't know what this is about, but if Mr. Rasmussen is in need of medical help, he is fortunate. This is my wife, Gretchen, an excellent physician."

"Oh, *ja,*" Gretchen said. "I would be most delighted to examine Mr. Rasmussen and give to him the treatment, even though he is somewhat older than my usual patients."

The contessa nodded and said to the uniformed men, "Bring them now."

Their hands were bound with tape, and they were marched out of the courtyard, through the house to the back entry, near the lake, and forced into a taxi van similar to the one in which they'd arrived. The van drove them along the western edge of the city and out onto the Desert Highway a short distance, to a spot where two Zodiaks, rubber rafts with Mercedes-Benz engines, were waiting. In the distance, what looked like a cruise ship wallowed on the sea as the waves billowed and crashed with the ever-increasing winds.

The thunder suddenly escalated from a grumble to a boom and crack as lightning forked across the water.

Not a great time for a cruise, Duke said.

* * *

The *ba* wandered restlessly over the yacht. She peered over the shoulder of Chimera as the scientist tinkered with Rasmussen's sample, trying to sculpt it somewhat to produce a profile less ruthless than the original. She followed Rasmussen's physician, observing the potions and machineries that were the tools of his trade. She studied Rasmussen, sleeping fitfully beside her own earthbound vessel.

She watched as the Zodiaks carrying the contessa and the ersatz Nucore security guards dropped away from the mother vessel like baby spiders leaving the web.

The weather had been clear then, even with the daylight ebbing. Since then had come the thunder, lightning, the rising swell of the sea.

The annual floods are beginning now, Cleopatra's *ba* said. *Some things never change, at least.* The queen had been saddened and silent to see, even at a distance, the ruinous remains of her once-beautiful city. The lighthouse was gone, the palaces vanished without a trace.

I don't know how to break it to you, Leda said, *but actually, since the Aswan Dam was built, the Nile doesn't really flood like it did in your day. And you remember Nubia? Well, it's a lake now.*

For the next hour or so, they watched the shoreline, illuminated solely by lightning. Leda saw the squat Fort Quait Bay, part of it crumbled away since the earthquake. Cleopatra saw in her mind's eye the wonder of the world that had been Pharos Lighthouse with its three-tiered tower and its brilliant lens that could be seen thirty miles out to sea.

Cleopatra beheld palaces where Leda saw tumbled stones and a lot of water.

Cleopatra saw a broad street with white columns and beautiful buildings surrounding it, a channel of the Nile connecting Lake Mauritus, an inland sea, to the River of Life. Alexandria of her time was all but an island.

Leda was still marveling at this when the specks that were men and women being carried across the sea in rafts began speeding toward the yacht.

By now the waves were so high that the Zodiaks played peekaboo with the larger vessel. Still, the high-powered motors of the small craft propelled them so that every time they reappeared, they were larger and nearer.

Suddenly, there was a flurry of noise and movement from below, unconnected with the rolling of the yacht in the swells. The *ba* located the source in Rasmussen's cabin. The man was a ghastly gray blue again. The heart monitor showed a flat line. His physician, several crewmen, Chimera, and Madelaine clustered around him. The physician pulled out the defibrillating paddles, told the others to clear, and applied them to the bared chest of Rasmussen. The physician didn't notice or didn't care that Rasmussen's left hand was still lightly resting against Leda's arm.

As Rasmussen's body jerked, the chest humping upward, Leda's spasmed, too. The *ba* found itself back inside Leda's body. As the paddles lifted, the connection stopped, and the truck Leda felt had hit her rolled back. The *ba* no longer saw or heard anything.

But Leda suddenly felt hands on her as she was rolled off the bed and thumped to the floor, the impact scarcely cushioned by the strong hands and small knees of her rescuer.

Chimera. Leda's eyes flickered open, and she looked into her friend's face. She was lying on the floor, Chimera bent over her, but she was awake again. She started to say thank you, but Chimera put a finger over her mouth and gave a barely perceptible shake of the head. Leda winked and allowed herself to relax and subside into a mock faint.

I thought they were going to mummify that hideous old

man, Cleopatra whispered inside her head. *Instead, they returned him to life. I would like to know how this is done.*

Electrical shock, Leda said. *We got some, too. That's why we're awake now—a bit early for a blending sleep. Who knows, maybe it will even cheer me up a bit.*

If Cleopatra was puzzled about the last remark, she let it pass.

Rasmussen's physician was still very busy. Chimera joined him, asking, "How can we help?"

"His heart will not last much longer," the doctor replied. "You see how erratic the rhythm is even now? But he wishes to see this thing done. So I will hook him to the life support so he may breathe and have his heart rate regulated. You must prepare your apparatus to carry out his wishes."

"It is ready," Chimera said without inflection.

The puff of the respirator, the beep of the monitor, were punctuated by booms of thunder and a grapeshot of rain on the decks above them. Something knocked against the hull. Voices hollered to be heard over the storm, feet ran to a single point on the deck, and there was a lot of groaning of wood and lines while people were hauled aboard. The voices, all male except for the contessa's soprano competing with the wind, became threatening. Some of the footsteps stumbled. The yacht listed so violently to one side that Leda's body rolled toward the bulkhead, away from Rasmussen's bed.

Either the stabilizers on this tub just went out or that was a hell of a big wave, she told Cleopatra.

The doctor yelled for help. Rasmussen, retching with the motion of the yacht, rolled away from his machinery. Footsteps clattered down the steps.

"Suction!" the doctor yelled and then after a moment or two of sickening slurping sounds that made Leda want to retch also, "Help me strap Mr. Rasmussen to the bed."

Big feet ran past Leda to accommodate. Then the contessa came down the ladder, Gabriella right behind. Leda could tell this because she slitted her eyelids and watched and also from the voices, the footsteps, the shoes. Next came a crewman, then Wolfe, followed by another crewman. Last came a small blond bombshell who looked only slightly like the Gretchen Leda had known in her youth. The crewman who came behind her ignored the blond. Probably figured she wouldn't do anything dumb because she was Wolfe's wife and yes, oh my yes, there were weapons drawn and pointed in Wolfie's general direction.

Gretchen knelt beside Leda. "Kid?" Gretchen felt for her pulse, but Leda grabbed the hand and mouthed, "Hi, Daddy." Then she closed her eyes again. "Possum," she mouthed before peeking again. Gretchen winked Duke's wink.

Rasmussen roused, and between respirations and compressions of his heart by the machines that sustained him, spoke. "Ah, Dr. Faruk. How. Nice. Soon. I. Join. You. Permanently. Wolfe! Chimera?"

"We are here," Chimera said from the doorway.

"Two. Blends. Faruk. And. Wolfe."

Madelaine's voice was tremulous as she answered. "Two are prepared, Mr. Rasmussen."

"Good. Now."

He sounded stronger all the time. Leda carefully inched her way toward the ladder, crawling. All attention was on the bed except Rasmussen's, which was on his intended victims. You had to hand it to the sick old man. He had focus.

Thunder shook the yacht so hard, for a moment no one could speak. Leda lay wedged between the stairs and the bulkhead, hoping anyone who noticed her change of position would assume she had rolled there with the movement of the yacht.

The deck shuddered beneath her like a washing machine with an unbalanced load. All she could see was feet,

the hems of the bedclothes, beneath the beds, and the base-
boards of the walls. If she escaped to the deck, what could
she do then?

Cleopatra, within her, saw the same things and sighed.
How unfortunate we have no venomous snakes . . .

We haven't lost our asp yet, Leda told her. Seeing
Duke's twinkle in Gretchen's eyes had cheered her consid-
erably. He seemed happy, except for the minor detail that
maybe he was about to get killed again, along with
Gretchen.

"Bring. Machine. Here. Now." Rasmussen said. "Girl.
First. I. Watch."

Crack! Came the noise of the storm, as if the deck were
breaking in two. The yacht bucked beneath them, and Leda
rolled as it subsided, thinking, *Nope, the stabilizers are
fine. This is just one hell of a big storm.*

She got stepped on three times, but when she stopped
rolling, her feet were beneath the head of the bed.

With an outstretched, seemingly limp arm shielding her
face, she could see the doorway through the bathroom,
where Chimera and Madelaine staggered, carrying the
portable machine and the computer.

"Help them!" the contessa commanded, whether for
the good of Chimera and Madelaine or for the good of the
equipment, Leda wasn't sure.

The computer and machine were both completely
portable and were set up quickly, bases secured with duct
tape by one of Rasmussen's flunkies.

Gabriella was forced into a chair, and people parted
from the foot of the bed, presumably at Rasmussen's command.

Chimera fitted the goggle-eyepieces over Gabriella's
face.

From the bed came a ghastly chortle.

*   *   *

Cesare Rasmussen knew he was dying, could feel his life return and recede with each puff of the machine inflating his lungs, each pump of the machine compressing his heart muscle. He could not complain, however. This was a fitting ending.

He would see himself transferred first into the woman, a willful, principled, beautiful woman he would enjoy conquering in every conceivable way. To begin with, he would see to it that she closed the permanent female tea party at her home and returned the women to their families and countries where they belonged. He had better plans for her.

And Wolfe! What a wonderful joke to have Wolfe under his control. Wolfe was still comparatively young, handsome even, and virile enough to keep the shapely blond who seemed to be his wife. He was also in control of the blendings. Rasmussen could extend his own power infinitely while controlling these two attractive young people—and have the little blond wife for an appetizer.

Wonderful that he had lived to such a great age that science could now preserve his essence this way.

The spittle that flowed down his chin as he watched the Faruk woman struggle with her bonds was not entirely because of the respirator. In another moment, he would be very close to her indeed, would feel her revulsion, and quell it.

What a horrible man, Cleopatra said. *He reminds me of an uncle of mine. I had to have him strangled.*

He's a honey, all right, Leda agreed. She had maneuvered herself so that only her head and arm were still exposed. The rest of her was beneath the bed frame.

There was a rasping whisper from the bed, then the contessa said. "Gaby, Cesare wishes you to know that the first thing you will do when you wake from the blending is begin negotiations to sell your refugees back to their families and governments for the appropriate disposition. He has other plans for the two of you—the three of us actually— and doesn't want you tied down, unless he arranges it."

"How could you, Ginia?" Gabriella protested, but the contessa didn't answer.

"Do it." Rasmussen's command was weak, and there was a lust as diseased as the rest of him in his voice as he said it.

Chimera sat at the keyboard and raised his hands.

Cleopatra's conciousness intruded on Leda's, which was firmly fixed on a course of action. *I sense we are about to do something, but why? Is this woman not your enemy? You hold her responsible for the murder of your father. If this man seeks to harm her, why should you care?*

Because he's the one that actually did murder Dad, and he wants to be to Gabriella what you are now to me. It's pretty complicated, but it wouldn't kill her, and it might make her worse. If she doesn't say thank you nicely when and if I pull this off, then we kill her.

And with that, her foot connected with a heavy cord. She bent her ankle and dipped it, winding the cord around her instep, and yanked. Nothing happened. "Must have been the one to the bed controls," she said.

Chimera's hands were on the keyboard. Leda wriggled farther back and felt with her foot again until she located another cord and yanked again.

The plug came free and smacked her ankle bone, but suddenly all that could be heard was the storm and the click of computer keys. The pumping and soughing of the life support machines was still.

Of course, nobody immediately thought to check and see if the machines were still plugged in, at least no one on Rasmussen's staff. They stood around with their faces hanging out, probably thinking *a short, the electrical storm outside, black magic,* whatever, but Leda was well out on the other side of the bed by then.

Gretchen Wolfe said in a sweet, concerned, doctorly voice, "Please to let me help. I am a physician also."

A question hung in the air. Then came the sound of slitting tape as the hands of the innocent-looking, helpful Gretchen were freed.

Leda hunkered up as close as she could to the under edge of the bed. Directly in front of her were the jogging shoes and uniform pants of one of the fake Nucore guards. He stood with legs parted, to maintain his balance on the rolling deck. She lowered her head like a charging bull, aimed her crown at his crotch, and shot forward at an angle that caught him where he lived.

The ship rolled again, and the guard was on his butt. Chimera lurched backward to the foot of the bed.

Lightning cracked, and Rasmussen's physician came up, holding the plug to the machines as if it were some decharmed snake. As he knelt back down to reinsert the plug, he fell against the bed. Meanwhile, using some moves that looked gratifyingly familiar to Leda from the police training films Duke had made, Gretchen took out the two guards closest to her.

The contessa jumped her.

Then someone fired a shot.

Everyone looked at everyone else. The guards fumbled to raise their guns, as if they'd forgotten about them.

"Drop it," a voice said from the top of the ladder. Pete stood there, with a gun of his very own. "This vessel is surrounded by the Egyptian Navy and will be impounded for violations of the maritime code occurring within Egyptian waters as well as the kidnapping of persons from Egyptian soil."

"I am the private physician of Mr. Cesare Rasmussen,"

said the man who was, "and these people are preventing me from caring for my patient."

"In that case, send them up here," Pete said. "Slowly, unarmed, I want to see Mr. and Mrs. Wolfe, Gabriella Faruk, and her aunts . . ."

"I'm here, too, Pete," Leda called. "And so is Dr. Chimera."

"And Madelaine," Chimera added.

"You guys, too, then, Punkin," Pete called.

CHAPTER 26

Fortunately for all of them, Pete didn't actually have the Egyptian Navy waiting topside to arrest the wrongdoers. What he had was the dam construction and diving crews from the dig in the harbor. They were much easier to deal with, Pete said, and they asked for less red tape. For this, Gabriella and her aunts were particularly grateful.

"My hero," Leda said, and she meant to make it a joke and bat her eyelashes satirically, but it came out more seriously than she intended. Pete did a double take.

"All I did was get some guys together," he mumbled. "You or your dad would have done the same for me."

Cleo! Leda said.

You didn't tell me we had such a handsome suitor at our command, the queen replied.

The yacht disappeared, and later, the contessa returned to Kefalos during business hours to have her blending reversed. She told them that Rasmussen's doctor had been unable to revive him. Once the blending had been reversed, she seemed relieved and ashamed at the same time.

"I will try to get his stockholders to agree to a Viking funeral for Cesare," she promised. "So . . . historical and appropriate, don't you think?"

Wolfe paid enough baksheesh to allow the refugees at Gabriella's house to be brought to Europe under false credentials.

The cofferdam was repaired and strengthened, and renewed excavations, under the leadership of Dr. Leda Hubbard, an American anthropologist with an astonishing intuitive insight into Egypt's past, took energetic and innovative new directions.

Nucore's interest in Egypt was, on paper at least, bought out by another corporation, Helix. Papers were shuffled, names and logos changed, and the Egyptian public settled back down, pleased with the knowledge that, for once, they had guarded their ancient trust from foreign interlopers.

In October of the following year, a new excavation uncovered a partially collapsed tunnel beneath the island that had contained the royal complex and the temple of Isis. This tunnel, once cleared, led inland, deep underground, to a secret tomb long buried beneath the building and grounds of the new Alexandria Library. In December of the same year, a huge news story erupted.

TOMB OF CLEOPATRA;
Instead of Fancy Jewelry,
the Queen Took Along Some Good Books

According to anthropologist Dr. Leda Hubbard, her team has recently discovered a mummy DNA tests have positively identified as that of Queen Cleopatra VII. Though the mummy carried none of the

treasures usually associated with such a royal burial, it was locked in an imaginatively engineered
and superbly constructed crypt apparently of the
queen's own design, Dr. Hubbard reported.

"The treasures Cleopatra chose to take with her
to this secret burial were intellectual. We found
cases and cases of scrolls we believe the queen rescued from the burning of the original library, in-
cluding some authored by Cleopatra herself, and
others by famous scholars of her day and earlier
times. These works should give us many insights
into the great mysteries of the ancient world, including, perhaps, the burial site of Alexander himself,
believed to be in Alexandria."

Dr. Peter Welsh, the engineer and hydrologist for
the expedition, credited Hubbard's intuition to the
unearthing of the queen's crypt.

The newly appointed antiquities inspector for
Alexandria, Dr. Gabriella Faruk (who replaced Dr,
Mahmoud Namid, arrested earlier this year when he
was found to have extensive holdings in brothels in
Thailand and the Philippines), says, "Leda's discovery is the most wonderful thing to happen to my
country in this century. It is as if Cleopatra herself
chose this time to reveal her great secrets. The
scrolls, of course, will remain in Egypt, as will the
queen's remains, though DNA samples have been
sent for analysis to the laboratories at the Hubbard
Foundation, established in honor of Dr. Hubbard's
late father, who died during the great quake of last
year."

EPILOGUE

The Christmas party was lavish but small, exclusive, and distinctly interdenominational.

Wilhelm Wolfe was an agnostic of Jewish descent; Chimera a Buddhist (or two Buddhists); Gabriella Faruk not a Muslim at all, as she seemed to be, but a Coptic Christian; Contessa Virginie Dumont a lapsed Catholic; as were Madelaine, Pete Welsh, and Duke Hubbard; and Gretchen Wolfe, alias Gretchen Graffin, a Lutheran. Leda Hubbard had been a Wiccan for many years, and Cleopatra Philopater was a time-lapsed worshiper and embodiment of Isis.

Nonetheless, everyone sang carols around the tree and exchanged gifts.

Pete had already received his from Leda/Cleopatra and sat with a deeply satisfied, dazed look on his face while nursing a 7UP. He no longer imbibed six-packs. Nor did Leda. The queen of the Nile, busily educating herself on all manner of modern discoveries, decreed that her father had been an alcoholic and Mark Antony more so, and she would not allow anyone she loved in this new life to destroy himself in that fashion. It amused Leda that Pete hardly missed what had been an integral part of his life as long as she'd known him. Cleopatra could be extremely persuasive.

And so was Duke Hubbard, apparently, for Gretchen had kept him with her long past the time when he could be removed. Neither she nor Chimera told Wolfe. If he was surprised when she chose her alias to work in the hospitals supported by the efforts of Gabriella Faruk and others like her, her husband didn't say so. He appeared to be as enamored and fascinated by her as Pete was of Cleopatra. Leda knew she had taken off the pounds, shaped up the bod, even improved the skin, hair, and teeth, but it wasn't the Leda material that bewitched Pete so much as Cleo's aura. Leda didn't really mind. She thought it was wildly funny to see old wandering Welsh so smitten with, well, her, that he offered to sleep across her doorway at night to protect her.

Privately, the Wolfes supported Gabriella's network to protect and shelter the endangered women of Egypt and the Middle East.

Chimera was refining the blendings so that the more toxic personality traits could be removed, the more admirable ones enhanced, but it was more art than science, finding the right blend.

Gabriella's new job gave her more clout and more ways to help her people.

But although she had reconciled with Ginia as a friend, she no longer trusted her aunt to help with the work they had formerly shared.

"Leda, you will be traveling, writing books about your discovery?" Gabriella asked. "When will you return to Egypt to look for Alexander?"

"I'm not sure," Leda replied. She wore a clingy, long-sleeved gown with a beaded collar her friend in Washington had made for her. Cleopatra liked it and declared it much lighter than the jewels she had worn in her former life. "It seems to me it may be the sort of thing that's best left to an Egyptian team. And, while part of me feels a real kinship with Egypt, I'm not, ethnically I mean. Besides, we've been there, been queen of that, and are feeling that it's time to move on now. There's been so much new knowledge in the years since Cleopatra's death that study and exploration are more interesting now than digging into a past we know already."

"I see. So you don't think you will return to Egypt soon then?"

"It all depends. But this is boring. Let's open gifts."

As the gifts piled up in front of her, Leda cried, "Tribute!" gleefully and opened them—some very expensive body oils and a negligee from Pete, *predictable but sweet,* a Christmas bonus from the company formerly known as Nucore, writings of the Dalai Lamas throughout history from Chimera, a copy of the scrolls authored by Cleopatra from Gabriella Faruk, and a pectoral of Bast, signed "Love, Dad and Leroy" on the back.

Leda gave Gretchen a speculum inscribed to her dad, knowing how well-suited he was for his new life and work.

Gabriella opened her gifts to find a bracelet from Virginie, a new maternity wing to her hospital from Gretchen Graffin, and a large donation to same from Wilhelm Wolfe. Finally, there was a custom-made T-shirt with a picture of Marvin the Martian, his space suit looking more Egyptian than Roman in the illustration, his eyelashes definitely longer and curlier, and lipstick adorning his Martian mouth. From Chimera, Leda, and Cleopatra, there was one more small package, a note saying that if she wished, Gabriella Faruk could receive the *ba* of Cleopatra Philopater with the blessing of the existing *ba* and its bearer.

Leda grinned at Gabriella's reaction. "It was Cleo's idea. She's completely given up trying to convince me to have you strangled and decided she likes you and admires what you're doing."

"It will be the first time we have used the same donor in two different blendings," Chimera said. "We will all be very excited to see what happens."

"I wonder," Gabriella said. "Do you think that even when you and I, Leda, are in different places, the *ba* of Cleopatra in me and the one in you will be able to communicate?"

"According to Cleo, yes. She says that is one reason she wishes it done. When she was queen, she always wished there was enough of her to go around, so she could be in two places at once. Finally, thanks to Chimera and us, her dream can come true."